The Not Quite Enlightened Sleuth

by

Verlin Darrow

The Wild Rose Press, Inc.
PO Box 708
Adams Basin, NY 14410-0708
Visit us at www.thewildrosepress.com

Publishing History
First Edition, 2024
Trade Paperback ISBN 978-1-5092-5419-4
Digital ISBN 978-1-5092-5420-0

Published in the United States of America

Dedication

To everyone. We're all in this together, aren't we?

Chapter One

I'd flown to San Francisco from Sri Lanka via Singapore and Honolulu, wearing civilian clothes for the first time in God knows when. After robes, they felt quite constricting. A hundred dollars sat in the back pocket of my knock-off jeans. I'd need to rely on the universe to raise the ground under my feet as I walked out of the temple grounds into my new life. I was curious to see how this would unfold.

My sister greeted me at the gate in the airport. Jan must've found some way to get through security. That was just like her. She could be a force of nature when she set her mind to it. In the past, this had created conflict and enmity between us. I hoped that wouldn't be the case now—that I could opt out of my side of our old dynamic, whatever she did.

Her smile widened as we drew closer, but tears simultaneously streamed down her lightly rouged cheeks. Our mother had suffered a stroke two days earlier.

Jan stepped into my arms with no hesitation and then let go a moment later. Her breathing was shallow and hurried, as though she were walking into a job interview with a trumped-up resume in hand. She was nervous about meeting me after all these years.

I'd forgotten how quickly everyone in the world moved from one thing to the next. In fact, the entire trip had overwhelmed me for a variety of reasons.

"Look at you, Ivy," Jan said, stepping back and struggling to sound like her usual self. "It's like you're a regular person again." She surveyed what I wore—flimsy jeans, a men's light blue work shirt over a black T-shirt, and the only white running shoes I could find that didn't sport a logo.

"It's great to see you, Jan, even under these circumstances. So you like my outfit? The Sri Lankan version of Goodwill offered very few options in my size. I'm a giant there." I spread my arms out to the side to display my wingspan, nearly striking a middle-aged woman in a navy business suit, who told me to watch out with an edge to her tone. Perhaps she was as exhausted as I was.

Jan wore a similar outfit to the aggrieved traveler, only her suit was burgundy, with oversized black buttons. Under that, a shiny white blouse with a scoop neckline highlighted her cleavage, completing the sexy businesswoman look. Either Jan had surgically modified her breasts or discovered the world's most aggressive push-up bra. An oversized gold purse almost matched her light-yellow heels. If I didn't know her, I might've thought she owned a chic clothing store or was bent on distracting an opposing lawyer.

Jan managed a half smile. "You look like an undercover cop on one of those shows where everyone's too good-looking to be real."

"Thank you. I was aiming for what everybody else looks like," I told her. "But I'll take that as a compliment."

"Let's get going." Her tone was dismissive, as if I were wasting time by responding to her. "We need to get to the crappy hospital up in the city near where Mom collapsed. She's hanging on to say good-bye to you."

We walked toward the airport exit.

"What do you mean?" I asked, my heart sinking. Jan's email hadn't hinted at a dire prognosis.

"She's in a coma now. She's not going to make it." Jan stopped suddenly, turned toward me, and studied my face, seeking visible signs of grief, but not finding them there.

"I'm sorry," I said.

"*Are* you sorry? Are you *really*, Ms. Spiritual?" Now Jan kept her gaze forward, even as her words shot sideways. Perhaps due to her bipolar disorder or a personality disorder, my sister's anger was almost always right below the surface. And Jan cast a critical eye on everyone. If the Dalai Lama came over for dinner, she'd admonish him if he asked for salt and pepper.

"Of course I'm sorry. She's my mother too, and I love her. I've just gotten off a plane after traveling halfway around the world, and I'm spent. I don't have it in me to live up to your expectations about how I'm supposed to grieve right now. Okay?"

I wasn't happy with this defensive response, which had become more animated as I spoke, but I couldn't think of anything to say to repair its impact. Jan was uncharacteristically silent.

We resumed our march to the world outside the airport, passing most of the others from my flight. My sister's breakneck pace was hard to keep up with.

The PA announcer's overly loud voice announced a last boarding call, and a couple to the side of us argued about money. I wasn't accustomed to so much auditory stimulation, and it took me a moment to get my mind back in gear.

"What else is going on?" I asked after several minutes of silence. "There's something else, isn't there?" I don't know how I sensed this—micro-cues that had been in Jan's tone or expression?

By now, we were passing the baggage carousels, where most passengers waited desultorily, with a few impatient types staring into the abyss where bags disgorged. The street was in sight through glass sliding doors. I hadn't checked any luggage; the entirety of my possessions filled half of my modest canvas knapsack.

"What do you mean by 'something else going on'?" Jan asked.

"Aren't you concerned about even more than Mom's health?"

"I was waiting to get into that later." Her tone was resentful. Why had I pestered her with this question?

"Okay. How are the girls?" My nieces were fourteen and sixteen.

We paused our conversation to cross the multiple lanes in front of the departures doors in a wide crosswalk, along with a cohort of younger travelers. Miraculously, all the cars immediately stopped, reminding me I was no longer in Asia, where, as a pedestrian, I often feared for my life.

"The girls are upset, of course," Jan answered. "But otherwise, they're thriving. Holly's a star on the volleyball team at school, and Dee's still the deep one in the family. I don't think I could stop her from reading everything under the sun if I tried. She'll probably grill you about the meaning of life or something."

"I wish I knew."

"Don't you?" Her tone was sharp again.

4

I just smiled as she opened the trunk of her gleaming, expensive-looking sedan and stared at me. She'd left her car in a no parking zone designated for hotel shuttle buses. One of them honked at us, leaning on his horn for several seconds.

Sitting behind the wheel, no longer angry—her moods changed quickly—Jan smiled back at the smile I still displayed. "I'm sorry. I'm on edge."

"That's understandable. No worries."

Jan began sobbing as we pulled onto the freeway a few minutes later.

"How can I help?" I asked.

"You can nail the son of a bitch," she managed to gasp.

"Who?"

"Dennis—Mom's husband. He murdered her. I know he did. She's not dead yet, but he murdered her."

That was all Jan would say. For the rest of the ride into San Francisco, she shook her head when I spoke, keeping her eyes glued to the road—well, to the cars ahead and around us. Who could see the road itself in so much traffic? Things had changed since I'd left.

Among other things, I spied far fewer full-sized trucks on Highway 101, but an army of mid-sized delivery vans swarmed around us. Upscale foreign cars competed with them to get to the city thirty seconds sooner. Most of these gleamed in the sunlight. Had they all been recently washed? When I'd owned my twelve-year-old subcompact, it had remained shiny for a week.

What had once been a verdant park near the bay was now a row of chain hotels. Another older hotel a few miles north was in the process of being demolished. I looked down at the scenario from the elevated highway.

5

A crowd had gathered on the street to watch the huge wrecking ball swing into the building's carcass, scattering the remaining metal beams and struts onto a pile of debris. The onlookers' proximity seemed quite dangerous, and clouds of dust and who knows what else drifted out of the site over their heads.

At that point, I noticed the negative slant to almost all my perceptions since deplaning. That wasn't who I wanted to be, but clearly, that was who I still was. I vowed to redouble my efforts to stay true to my Buddhist values.

Then I considered what Jan had told me. Why would Jan want *me* to hold Dennis responsible? What about the police? Why me?

I'd never even met my current stepfather, but Mom had always been drawn to the sort of man who'd take money out of the collection basket at church. If caught, Mom's partner would explain—in condescending fashion—why he was justified in doing so. And he'd believe it. None of her husbands had been evil or even immoral per se, just high achievers in the self-deception department. Having convinced themselves their self-serving bullshit was true, they spoke from a seemingly honest place.

****

The Catholic hospital sat on a steep hill overlooking the Haight-Ashbury neighborhood in San Francisco. If it could've expressed its disapproval of the neighborhood's history, I'm sure it would've.

A ten-story concrete monolith, as featureless as anything Mussolini had ever designed, Saint Brigid's homeliness was accentuated by the color scheme—dark brown with a black portico over the sliding glass doors.

A tall, bedraggled hedge lined the base of the elderly hospital. On the other hand, additional attempts at landscaping were far more successful. A garden of mature lavender sat by the side of the parking lot, and several apple trees sported pink flowers by the sides of the entrance.

The fiftyish receptionist in the center of the cavernous, hard-surfaced lobby managed a fair imitation of a parochial school nun, although her wedding ring indicated she wasn't one.

Her graying hair, pulled back tight against a pale, wide face must've been bound in a bun in the back of her head since she wasn't the sort of person who'd opt for a ponytail. Set deep under perfectly plucked and arched eyebrows, her dark eyes narrowed as they peered at Jan.

When it became apparent we weren't stopping to chat with her at the circular island counter, she barked, "May I help you?" Her alto voice echoed off the gray stone walls. She pursed her lips in almost cartoon fashion.

I was surprised by her behavior. Despite her severe appearance and whatever negative judgments I'd already made about her—another bad habit of mine—I still expected her to greet visitors in a friendly fashion. That was her job, after all.

My sister Jan slowed and responded before I could. "Give us any crap today, Louise, and I'm talking to Sister Diane."

"Please! This is a sacred space. Show some respect."

"Screw you," Jan growled, and we marched to the elevators in the corner of the lobby.

"What was all that about?" I asked her while we waited to ascend.

"Louise and I have history," Jan replied, with no evidence of lingering ill-will.

One elevator sported a hand-drawn out-of-order sign. The wielder of the black marker had tried and failed to add whimsy to the announcement, varying the font and adding curlicues, which only served to obscure the words. The other elevator was currently on the seventh floor, according to an old-fashioned semicircular dial above the door. A reflective panel separated the two sets of doors.

The area smelled strongly of floor wax, and I caught a whiff of cigar smoke. Who would smoke a cigar in a hospital? Perhaps someone had snuck in a few puffs while sequestered in the elevator.

At first, while we waited, I stared at the polished stainless steel elevator doors blankly, ignoring my sister. I felt emotional, but in an undifferentiated, surreal kind of way. Whatever was happening within me seemed as though it were happening to someone else.

The vertical panel between the elevator doors reflected Jan's countenance. The image was blurry—it wasn't a mirror per se—but I didn't have an urge to turn and look at her directly. I'm not sure why. Perhaps in my dissociative state, I was trying to minimize my dosage of reality.

Her long, narrow face sat below dense, wavy hair she'd piled on top of her head like a fraying turban. Indistinct tears squeezed out of the corners of her dark brown eyes, dragging more visible dark mascara with them.

I'd decided when I was eight that, if Jan were an animal, she'd be a coyote. Of course, this was based on Roadrunner cartoons—I'd never seen the actual animal—and was probably biased by Wile E. Coyote's attempts to annihilate the roadrunner, whom I identified with.

Jan's pointy nose was the most coyote-like part of her. It began its descent from above her brown eyes and stopped just short enough above her upper lip not to distract the viewer from her otherwise attractive looks.

Although she'd filled out at thirty-six—verging on wolf status now—the physical resemblance still fit. Behaviorally, though, you'd have to force six cups of coffee down a coyote's gullet to simulate Jan. My little sister lacked the slow, loping grace of the animal, to say the least.

We looked nothing alike. Growing up, Jan wanted to look like me, and vice versa. I guess anyone with a narrow face and a long nose would prefer my ordinary proportions, and many would covet my best feature—my pale green eyes. For my part, I wanted her hair, her sensuous lips, and ears that didn't look tacked on.

The ride up to the fifth floor confirmed my cigar theory. The air in the car was rank. Jan and I made faces at one another. Hers was a scrunched-face scowl, accompanied by a slow head shake. I can only guess how my expression came across. I still felt removed from what was happening.

At the end of a long, stark hallway on the brightly lit fifth floor, past three manned—or actually womaned—nurses' stations, a glance into our mother's intensive care room didn't inspire hope. The usual array of monitors huddled beside her motionless body, beeping listlessly as though they were ready to lapse into a coma, too. A squat, black ceramic vase of droopy white lilies perched on the low Formica table by the bed, and a lone card formed a miniature pup tent on the wooden shelf under the flat screen TV.

The scene made it hard to visualize anything ever happening in there that might help someone, let alone instill hope. A leaden feeling spread from my chest to my limbs, and I looked down at my shoes. I had to force myself to keep moving. As I trudged through the doorway, Jan remained standing in the hall, hugging herself as she cried quietly.

I sensed my mother's weak, fading energy as soon as I crossed the threshold. She was barely there. I perched on the elderly chair beside her, held her hand, and opened my heart chakra. Perhaps I could feed her enough healing chi to animate her for a proper goodbye.

Mom's thin strawberry blonde hair showed gray roots and dangled over her shoulders, partially covered by the bedsheet, which nestled halfway up her neck. Her head rested on three pillows, propping her up in an unnatural position. Were she to open her eyes, she'd be peering at a painted wooden cross high on the wall above the TV. That wouldn't have suited her. One of her crosses to bear was, in fact, crosses—she was virulently anti-religion, including mine. In fact, Buddhism might have been her least favorite. She steadfastly believed that the Buddha had taught his followers to be passive fatalists, no matter how many times I explained this was not so.

Apparently, Mom had let go. As Jan had told me when she'd met me at the airport, our mother was staying alive for my sake, and now here I was. I would've liked to have seen her clear hazel eyes one last time or heard a few words before she passed. But my attempt to energize her failed. Within a few minutes, she was gone, her last breath an unnerving rattle. For some reason, the monitoring equipment failed to sound an alarm.

I continued to sit as my feelings arose—now all too nameable as raw grief, tears streaming down my cheeks. The tears morphed into sobbing. I hunched over, my head bobbing involuntarily over my knees. I was conscious of nothing but sadness.

After a time, my thoughts intruded. I would never be able to say goodbye—to tell Mom I loved her. I hadn't even done it while she lay in a coma in front of me!

I'd been busy with my self-absorbed chi nonsense. I'd put my need to interact with Mom ahead of her need to hear me say I loved her—to say good-bye. Coma or not, someone in her failing body was yearning to hear exactly that.

If I couldn't muster compassion for a loved one on her deathbed, what did that say about me? Were my years as a Buddhist nun wasted? And here I was now, *still* focused inward as I beat myself up. Minutes after my mother passed, I was back in Ivyville, the home of Ivy Lutz, the bad Buddhist.

The distraction my thinking provided did stop the tears—for a minute or two. And that was a relief. Then I began to sob again. The grief washed away the self-pity. Jan must've heard me, because a moment later, her hand landed on my shoulder and her sobs joined mine.

"She's gone," I managed to tell her, watching our mother's slack-jawed face.

"At least you got to say goodbye," she replied.

I cried harder.

Chapter Two

After Mom passed, standing by the nearest nurse's station with Jan, waiting to find out what we needed to do next, I wondered why my mother had been alone. Where was Dennis or her brother Brian? Or even a nurse? Was this any way to treat a stroke victim?

A huge clock on the wall ticked loudly, and a pungent antiseptic odor stung my nostrils. These, along with the insipid pop music from a radio on the desk behind the counter, irritated me. Life felt like my adversary, not the friend it had been a few days before.

Between bouts of tears, Jan explained that Dennis lay in another hospital bed downstairs, the victim of a woodworking accident. Uncle Brian had been working in Africa, so his flights wouldn't bring him into town until the next day. She didn't know where Mom's male nurse was.

"He's a nice guy," she told me. "Maybe he's off today."

If he'd passed muster with Jan, he was probably a saint.

"What has Uncle Brian been doing overseas this time?" I asked. We'd lost touch the last few years.

"He's been doctoring at a village medical clinic in one of those Central African places," Jan said. "You know, where wars killed off all the professionals."

"Isn't he a bit old to be doing something like that?

He must be in his early seventies."

"Hey, try telling him that when he gets here. You'll get an earful." She grimaced, perhaps remembering when she'd tried.

We tabled further discussion as an anorexic-looking young nurse approached us to tell us what happened when someone died in a hospital. Later, after signing various papers, we regrouped in a surprisingly upscale coffee shop in the basement. With dark brown, leather-clad booths and peppy young servers wearing black from head to toe, it was as if someone had transplanted a mid-level hotel restaurant into Saint Brigid's. Perhaps Catholic financial priorities were skewed toward food service, although I couldn't imagine why.

The air was redolent with artificial floral fragrance, spiked with the odor of bacon. The other diners in the sparsely filled room spoke in hushed voices, except for one disheveled teenaged girl who began wailing shortly after we were seated. Her mother attempted to soothe her with quiet words. When that didn't work, she placed her hand over her daughter's mouth, muffling, but not stopping the heartrending sound. A few seconds later, the mother hurriedly pulled her hand back. Perhaps the girl had bitten her, which I certainly would've considered doing.

Jan had used up her tears for now. She sat demurely, allowing me to begin our conversation once we'd ordered—coffee for her, tea for me.

"Did Dennis lose a limb or something?" I couldn't imagine what sort of woodworking accident would necessitate a hospital stay.

"No. It's all bullshit. His sister is the head administrator here—Agnes Somebody."

"Well, he must have a major injury of some sort."

Jan shook her head. The loose bits of hair on top of her head rocked sideways in unison, distracting me for a moment.

"His sleeve got caught in a lathe and pulled his forearm into a chisel," she told me. "Apparently, it gouged him down to the bone, but that's no reason to be here. He was here to make sure Mom didn't survive, and I don't know how he did it, but he found a way."

"So you think he hurt himself on purpose to have better access to Mom?"

"I know how that sounds, but I do think that, even if maybe she *did* have a stroke in the first place. She was getting better. The initial stroke wasn't going to be fatal. Then all of a sudden she took a turn for the worse. Then it was just a matter of time. You're going to prove Dennis killed her, Ivy. You owe the family that."

My hands fanned out of their own accord. "Why in the world would you think I'm qualified to do that?"

Jan reached across the table and took my hand. A first.

"I know we don't see eye to eye on much, and I know I can be a hothead. But you're a remarkable person, Ivy. You don't get upset, you know things you have no business knowing, and you're the smartest person I've ever met. I mean it. Half the mean things I've said to you over the years were nothing but envy."

I teared up again and squeezed her hand. "I appreciate this, Jan. Years ago, I yearned to hear it. Why the turnaround?"

"I'm a Unitarian-Universalist now."

"Good for you."

I didn't quite see how that would've gotten the job

done, given Jan's impulse control problem and emotional reactivity—symptoms of her mental health diagnosis.

"But I still don't see how I'm qualified to play detective," I protested. "Why not talk to the police?"

"I tried. That went nowhere. Listen, let me ask you a few things, and please answer honestly."

"Okay." I couldn't remember the last time I'd lied.

"Can you sense people's energy—what's going on inside, behind what they say?" Jan leaned forward, eager to hear my answer.

"Well, yes. Sometimes. But it's not a life skill that's particularly—"

"It's because you're spiritually advanced, right?" Jan prompted. Her energy was ramping up with each question. It was hard to get a word in edgewise now.

"No. I've explained that before. Remember? It's not because I have some vaunted status. It's just a side effect of meditating a lot."

Jan waved her hand, dismissing my assertion as false modesty. "So maybe you have other powers I don't even know about," she said, leaning even farther forward as if this might influence me to reveal them. "Maybe you're like a spiritual superhero or something."

"Absolutely not. I don't know where you're getting this from. That's not the way it works."

"Well, I'm sure you see what I'm saying. However snotty and annoying you can be, there's something special about you. Maybe Dennis can charm the police out of considering him a suspect, but he can't fool the likes of you."

I paused to consider how to respond. "Thank you for thinking so well of me, Jan. I appreciate that. But let me ask you this. Is there any physical evidence that Mom was murdered?"

"No, that's the problem. See? You focused on it right away. You're getting the hang of this already."

An unspiritual sigh leaked out of me. "All right. I'll talk to Dennis and see what I can find out. That's all I'm promising."

Jan clapped her hands together and then immediately pulled them down to her side, as though she were betraying Mom by not being sad.

I took a sip of the weak, awful tea that had finally arrived. Apparently, the hospital's food-service priority was limited to decor.

I stepped out of the moment and took a look at the situation from a more global perspective. Unless I did this periodically, I lost track of the values and principles I tried to live by. Adherence to these wasn't on autopilot the way it was for my teacher.

This was what the universe had presented, like it or not, I realized. My job was to cooperate with how things needed to be, and apparently playing detective was just that. For now.

****

"Let's go see Dennis," Jan said when we'd finished eating. "I want to see his face when we tell him Mom passed—you know, like on TV where the detectives see if the perp's reaction is authentic. Plus you need to get to work checking him out as a person."

"I'm pretty worn out, Jan."

"Oh, come on. We're right here in the hospital."

"All right," I agreed. Someone else would've registered my tone and backed off.

When I stopped to assess him from the hospital

hallway, my first impression of Dennis was positive. Sturdily built, with a barrel chest, he sat on the side of the bed, dressed, as he looked down at his phone. His bandaged forearm was visible. He wore a short-sleeved blue dress shirt and old-man jeans—the baggy kind that no millennial would be caught dead in. The white wrap on his arm extended from just below his elbow to several inches above his wrist. When I imagined what kind of down-to-the-bone wound might be that long, I shuddered.

Dennis's face was squarish and lined with age and sun damage. He looked to be in his late sixties. His attempts at disguising his balding pate were partially successful. He hadn't gone for a combover. Instead, he'd opted for a gelled comb forward, his graying brown hair frozen in place.

When he became aware of us and glanced up, his smile exuded confidence, and everything else about him beamed goodwill. His eyes looked out of place sitting atop his snub nose and wide mouth. They belonged on a woman, or at least most women would've been happy to have them. Big, brown, and alert, they were certainly his best feature.

Dennis rose and strode forward as we walked into his upscale hospital room. He held his meaty hand out to me, ignoring Jan, and I shook it.

"Dennis Sorenson. It's pleasure to meet you, even under these circumstances. Your mother is very proud of you."

He turned to my sister. "Hello, Jan," he intoned without warmth once he'd released his hand. "How is Lois? Any improvement? I just got permission to head up there."

17

"She's dead," Jan told him, keeping her voice neutral.

Here was the moment of truth. How would Dennis react?

His features froze, all traces of bonhomie gone. Then he blinked furiously and fell back onto the unmade bed.

"Jesus," he exclaimed. "Jesus Christ. I thought she was getting better."

"She was," Jan told him, "then she wasn't."

He crumpled into a ball and began crying, his head in his hands. "I knew something was going to happen," he muttered. "I knew it."

I could barely hear him. I glanced at Jan, who was glaring at him, the outside corners of her eyebrows raised, forming arrow-like lines aimed at her intense eyes.

"What?" she asked, raising her voice. "What was going to happen? Who did this?"

"I knew she wasn't safe up there. I knew it, and I didn't do anything." Then Dennis abruptly gathered himself, sat up, and dabbed at his eyes with the bandage on his arm. "Don't worry," he told us. "I'll take care of this."

"Take care of *what*?" Jan asked, raising her voice.

"Don't worry," he repeated.

Then his head snapped up, and he looked me in the eyes, all traces of grief gone. He was taking my measure, much as I was his.

I saw that Dennis may not have been who he seemed to be at first. His eyes betrayed him. Their cunning—now obvious—didn't match the rest of his face.

"As I said, I'll take care of all the arrangements,"

Dennis told us in a hale and hearty salesman's voice. "Louise was well loved. A philanthropist. A wonderful, wonderful woman. We'll have a big crowd at her memorial."

"That wasn't what you meant!" Jan told him. "You know something. What is it, you bastard!"

I grabbed her arm as she lunged forward, intent on God knows what.

"Jan, why don't you meet me out by the car. I think Dennis and I need to talk this over."

Her arm vibrated with energy as though she were plugged into a charging station. Her face was contorted with rage.

Surprisingly, she turned on her heel and stalked out without a word.

"Your sister and I have never gotten along," Dennis told me when she was gone, frowning and trying to run his fingers through his hair. There was no give. His fingers bounced off. Perhaps the hardened gel was confounding an old habit. "I'm not sure why," he added.

"You might take a look at your side of the street," I suggested. "How might you be contributing to the problem? That's usually a good approach when you're trying to understand a problematic relationship."

He nodded insincerely, as though he'd get right on it as soon as I left. I was tuning into him more and more as we talked.

"Be that as it may," I continued, "why don't we actually discuss the memorial service?"

I wanted to keep him talking, and a topic he'd introduced himself seemed as though it would have legs. I was curious to see if he'd keep projecting the same persona or try someone else. What would his behavior tell me?

"Good idea. There's a beautiful room at my country club, and I can get a discount since I'm a long-standing member—as was your mother. That's where we met."

"That sounds fine."

"Another piece of business is the reading of her will." He zeroed in on my eyes again as he told me this.

A chill ran up my spine. This time, his energy, reflected in his eyes and now radiating out to me, scared me. I'd only run across its like once before, when a pedophile had visited the temple.

I plunked down in the black leather armchair behind me—just inside the doorway. Somehow, I felt safer sitting, although nothing was likely to happen to me in that room.

It was a much nicer space than my mother's, the kind you paid a lot extra for. The exterior wall was all windows, with vertical wooden slats that were tilted open. I could see down the hill across the historic San Francisco neighborhood to the towers on Twin Peaks.

The door to the bathroom on my left was open; a burgundy ceramic basin perched on an almost-matching slab of granite. The floor looked to be white marble, which I would've thought presented a dangerous surface for injured patients.

A green leather recliner sat in the far corner of the hospital room, and the biggest TV I ever saw spanned the wall beside me, dwarfing everything.

"I believe Lois left almost everything to you, Jan, Jan's kids, and several charities," Dennis told me.

"No provisions for you?" I asked as sweetly as I could.

"Just a bit. She knew I'm doing fine. I retired with a

hefty pension, and I own an apartment building in Denmark. I have family over there who manage it for me. I hope you don't mind me talking about these things."

"Not at all."

Of course, it was actually weird to jump to these topics when Dennis had just received the news of his wife's death minutes before. Clearly, he was uncomfortable being vulnerable—exposed. He wanted to distract me away from the man who'd cried.

I thought about what he'd just told me about the will. Dennis was saying he didn't stand to gain from Mom's death. That was salient.

"I understand you're some sort of Buddhist?" he asked out of the blue.

"Yes," I answered.

"Does that make it easier for you when someone dies?"

I was struck by the way he'd phrased his question— leaving my mother out of it. He'd removed us from the here and now and brought us into a general, abstract topic.

"Yes, actually. When you believe in reincarnation, you believe we're just moving from one state to another when we drop our bodies. I may not meet my mother when her essential self comes back in a new body, but I know she has more karmic business to work out, so I know she's not done."

"Hmm, interesting. Aside from that, what's it like being a Buddhist?"

"I'm much happier than I used to be. And I'm more willing to be who I truly am."

"That's great. Good for you."

"I think that becoming our authentic selves is a

worthy goal," I added in my role as amateur sleuth. I was hoping his response would indicate his level of self-awareness.

Dennis flicked his eyes to the side, frowned briefly, and then produced a broad, insincere smile. I could almost see the gears whirring in his head. Was I onto him? Did I know there was an inner Dennis pulling the puppet strings of the guy in front of me?

I try not to judge people, especially in the first few minutes of meeting them, but even if Jan hadn't asked me to, I still couldn't have helped zeroing in on Dennis's song and dance as we continued to converse. Both his energy—his chi—and the incongruous expressions on his face as he continued to speak told the tale. For that matter, his body language seemed staged, the way a less-than-professional actor would hold himself in a play.

I was sure his current persona was nothing more than a collection of self-serving behaviors someone else inside him had adopted. He wasn't glad to meet me. He wasn't interested in Buddhism. He wasn't charming. He'd decided to act as though he were. That I perceived all this in a few minutes was a testament to the magnitude of Dennis's narcissism.

"I agree," he responded. "Integrity is the key, especially in business."

"What business are you in?"

"I'm retired. I sold medical supplies to big outfits—hospital chains, the military—you name it. Commissions have been kind to me. What about you? Did you have a profession before you started chasing nirvana?"

I was struck by the fact that his occupation represented a bit more weight on the guilty side of the balance scale. Dennis possessed medical knowledge. If my mother had been murdered, it would've been while she was in the hospital.

"Chasing nirvana" was certainly an offensive way of characterizing my spiritual path, but I attributed this to ignorance. Most Americans seemed to think that Buddhism embodied an ego-based goal—a permanent stay in Blissville.

"Years ago, I was interested in psychology," I told him, "and I still am, especially personality disorders."

That last part was a stretch, but I wanted to test the waters around his sense of self again. Some narcissists are fully aware of their diagnosis, although they certainly don't want it ferreted out by a professional.

His face betrayed nothing. He held his features still.

"I was in graduate school to become a therapist," I finished.

As I thought he might when I finally struck a sensitive nerve, Dennis told me he had something important to do in the administrative office of the hospital, and hustled me out the door.

****

"So what do you think, Ivy?" my sister asked as soon as I'd joined her at her car.

She leaned against the hood in sunlight, her arms crossed, before she raised one to shade her eyes.

"About Dennis?"

"Yes, of course. About Dennis."

Jan was still worked up. She pushed herself off the car and gestured emphatically back at the hospital entrance. Her dark, wavy hair swayed on top of her head without quite returning to vertical. The asymmetry distracted me.

"He's manipulative and quite good at it," I said as I

climbed into the passenger seat. "What he says and does is self-serving. There's a guy in there who is anything but charming."

Jan clambered into the driver's seat and exclaimed, "Yes! Exactly! Do you think he's capable of murder?"

"Probably not, Jan. People like that operate so much out of self-interest that the risk-reward has to be overwhelmingly tipped toward reward to act, and he told me he's getting very little from Mom's will. Plus, did you see how he reacted when you told him about her?"

"Maybe he's a great actor. And isn't he arrogant enough to think he could get away with it—that he's smarter than the cops?"

We'd both turned in our seats to face one another. Since Jan hadn't started the car, it was uncomfortably warm and stuffy. I knew that if I asked her to do something about that, she'd hear it as criticism—my saying she was doing something wrong.

"He probably does think he's smarter," I answered, "but I can't imagine that's enough of a motive by itself."

"Well, we don't know the whole story about the money," she protested energetically. One arm snaked out to gesture, but smacked with a thud against the steering wheel.

"I'm certainly not ruling him out just because of what he said to you," she continued. "Anyway, if he didn't do it, it sounds like he knows who did." She turned her head and frowned at me as she started the car, raising her voice as she continued, as if the muted engine noise required that. "We caught him off guard. I think he blew it and showed us he's mixed up in this. And what he said proves *something* bad happened. Mom didn't just fade away."

She glared at me as though what she'd said refuted a competing argument I'd just made.

"I'm just answering your question, Jan—giving you my inexpert opinion. I'm not trying to tell you what happened or what to think."

"Yeah, okay. What else did you two talk about?" Her tone was almost back on an even keel now.

"The memorial arrangements. And this and that. I asked a few telling questions to test my first impressions of him."

"I was thinking the country club might be a good place—maybe on Saturday if we can get the room on short notice. Mom loved it there."

"Sounds good. That's one thing you and Dennis agree on."

Chapter Three

Jan had won her family's home in a contentious divorce a few years earlier. Her ex was an ordinary guy who'd hit his limit with her reactivity. Splitting up hadn't brought out the best in either of them. If Brad had kept his inheritance separate instead of in a joint account, a great deal of suffering could've been averted. As it was, my sister lived in the splendor to which she was accustomed.

Jan's two-acre estate in Woodside, an aptly named upscale community a half hour south of San Francisco and a few miles west of Palo Alto, included a guesthouse—my lodging. The girls were asleep by the time we arrived a little after midnight.

As soon as I crossed the threshold of the guesthouse, I tossed my backpack onto the plush carpet in the living room, stumbled to a king-size bed in an adjoining room, and immediately fell into a deep sleep, waking up at six. Wherever I was, I woke up at six, local time. I guess my internal clock featured an automatic time-zone setting.

I found myself in an expansive bedroom, still fully clothed as I lay on my back, extremely thirsty. After peeing, I filled the glass next to the voluminous sink in the adjoining bathroom and gulped it down.

I looked around. A deep freestanding bathtub sat alongside one wall, its sides clad in copper, which clashed with the ochre Mexican tile behind it. Across the room, a glass-walled shower stall invited me to visit and wash off the accumulated grime from my trip.

I did so, which was delightful. The water pressure alone was a treat. On the other hand, climbing into my soiled clothes afterward served as a disappointing conclusion to the process. At least I'd brought a change of underwear, I thought—until I tried on my new bargain bra and panties. They itched as though they'd been created by a passive-aggressive, misogynist designer. I checked the tag inside my bra. Ninety percent polyester, ten percent cotton. The sign on the bin at the stall in Kegalle had read "The finest cotton underwear." I should have known better.

Could I tolerate itching? Was it preferable to feeling dirty or going braless and enduring men's ogling? I decided it was. I'd gotten used to worse during my sojourn overseas.

Next, I explored the rest of the guesthouse. Across from the bed I'd stumbled onto, a green marble fireplace soared higher than my head. Perched above that, another monstrous flat-screen TV was attached to the light gray wall, with no wires showing. Did it run on batteries? And who would want to lie in bed and crane their neck to watch it? The oil painting over the bed was in the style of Monet, only this lily pond encircled a tall, white obelisk, replete with a vertical row of hieroglyphics.

The living room of the guesthouse was more modest, with a pale blue loveseat and two matching armchairs surrounding a wrought-iron coffee table. Its glass top reflected the high, beamed ceiling, looking as though it were an entryway into a mirror-image basement.

I trod toward the kitchen in my stocking feet, slow

going given the thick, spongy gray carpet. I wondered why someone would intentionally make it difficult to move through the guesthouse. And why would someone want the carpet and walls to match? For that matter, gray certainly wasn't a cheery color to wake up to.

Noticing all this critical judgement, I took a few deep breaths. Of course it wasn't surprising that whoever built the estate had different taste and priorities than I did. I'd been happily living with a roommate in a tiny cell-like room with only one small window. Even in the States, before venturing to South Asia, I'd lived in cramped apartments, which were all I could afford.

I felt most comfortable in the kitchen. A small round oak table sat exactly in the middle of the square room. The appliances were basic contractor models, and the cream-colored composition counters were scarred by parallel knife marks beside the stainless-steel sink. The kitchen proved that someone else had actually stayed in the guesthouse.

After meditating for an hour on the living room floor—most of which entailed no thought whatsoever—a blessed relief—I strolled around the property in the flattering early morning light. It was cooler than it had been the evening before. I'd seen a hooded raincoat hanging on the back of the front door, and I wished I'd brought it, but not enough to go back and get it.

Jan's faux-Tudor two-story home would've dominated a typical lot. It was at least five thousand square feet, and my quarters to the side of the pool was probably another thousand.

The acreage was divided into sections. In front of the house, a drought-defying bright green lawn was bisected by a long asphalt driveway, which terminated in a wide arc that could've fit four or five cars. None were visible. Jan had parked the night before in a three-car garage beside the driveway.

An English-style garden decorated the near side of the house. It was immaculately groomed, with perfectly shaped topiary and colorful flower beds. Since it was April, the gardener's work was on glorious display. Jan hated to get her hands dirty, so I knew the display wasn't her handiwork. I especially liked the array of orange and red tulips which seemed to be competing to be the tallest flowers among the varieties surrounding them. Only a foot and a half tall, they nonetheless seemed to soar, filling the air with color.

A brick patio with upscale lawn furniture and a fire pit stretched across the width of the house at the rear, and a good-sized kidney-shaped swimming pool gently sloshed behind that. The shimmering patterns of light on its surface varied as the wind shifted nearby tree branches that were in line with the rising sun.

I ventured beyond the shoulder-height hedge that formed a border beyond the pool into my favorite part of the property—a grove of live oak, bay, pine, and madrone trees. I could barely see a neighbor—just one modern white home through a tangle of live oaks. I've always loved the patterns that tree limbs create, especially in collaboration with other trees. It's as if they know what would constitute a pleasing scenario.

When I was ready to face the world, I opened the sliding kitchen door at the rear of the house that overlooked the patio. My younger niece Dee—the fourteen-year-old—sat at one end of a long teak table, reading a Pema Chodron book. I hadn't seen her in person since she was an infant, but it was easy to recognize her from recent photos. Short, with long honey-blonde hair, and a bit overweight, she radiated alertness when she looked up. I'd met a few teens at the temple who naturally lived in the moment. Was my niece another one?

I immediately felt a sense of kinship with Dee. Perhaps she was an old soul in a young body—the product of countless lifetimes. Old souls, after all, could wear faded denim overalls and purple ski caps the same as anyone else.

"Aunt Ivy, I presume." She rose and shook my hand as I approached her. Hers was small, warm, and surprisingly firm. I smelled coconut, which I assumed was the fragrance of her shampoo or conditioner. Her hair glistened with moisture from a recent shower. She was barefoot.

"Indeed. And you must be Dee, my new favorite niece."

"Don't let Holly hear that. Her sense of humor is rather stunted."

She emphasized the word "stunted," as though she wanted to make sure I noticed her vocabulary skills.

"I'll keep that in mind. Is there any tea?"

"Of course. Let me get it for you."

When she rose and turned around, Dee's denim overalls didn't turn all the way with her. There was room enough in there for two nieces. Was she hiding her figure as I had at her age? I hoped it wasn't a response to sexual trauma.

Dee bustled at the counter across the table from where I'd sat down. I asked her how she liked the Chodron book.

"I'm reading it in preparation for your visit," she

told me.

I looked at her progress in the bookmarked paperback on the table. "You're almost all the way through it already? Or did you know something I didn't about my coming here?"

She turned and smiled. "Actually, it's slower going than most of what I read because it's so thought-provoking." Once again, she seemed proud to be able to say that. "Does she speak for all Buddhists?"

"No, but her take on things is more universal than most. I had an opportunity to meet her. She's a delight."

"Is there some conference where all you bigwigs go and hang out?" Her eyes reflected her interest in my answer. She wanted me to have hobnobbed with celebrity spiritual teachers.

"I'm not a bigwig, Dee. Where did you get that idea?"

"From Mom. You're enlightened, right?" Now she returned to the table while the water worked its way toward a boil.

"No. And I'm not sure that word has any meaning."

Dee considered what I'd said while I looked around the kitchen. Everything was exactly in place, as though an OCD maid had finished her work a few minutes previously. A six-slot toaster squatted on a black stone counter next to an enormous wood-clad refrigerator. Perfectly positioned beside that, its edges exactly lined up with its neighboring appliance, a tall, expensive-looking blender proclaimed that food could be torn apart at twelve different speeds. Even the tall, stainless steel trash bin gleamed back at me from a perfect ninety-degree angle beside the far wall.

"That's a very unsatisfying answer," Dee finally

said. "How could a word not mean something?"

"I imagine you're accustomed to being dissatisfied with the answers you receive from other people."

She nodded. "That's astute." Then she cocked her head and studied my face. "But I expected more from you."

She headed to the counter to procure the whistling teapot, and then poured hot water into my mug upon her return. A sad-looking teabag bobbed in there. My disappointment clued me in that I had become a tea snob. The fantastic brews from nearby tea plantations in the Sri Lankan highlands had spoiled me. The day before, at the hospital, I hadn't minded the pallid flavor as much as I anticipated I would today.

Dee nodded vigorously. "Maybe the problem here is that you're not matching the template I constructed in my head."

"Are you really fourteen?"

"Yes." She paused again, a wide smile splitting the bottom of her face. "I'm told I'm unusually gifted." She tucked a strand of blonde hair behind her ear.

I sipped my tea, which, of course, was awful.

Jan ambled into the kitchen wearing a fuzzy white robe—the kind expensive hotels hung in guests' closets. Her hair cascaded onto her narrow shoulders, framing her similarly narrow face. She wore no makeup. To my eyes, she looked better that way. Jan yawned before speaking.

"Brainwashing my daughter? Turning her into a cult robot?"

We both stared at her.

Jan laughed. "Just kidding. Don't let me interrupt."

"No worries," I told her. "Good morning."

My sister continued as if I hadn't spoken. "I can't think of anyone less likely to be brainwashed, Ivy. I haven't even been able to convince Dee to wear normal clothes."

"Mother, what constitutes normal? That's a completely subjective term, in my opinion." Dee asserted this while gesturing with her right hand. She held up her index finger as though she were indicating the first item on a list.

Jan turned to me, her hands on her hips. Her robe was threatening to gape open, and apparently she was nude underneath. "See? You see what I'm dealing with?"

"I see a delightful, curious free-thinker," I responded. "That's my experience."

"Thank you," Dee said, smiling broadly.

Validation was probably in short supply in her life, especially from her volatile mother.

"That's easy for you to say," Jan responded, addressing my positive description of Dee. "Try being her mother."

She clasped her robe closed and glared at me. For some mothers, complimenting her child was tantamount to complimenting them. For Jan, it represented an annoying challenge to her negative assessment.

"Try being your daughter," my niece replied.

The strand of nair she'd tucked earlier flopped off the top of her ear back onto her cheek. This time she left it.

"It all depends on your vantage point, doesn't it?" I said, attempting to divert what might be revving up into a full-scale argument.

"That's what I was saying," Dee said. "You know, about the word 'normal' being subjective."

"Whatever." Jan waved her hand airily. "Is there coffee?"

"Not yet," Dee answered.

"Why not?" Her tone was inappropriately sharp.

"I didn't know when you'd get up or if Aunt Ivy drank it," Dee replied hurriedly.

Jan shuffled in her blue quilted slippers to the other side of the room and opened and closed several cabinet doors emphatically as she hunted for coffee-making gear. It seemed odd she wouldn't know where things were in her own kitchen.

"Has anyone seen Holly?" she asked.

"She was still in bed when I checked a while ago," Dee said.

"Well, go get her up. We have a lot to do today."

Dee wandered away, and Jan sat down next to me at the table after starting the coffeemaker, an anomalously modest device next to the twin stainless-steel sinks.

"I'm glad you're here. These girls haven't had a male role model for years, and you're probably the next best thing."

"I'm finding it hard to take that as a compliment," I told her. "What about their dad? My understanding is he lives nearby."

"Brad is useless as a role model, unless you want your kids to be lying cheaters who always put themselves first. The girls are old enough to see this for themselves, so they don't spend much time with him."

"That's a shame."

"I thought you didn't believe in shame—or even anything ever going wrong. Isn't that part of Buddhism—that everything happens the way it's supposed to?"

She wasn't angry—just curious. "'It's a shame' is just a figure of speech, Jan. What I meant is that I feel compassion."

"Including for Brad?"

"Yes. It's probably even less fun being him than being around him."

She thought about that. "I'm sure that's true, but I don't care."

Jan sighed heavily as Dee and Holly trooped into the spacious kitchen.

I stood. "Hello, Holly. I've been looking forward to seeing you again."

"Yeah, me too," she said without conviction.

She hugged me perfunctorily and plunked down in a chair across the table from me. "What's for breakfast?"

"Why don't I make something?" I said. "I need to earn my room and board."

"I'll have scrambled eggs," Holly said. "And bacon and toast. Can you do that?"

"Sure. I'll just need some help finding things."

"I'll help," Dee said.

"Any other orders?"

Jan and Dee settled on the same breakfast, probably to make things easier for me.

Holly typed on her huge phone as Dee gathered cooking gear. My older niece slouched in an elongated C shape, her slender but strong-looking legs straight ahead of her under the table. She wore khaki shorts and a cream-colored T-shirt with "Get a Life" written across her modest chest. A pixie-style haircut constituted the only evidence of playfulness or youth. It softened the scowlish set of her wide mouth, and the studied indifference of the rest of her long face. I liked her eyes, which were a startling shade of blue.

I wondered why Holly was being so hostile. Was it about me in particular or just any adult? My older niece and I had so little history with one another, it was hard to imagine she resented me.

As Dee pulled ingredients out of the fridge, she turned to me. "Are you going to be grossed out by bacon? You're a vegetarian, right?"

"I'll manage."

"No, really. We can skip it if it's going to ruin your day."

"I appreciate your concern." I glanced at the others. Both were on their phones now, and Holly continued to type furiously. "But if I can't put my own needs to the side in a situation like this, what then? Next thing you know, I'll be making everyone live exactly the way I do."

"Would that be so bad? Isn't your way a good way?"

"For me. I don't know that good or bad applies to the variety of other people's life experiences."

Dee handed me the eggs and shoved a blue ceramic mixing bowl across the counter. I cracked open the last of the eggs and began whisking.

"I don't understand," she said, her face reddening. "Why wouldn't it?"

"Hallelujah!" Jan crowed from behind us at the table. "There's *something* she doesn't understand."

I hadn't realized that Jan was tracking our conversation.

"You don't have to understand everything, Dee," I told her. "Rest in your confusion."

"I don't understand that, either. That doesn't make sense. It fact, it sounds stupid. *Rest in your confusion.* That's fortune-cookie crap." Her voice rose as she spoke.

Breakfast was almost ready. "Why don't you grab the plates and silverware?" I suggested. "We'll continue this conversation later."

"No! I want to know now! What did you mean?"

"Sorry."

"This isn't fair!"

"No, it isn't," I agreed amiably.

Her mouth formed a classic childish pout, and she stomped to a cabinet and noisily gathered plates. After she set the table in emphatic fashion and helped herself to eggs and toast, she resumed stomping, all the way out the door of the kitchen, her plate in her hand.

"She's still a fourteen-year-old at heart," Jan said. "And sometimes a ten-year-old. Don't take it personally."

"Of course not."

"She's not the worst little sister in the world," Holly added, looking up at me for the first time. "But you should see her at school. It's embarrassing. One minute, she's Einstein, which nobody likes, believe me. She makes everybody feel dumb. Then the next minute, she's like a little kid—so immature you wonder where her big brain went."

"It must be hard for her," I said.

"Well, sure. But what about me?" Holly pointed at her chest and jabbed, stopping just short of spearing herself. "She likes being like that. I'm the one who's stuck with it. You hear about kids trying to live up to their older sister's grades and all. This is the other way around. Teachers who have never even met Dee expect me to ace all their tests."

"So do you have difficulty getting along with one another?"

"Sometimes. We're just so different."

"I get it. Your mom and I are really different, too. Growing up, we didn't always get along."

During the meal, I tried to draw Holly out. "Tell me about yourself."

"Why?"

"I'd like to get to know you."

"You've had plenty of chances for the last fifteen years, haven't you? I didn't see you bothering when I could've used an aunt in my life." Her scowl took over her face.

There was my answer. She resented my absence, perhaps fantasizing that everything would've been all right if I'd only stayed in town, which certainly wasn't true.

"During the divorce, you mean?" I asked.

She nodded. "Mom was an even bigger basket case than usual back then."

Before Jan could react, I spoke again. "I'm sorry. I can see now that hiding in a religious community was a disservice to my family."

"Damn straight. And now it's too late. I'm doing just fine, and I don't care about all your mumbo jumbo."

Dee came back with her empty plate. "Sorry, Aunt Ivy. I get frustrated."

"No worries. Me, too."

"You probably don't act out and then run out of the room, though, do you?" Jan asked.

"Not lately."

"Anyway," Dee continued with an edge to her tone, "I said I was sorry, so let's forget about it, okay?"

"Sure."

Jan assigned the clean-up to her daughters and

invited me to take a walk with her around the neighborhood.

I knew Woodside, but since I'd last visited, Silicon Valley tech workers had been buying homes, knocking them down, and then constructing sprawling estates that almost filled their oversized lots. My sister gestured emphatically at a few prime examples as she decried the changes.

"These monstrosities are just so ugly. I know they add value to the neighborhood and they're good investments, but honestly, can you imagine building any of these? Look at that squatty one with all the round windows. What were they thinking?"

As a real estate agent, Jan's commentary eventually shifted to all the sales commissions she'd lost to other agents.

"I live here. These people know me—well, some of them do. Why are they going to strangers in Palo Alto?"

I should've left that alone, but I'd always been a sucker for a rhetorical question. "So you get along well with your neighbors, Jan?"

I knew that wasn't the case. She never had, since it didn't take much to trigger her wrath. A poorly mowed lawn, Christmas lights she deemed too gaudy, or even five minutes of a dog barking, and she banged on doors.

"They don't have to like me," Jan said, glaring at me. "Liking people isn't always what something is about, Ms. Popular." Jan was simmering but not boiling yet.

I tried to head that off at the pass, despite an urge to point out I'd never been particularly popular. "Sorry. You're right. It's about how good a job you'd do, and I have no doubt you're really good at your job."

"I am."

To my eye, most of the new homes embodied creative, eye-catching architecture, and some owners had matched their home to the land surrounding it. I rather liked the majority of them, not that I voiced that in response to Jan's rant.

"So what's next?" I asked her when she seemed to have calmed down. "What's our day look like?"

"We're having lunch with Uncle Brian, and I called Dennis first thing this morning and arranged for us to meet him at Mom's this afternoon. I told him it was about planning the memorial service."

"Sounds good."

She raised her voice. She was still upset. "That doesn't mean anything, does it? Everything sounds good to you."

"Jan, let's try to clear the air." She sped up and I quickened my pace to stay beside her. "What's your problem with me? Honestly, why all this hostility? One minute you're complimenting me, the next you're attacking me."

She stopped suddenly and turned to face me as a car drove by. "You want to know? You really want to know?"

I nodded.

"I suffer, Mom suffered—everyone suffers. Except for you. You breeze through life. It all goes your way. It all falls into place."

I'd expected anger behind her words. Instead, I felt her hurt and her envy, which I realized were her primary emotions. Jan usually jumped from uncomfortable feelings to one she liked better—anger. Not this time.

I paused to craft a thoughtful response. "It hasn't

been an easy path to get to where I am now—to where there's truth to what you're saying. True, life isn't the sort of struggle for me it was when I was younger. But I don't want to compare suffering."

"I'll bet you don't. Because you'd lose, big time. Here I am, raising two kids as a single mother and fighting off diabetes. You didn't even know about that, did you? My blood sugar is all over the place. And you know about my bipolar."

"I'm sorry it's been so hard for you, Jan."

"You just skated through the whole thing with your nun deal. It's like you're a life dropout instead of a college dropout. We're all playing the game by the rules, and you're doing whatever your so-called teacher tells you to do without a thought about anyone else."

"Not exactly."

"So what is it instead?" Her voice softened. "I'd actually like to know, because I know you're not a selfish jerk at heart, Ivy. I do."

"Let me start by acknowledging the validity of much of what you said." We began walking again. "I did drop out of ordinary life, and I can see now that when I joined the sangha, I was trying to escape my problems instead of solving them. As the years went by and I made progress, I never truly reevaluated my original decision to be there since I could see how Bhante was helping me."

Jan pivoted and started back to the house. I hustled to keep up.

"The main thing I got from all the meditating," I continued, "is a commitment to kindness. Not just kind acts, but an internal positive regard for everyone and their circumstances. I struggle with it, but that's my orientation, and I can't imagine anyone having a problem with that. Should I be less loving, less accepting? How would that serve anyone?"

"Maybe I want that too, but I can't have it."

"Why not?"

"Because I have a *life*!" Jan exploded. "How do you have kids and a job and have the time to get all the good stuff you've got? Do you think I like being so angry? Do you think I even want to be having this conversation? I know I'm being unreasonable. I know it's envy. I can't stop."

"Have you tried therapy?"

"No, actually."

"Why not? It helped me a great deal."

"I'm scared. What if I find out I'm even worse off than I think? A shrink is bad enough. I don't need a therapist, too." My sister turned to me, hoping I'd agree with her now that she'd explained.

"Jan, I can't put myself in your shoes, and I don't really know what you ought to do. I just want to help in whatever way I can. I'm sorry if I do that poorly sometimes."

Jan reached out and hugged me. "I know you do your best," she said between sudden tears. "I think I'm pissed off about Mom more than anything."

"That's understandable."

I held her while she cried. Then we trooped back to the house.

Chapter Four

Uncle Brian had picked the restaurant for lunch—an upscale Cambodian place in downtown Palo Alto, a few blocks from the Stanford campus, and a mile or so from where I'd grown up. As Jan and I walked in, the ornate decor distracted me from picking out Brian from the other diners.

A tall, carved teak folding screen sat diagonally a few steps into the Mekong Joy, shielding us from an empty room to the left of the main dining room. Through cutouts in the floral design, I spied colorful paintings of Buddha and his followers on its walls. In Southeast Asian style, he was portrayed as slim and somewhat androgynous.

Photo murals of Angkor Wat and several other ruins I didn't know lined the walls of the main room. In the murals, a few people stood by the monuments, peering out at the diners as if to say *they* were the ones having the authentic Cambodian experience.

The carved tables and chairs matched the folding screen, although glass tops had been affixed to the tables. Persian-looking carpets were scattered on the wood floor, looking as out of place as we were in the decidedly Southeast Asian environment.

Jan took my arm and directed us to a table near the back, against the side wall. Brian stood and smiled. About six foot three, half a head taller than my five foot eight, his fit, lean frame bespoke a much younger man. Only when we were shaking hands could I see the deep lines around his eyes and mouth that few septuagenarians could avoid.

He was still movie star handsome, with gleaming white teeth, and a cleft chin. His pale blue eyes flanked a long, aquiline nose—somewhat like a slightly truncated version of Jan's. His head of brown hair was exactly that—a full pate with no sign of retreat. A royal blue fatigue sweater fit him perfectly, as did black slacks. He wore a pair of well-worn tan hiking books.

"It's great to see you both," he said as we all sat, which our diminutive hostess had been patiently waiting for us to do. After she'd handed out oversized, rattan-covered menus, she bowed and sidled away. Her formal behavior reminded me of several Sri Lankan nuns at the temple. Only time and gentle humor had melted their adherence to traditional gender roles.

"How long has it been since we've all been in the same room?" Jan asked, stroking her menu as if it were a pet.

"I have no idea," Brian replied.

"Fourteen and a half years," I said. "Christmas at Mom's."

"How are you two holding up?" Brian asked.

"I'm very upset and I'll tell you why in a moment," Jan said. "It's not just Mom passing."

Brian took this in stride, turned to me, and raised an eyebrow. "And you, Ivy?"

"I'm fine," I said.

"Your training gives you a non-mainstream perspective on death, eh?"

"Yes. How were your flights? You must be

exhausted."

"I am," he said, although I could detect no sign of this. "African airlines are a bit terrifying. The plane was old—no longer safe to fly in its country of origin. Water dripped down from fissures in the ceiling, and my seat wobbled. But once I was ensconced on a British Airways flight, it was only tedium I faced."

Sometimes Brian spoke as if he were still lecturing other physicians about ethics. Spending time in developing countries seemed to expand his working vocabulary. Perhaps the scarcity of opportunities to use GRE words made proper English a treat for him.

"Let's get to the business at hand," he said. "Jan, I presume you're upset about the nefarious Dennis. Tell me why you suspect him of foul play."

"How do you know about that?"

"A little bird told me."

"Dee?" I asked.

Brian nodded.

"I should've known she'd figure it out," Jan said, shaking her head with a mixture of pride and annoyance. Then she stared off into space.

"Let's look at our menus," I suggested. I could see Jan wasn't ready to talk about Mom yet.

The name of every item was not only in Cambodian, but the descriptions of the dishes were as well. I glanced around the crowded room. Everyone else was Asian.

"I recommend number eleven," Brian said, "although I can't say the name of it without revealing my abject ignorance of the language. It's something like a curry. Vegetarian, Ivy."

"Great." People tended to focus on my diet more than anything else about my religion. Perhaps, deep down, they felt uncomfortable devouring animals.

"I think I'll quiz our server," Jan said. "I need meat."

Another tiny Asian woman scurried up to our table. She must've been standing a few steps behind me. "Meat. Yes, we have meat. Pork, beef, you tell me what you want."

This striking young woman bowed, too, which seemed unnatural in her case. Perhaps the manager demanded that all the employees honor diners this way.

What stood out for me in the server's face was a combination of a model's high, distinct cheekbones, with very soft-looking skin stretched across it. Her skin tone was darker than the Cambodians I'd met overseas. And she wore a pendant I was familiar with—a silver flower of life in the South Indian style.

I took a chance and spoke Tamil to her. "You're not Cambodian, are you?"

She smiled radiantly. "No. How wonderful to hear my language. I'm from a village near Goa," she replied in Tamil.

"I love Goa," I told her. "At least, away from the tourist beaches."

"Yes. It is very beautiful, but the city people are mean—like here."

"Why did you come?"

Jan and Brian watched me. The former with impatience, the latter with interest.

Our server sighed. "Love, or so I thought."

"Hang in there. When I moved to Asia, it took time to adjust."

She nodded, and looked at Jan, who was obviously agitated at this point—ready to order.

Jan engaged the young woman in a long discussion

about the carnivorous options. Some of their interaction resembled an Abbot and Costello routine. After our server had taken all our orders, relieved to simply hear the number eleven from me and Brian, Jan spoke again, looking at our uncle.

"First of all, Dennis is a narcissist and maybe a sociopath. He's charming, or so it seems, but behind closed doors with Mom, it was a different story. He supposedly has money of his own—I checked him out when they became engaged—but I'm not sure that's true. He may have corrupted my investigator or lost his money since he married Mom. I know he has a gambling problem. And his first wife died, too."

"Under what circumstances?" I asked.

"Well, they say she had cancer, but you never know."

"I don't like the sound of him," Brian said. "Tell us more. How do you know it wasn't natural causes with Lois?"

My uncle's use of my mother's first name reminded me that neither Jan nor I had used it so far. She was Mom to us—her role trumped her name.

"Mom was healthy," Jan replied. "She had a physical a few months ago. Her doctor said that strokes can just happen with no precursor conditions, but I've never heard of that. And they said in the emergency room that she'd recover after they did a bunch of tests. She might need rehab, this Indian doctor told me, but we could expect to bring her home in a day or two."

"What happened?" Brian asked.

"While she was supposedly alone in the ICU, she suddenly got worse," Jan told him.

"Did they say why?"

"No, nobody could explain it. Not medically."

"What do you think, Brian?" I asked. "As a physician, I mean."

"It *is* possible to have a stroke without a known pre-existing condition," he said, "but that's not the norm. And sometimes an initial stroke makes it more likely to have another, bigger one. Once again, *that's* not common. Put the two circumstances together and you have a puzzle. If Lois initially endured an atypical stroke that didn't involve a history of a blocked artery or a compromised blood vessel, she shouldn't have had any follow-up strokes."

"I knew it!" Jan exclaimed.

"What else can you tell me?" our uncle asked.

"Dennis could've been alone with Mom in her hospital room because he was in a room nearby."

"Why's that?"

"He gouged his arm on a chisel. That's no reason to be overnight in a hospital, is it? You're a doctor. I'm right, aren't I?"

"It depends. Any deep wound from a non-sterile blade is at risk of infection. Sometimes it makes sense to hold someone for observation to head off a serious infection like sepsis."

Jan frowned, and her eyes glowered. Apparently, Uncle Brian was supposed to agree with her, no matter what his actual medical opinion was.

I remembered when we were kids how Jan would demand instant compliance from me if something was important to her. Our mother had tried to talk to teen-aged Jan about her entitlement issues, which, ironically, triggered her to become more entitled. She didn't deserve criticism from her own mother, she told her. She was entitled to be left alone to do her life her way.

"Well, he is her husband, Jan," I said. "If he visited Mom in her room, wouldn't that be normal behavior?"

"Maybe. But what are we supposed to look at when there's a murder?" Jan asked. "Motive, opportunity, and something else I don't remember. I looked it up. So his being there is the opportunity part."

"Let's stipulate he had opportunity," Brian said. "What about motive?"

"I haven't seen Mom's will, and I don't know if there was a prenup or a life insurance policy, but either of those would be a motive," Jan told him.

"Did the police check into those when you raised your concerns?" Brian asked.

"They said they did, and that Dennis wouldn't get much, but you never know. Nobody let *me* look. Don't you think that's suspicious?"

"Not necessarily. We'll find out more soon," I said.

"Why are you two being like this?" Jan asked without the emotional heat I'd come to expect.

"How are you experiencing us?" I asked. "I'm not sure how to respond."

"It's like you're defending Dennis. Everything I say, you and Uncle Brian push back. Well, except for the part about strokes. I told you what I need—how you can make up for your ditching our family, Ivy. Nail the son of a bitch!"

The anger was back—displaced and aimed at us since Dennis, the real target, wasn't available. Putting aside Jan's personality, some people with bipolar disorder rapidly shift emotions in unpredictable ways. Jan, at least, could be counted on to alternate between just two—reasonable and enraged. You'd get one or the other. All you could do was hope the dice would come up reasonable more often than not.

"We're all on the same side here, Jan," I told her. "Brian and I are just trying to understand."

He nodded. "All is well. Let's move on. I suggest I do a bit of research about how someone could murder a stroke victim without leaving any traces. I know a fellow physician who does forensic work. Perhaps he could lend some relevant insight."

Jan smiled. "Now we're getting somewhere. What should I do?"

Unleashing Jan wasn't likely to help matters. "I suggest you lay low until Brian and I get more information," I told her. "We don't want to tip off Dennis that we're investigating him."

I glanced at Brian, and he winked. We both knew that keeping my sister at bay was a good idea.

Our food arrived, and as promised, it was delicious. Brian regaled us with stories about his stints at clinics in Peru and Malaysia. Most of these centered on novel medical solutions when supplies weren't available, but several detailed romantic encounters, which seemed inappropriate to me. Perhaps he was trying to emphasize his vitality now that he was older. Vital or not, why would someone tell his nieces about a one-night stand with a twenty-six-year-old nurse?

On the way out, I heard my name called by a familiar, high-pitched voice.

"Ivy! Over here!"

"Sue!" I called back, and hurried over to her table. She must've come in while I was sitting facing away from the door.

Sue had been my next-door neighbor for most of my

childhood. All these years later, she still layered on her makeup with a trowel, especially the purple eyeshadow above her deep-set brown eyes. An obvious dye job and perm had transformed her into a curly-headed platinum blonde with non-matching eyebrows and skin tone. Sue's sleeveless top also revealed the top of her substantial bosom, split by a green crystal pendant.

Sue had expanded, especially in the middle, but her wide, toothy smile and crinkles at the corners of her eyes lent her an attractive female Santa look. A stranger would expect her to be jolly—or at least merry, assuming there was a difference between the two.

"Sit, sit." Sue gestured as though she were offering me the throne of a good-sized nation.

"I'm with my sister and my uncle." I glanced at them through the window. They were chatting on the sidewalk.

"Come on. Sit. I'll give you a ride wherever you want when we're done. We *have* to catch up."

I was fond of Sue, despite her quirks, and once again, here was what the universe had placed in my path. The very unlikeliness of our running into one another hinted at the possible significance of the meeting. I'd noticed that the more the universe had to work at setting something up—the more amazing a coincidence something was—the more it was worthy of my attention. Why bother orchestrating something so elaborate unless it mattered?

"Hold on," I said, and strode out to my family. I explained the situation.

"Just meet us at Mom's house at three, Ivy," Jan said. "That's when we see Dennis."

"Sure."

I returned and sat across from Sue, who slurped soup as nearby Asian diners shot her disapproving glares.

"So, this is what a Buddhist nun looks like? Honestly, you could wear a jail jumpsuit and look better than me. Look at your complexion. And those eyes. But it's all a waste, isn't it? No men for you."

"We'll see," I said.

"What do you mean?" Her raised eyebrows and head tilt indicated her particular interest in the topic. Sue was a very sensual person, which had gotten her into a lot of trouble in high school. Unfortunately, I'd heard that her reputation had followed her to college in Southern California.

"I'm back in the world with no restrictions, Sue. I have no idea what the future holds."

"That's great! So let's get drunk, shoot some heroin, and hire male hookers. After that, we can stick up a convenience store."

I laughed. "Sounds like a plan."

"Why the change of heart? Oh, and by the way, I do mindfulness now. It's great!"

"Good for you. We can all learn to pay more attention to our own experience, can't we?"

"You're just chock full of wisdom now, aren't you? Tell me more. And I still want to know why you left Sri Lanka."

"My mother just died, actually." I felt a tear leak out of one eye, surprising me.

"Oh, I'm so sorry! Lois was the best. Remember all those times she let me stay over when my parents were fighting, and she even brought me along on that trip to Disneyland. You know, when I threw up all over the park?" Sue smiled. The once-embarrassing memory had morphed into an amusing anecdote.

"Who could forget that? It was epic, Sue."

She laughed. "If a job's worth doing, it's worth doing well. Your mom taught me that, actually."

"I'm not sure she had vomiting in mind."

"Whatever." She paused to slurp her soup. "This is *so* good, Ivy. I come here at least once a week for this soup. Ask for number thirty-eight. I don't really know what it is. My hairdresser turned me on to it."

"Thanks. I'll try it next time."

Back to slurping.

"How did she pass?" Sue finally asked, lowering her spoon sloppily, spilling what remained on it onto the glass tabletop.

"A massive stroke." The words made her death even more final. I repeated them in my head.

"Well, at least it was painless, and who knows? Maybe she's better off with the way the world's going."

"How's that?"

"You know. The environment. All the rotten kids with their devices stuck to their ears." Sue held a hand up to her own ear in such a practiced fashion that I knew she was no stranger to smartphones. "This is the generation that's going to run things someday?" She shook her head and rolled her big brown eyes, drawing my attention to her false eyelashes.

I'd tried enhancing my eyelashes once. Just once—the same number of times as high heels. Jewelry lasted a little bit longer. So many women's efforts to fool the eye result in them not only looking less like themselves, but also less like *anyone*. Even shaved legs look plastic to me—as though someone lost theirs in a terrible accident.

It's like my least favorite aspect of Catholicism—

original sin. Apparently, Americans believe we're born with original ugliness. In both cases, if we buy into the paradigm, we have to work hard—and spend money—to become okay.

"What's new in your life?" I asked.

"I just split up with the latest loser. Can you believe it? He wanted to have a three-way with my sister."

"Claire?"

"No, the other one—Hannah. He even talked to her about it. That's how I found out." She shook her head and held back tears. "I thought he was the one."

"How disappointing—and hurtful. I can't imagine."

I truly couldn't. Sue lived in a different universe.

"Otherwise, things are good," she continued. "I got a promotion at the office, and I'm working on a book. A mystery." She grinned with pride. Her version was more overt than Dee's had been.

"You're writing now?" I was surprised. Sue hadn't been at all successful in school, except as a softball pitcher.

She nodded. "I love it. I'm going to self-publish."

"What's your book about?"

"There's this woman who's a sculptor and her husband is the main suspect, but he didn't do it."

I thought I may have discovered why we'd run into one another. "Did you do research about murder methods?"

"Yes, a lot."

"What do you know about how to make a murder look like a stroke?"

"Nothing. My victim is poisoned by the murderer putting this toxic powder on her steering wheel. Why do you ask?"

I started to answer.

"Wait a minute," Sue broke in. "You think someone killed Lois?"

"Jan does. I'm not sure."

"Wow. I don't know what to say." Her jaw actually dropped, exposing uneven lower teeth.

"So far, the police haven't been a help," I added.

"You should call Rick Foster—remember him? He's a cop now. We went out for a while about five years ago. He's a straight shooter, but he was hopeless in bed. Plus I think he has PTSD from some police thing he was involved in. They've got him sitting at a desk now. Poor guy."

That was interesting. I'd dated Rick in high school myself. Was he making the rounds of the social clique I'd belonged to back then? And did Sue have unrealistic bedroom standards? I'd been happy with Rick's performance, albeit based on a single digit sample.

"Maybe you can drop me off at the police station when we're through," I said. I knew it was harder to say no to a request in person, and it would be nice to catch up with Rick in any case.

"Sure."

She'd steered me to Rick. That was what this was about.

Sue finished her meal while we discussed mutual friends and how the town had changed.

Sitting up high in Sue's mammoth SUV on the way to the police station was a new experience for me. I liked being able to see more. Most of the other vehicles I spied on the way to the police station were also SUVs. That was new, too.

Chapter Five

I needed to climb a flight of steep stairs to reach the doors of the modern white building that housed the Palo Alto police department. Narrow vertical windows marched across the face of it, and my overall impression was that the city had been more interested in innovative architecture than providing what the force might need.

The empty lobby was smaller than the ones I'd seen on TV, with a row of empty airport-style attached chairs against a side wall. I stepped forward, slid, and almost fell on the freshly mopped beige linoleum floor. A yellow plastic pylon announcing the danger in English and Spanish lay tipped over in front of one of the chairs. I detoured to right it and move it to a more visible spot.

As I was doing so, a tall uniformed woman exited a door I hadn't noticed to my right.

"Good for you," she said. "It's a favorite pastime for perps leaving the building—kicking things."

I smiled and nodded. She smiled back. So far, so good.

The slender Asian man manning the glass-enclosed counter greeted me with a big smile and a howdy.

"Howdy back," I said. "You make me think of the old westerns I used to watch with my dad."

"I'm trying it on for size. I went with 'good day' last week, but people didn't seem to like it. What can I do for you? Here to turn yourself in for some heinous crime?"

"That's right. I stole the Golden Gate Bridge, and now I see the error of my ways."

"Splendid. Any other business?"

"I'm an old friend of Rick Foster, and I'd like to say hi."

"No problem. Let me give him a call. I can't let you back there, but he can come out here."

The phone interchange was brief. Thirty seconds later, Rick strode through a different door into the antechamber.

He'd weathered the intervening years well. Rick had always been good-looking, but in high school his reddish hair, fair complexion, slender frame, and smallish features hadn't been macho enough—not what a young male was shooting for. Now, filled out and obviously muscular—he wore a white polo shirt displaying his biceps—I could see why a looks-oriented woman like Sue would go for him.

"Ivy! Great to see you. I didn't know you were back. Let's get coffee."

He thought about hugging me and then shook my hand vigorously. I remembered how he'd always smelled like leather back in high school. He didn't now.

We walked out of the station and around the corner to an old-fashioned coffee shop. Several tables of uniformed police and a few civilians half filled the room, which smelled like burnt toast. The woman from the station was one of the officers. She gave me an even bigger smile and a thumbs-up. Perhaps she thought Rick and I were dating.

After settling into a cozy booth and ordering coffee and tea, we briefly caught up on our lives. Then I launched into why I'd sought him out. He probably couldn't be away from his desk for long.

"My mother just died, and my sister suspects it's homicide. I'm hoping you can see what the San Francisco police did when she approached them about this."

"Sure. No problem." Rick nodded vigorously. His gestures and mannerisms had always been larger than life, something he'd learned from his actress mother. "If there were an ongoing investigation up in the city, I'd know about it since your mom lives here, so my guess is they checked things out and she's wrong. This happens all the time. People watch crime shows on TV, and next thing you know, everyone's getting murdered."

"Thank you so much. You won't get into trouble?"

"No, no. Part of my job is doing things like this, although it's usually for someone within the department. I'm like a professional double-checker—wrapping up loose ends."

"Do you like it?"

"No, I sure don't. I want to be back on the front line. Did you know I'm a detective now?" He leaned back and spread his hands with a flourish. His movements didn't always correlate with a given situation. He just felt obliged to punctuate most of his speech with some sort of movement.

"Yes, I did."

"I'm the only desk-bound one on the force. It's a waste of my talents."

"Why did they assign you to that?" I sipped my barely palatable tea. Maybe I'd switch to sparkling water next time.

"Well, the chief had his reasons, I'll grant you that. I freaked out at a crime scene a few months ago when it was a lot like a nasty earlier case. So I'm stuck in therapy and exiled to a desk. I guess I need to prove I'm okay, but what chance do I have to do that sitting around all day in the station?" Rick threw his hands in the air as though he were stumped while appearing on a quiz show.

"I'm sorry to hear that." I reached out and placed my hand on his forearm without thinking. Other than a perfunctory handshake with my uncle, this was my first physical contact with a man in years. Bewildered for a moment by the intensity of the experience, I reclaimed my hand, and then asked Rick if it would help to hear more details about my mother.

"Sure. Go ahead."

I filled him in, and he proved to be an attentive listener. This wasn't the guy I'd dated all those years ago. Sixteen-year-old Rick loved the sound of his own voice. He'd been perched above me in the high school pecking order, which rendered him desirable until I'd put in my time listening to him.

He responded the moment I'd finished. "It doesn't sound like there's much there. We run into medical mysteries all the time—weird stuff you don't find if you look something up online. Once we didn't bother to hold a perp because his oncologist was sure he only had a few weeks to live. After a spontaneous remission, the creep is still on the loose somewhere in Ohio. But I'll check. I'll probably have a chance later today. That's another thing. I'm not nearly busy enough, so the time drags. You know what I mean?"

"Like in Mr. Mason's math class?"

"Exactly. That was the slowest clock on earth, wasn't it?" He pointed to the wall to our left, where I expected to see a clock when I looked. There wasn't one.

I nodded.

"Listen, Ivy. I've got to get going. Lieutenant Cline is old school in a lot of ways. If you're awol for more than a half hour or so, you get reamed out like you're in boot camp." Rick lowered his voice and looked me squarely in the eye. "And be careful, Ivy. If there's a murderer out there, you don't want to forget that for a second."

"I will be. Thanks."

I borrowed the pen Rick had clipped to his shirt pocket and wrote my phone number on the back of a business card I'd found on an empty seat next to me in the Singapore airport. I'd meant to throw it out, but I'd forgotten.

"I'll stay in touch," he promised as he rose to leave. "Finish your tea. I'll get the bill on the way out. And people can just put numbers into their phones now."

"I'll remember that. Thanks."

I used the restroom, and it wasn't until I found myself out on the sidewalk that I realized I had no way to get to my mother's house to meet Dennis. I called Jan.

"I've stranded myself," I told her.

"Ivy! I thought you had a ride. Where are you?"

I told her.

"You're not on the way at all. Why don't you Uber it?"

"What's Uber?"

"Jesus, you're hopeless. Tell me where to pick you up. Let's get this show on the road."

I was thankful to have some time to myself while I waited on an empty bus bench for Jan and Brian. The temple had been a haven of silence and time alone. At first, this had constituted a hardship, but that gradually shifted into something wonderful—the space to go deeper and deeper into myself.

So far, things continued to move faster in the world than I could process in an ongoing way. I knew that most of the curriculum embedded in my post-temple experience was passing me by. I hoped I could play catch-up at some point.

Jan had calmed down by the time she arrived, and Brian was positively buoyant, speculating whimsically on the backgrounds and academic majors of likely Stanford students he spied on the way to Mom's house.

"See that one with the porkpie hat? He's a grad student in waffle technology, hailing from the Yukon. That young woman on his right? A sophomore from New Jersey focusing on Mafia studies, with a special emphasis on pizza toppings. That's how the two got together—their love is grounded in their passion for wheat-based foods."

"Someone's hungry," Jan commented.

I just listened. Why Brian seemed to be in such a light-hearted mood was a mystery to me. If he were a teen, I would've suspected drugs. After all, we were on our way to evaluate a potential murderer, not driving to the beach.

Jan avoided the Camino Real, the main business artery through town. This road retraced the original route of the Franciscan missionaries who'd pushed the Spanish presence north from Mexico. Instead, she wound through established neighborhoods and pointed out homes she'd sold (a few), nearly sold (a few more), or believed to be inhabited by jackasses—that is, people who'd refused to list with her (lots.)

I enjoyed viewing the majestic sycamore trees lining

most of the avenues. Palo Alto had been named after one of the few trees in the area when the town had been founded—a soaring redwood beside a creek. Almost all of my hometown had been grassy meadow until city hall had decided to create what they called an urban forest, beginning in the 1890s.

A lone, odd-looking pine caught my eye as we cruised through a neighborhood of older, relatively modest homes. Its remaining branches meandered sideways from the top quarter of its fire-damaged trunk. Diminutive needles bunched at the ends of the otherwise bare branches, and woodpecker holes created a connect-the-dots pattern on many of them. This tree was a survivor—a testament to the commitment of living things to endure.

Mom's house—a Spanish-style hacienda—was set back from a quiet street of similar tile-roofed adobe wannabes. The stucco walls of these sprawling one-story estates were various shades of ochre, burnt orange, cream, and light yellow. Mom's was the darkest color—nut brown, with light green trim.

Dennis met us at the arched mahogany front door—had he been gazing out the window, watching for us?

"Come in, come in," he implored.

Mom's incongruous English furniture filled the surprisingly compact living room. I'd remembered it as twice its size. I could see no evidence that Dennis had contributed any pieces to the ensemble of Victorian antiques. He'd probably tried. Mom had never tolerated any dilution of her personal style, however much she'd appropriated it from other eras.

"Please sit," Dennis said. "Can I get anyone anything? Something to drink? A snack perhaps?"

We all shook our heads. I glanced at Brian. He seemed entranced by Dennis's uber-host behavior.

I settled onto a plush button-tufted loveseat, its pale lavender matching the trio of armchairs the others chose. I faced the interior of the room while the others viewed me as backlit. The picture window at the front of the house scattered sunlight onto the scene.

"So what thoughts do any of you have about the service?" Dennis asked.

I'd forgotten this was the pretense of our visit. Pretense or not, we needed to decide.

Jan spoke up. "I never heard her express a preference, but my guess is she wouldn't want anything too grand."

"I agree," Brian said. "Perhaps a simple ceremony with a few eulogies. Then a trip to the cemetery to inter the body."

"Well, that would be a problem," Dennis said smoothly, anticipating upcoming conflict. "She told me she wanted to be cremated, so I've gone ahead with that."

"*You what!*" Jan exclaimed. "*Already!* How is that even possible? What were you thinking? I can't believe this!"

He held his hands out, unconsciously warding off her energy. "Calm down, Jan," he implored. "It's what she wanted. She even told me what kind of urn she wanted. Want to see it? It's beautiful."

Jan stood and began pacing. "Of all the high-handed...You really are a piece of work, Dennis. What's next? Shipping her urn off to Alaska so Eskimos can do the memorial?"

"Inuits," he replied smugly, unfazed by her outburst. "You don't call them Eskimos anymore."

Jan screamed, a high-pitched sustained sound, and rushed him. Brian grabbed her around the waist and pulled her into the front hallway. A moment later, I heard the front door open and close.

"I've never seen her this bad," Dennis said, frowning and trying to run his fingers through his hair again with no luck. This time he pulled his hand down and stared at his fingers as though they were the problem.

"Her mother never died before. And she never suspected her stepfather of killing her."

I'd decided on a frontal assault once I'd seen Dennis's smug expression.

He paused and assembled his features into what passed for humility—with most people, that is. His eyes reminded of a hound I'd known—a conniving creature who was always stealing his sibling's food.

"I loved your mother very much, and God knows why, she loved me back. I would never harm a hair on her head. Truly."

"I'd like to believe you, but what you said back in your hospital room was alarming," I told him.

"Look," he began, leaning forward, "I can see you're sharp, and you know I put up a front sometimes. It's hard for me to let people in—let them see who I really am. But I'm leveling with you here. I did *not* kill your mother."

"But you think someone else did? Is that what you were saying yesterday?"

He leaned back again and crossed his arms. "I said I'm taking care of that, and I will."

"You think there was foul play?"

"I do." He kept his face studiously neutral.

"And you think you know who it was?" I asked.

"I do."

"Why not just go to the police—or tell me, at least?" I asked. "Don't I have a right to know?"

"It's complicated. I need you to trust me."

"Dennis, you're the person I trust least in the world right now. Everything about you seems to be inauthentic."

He wasn't offended. In fact, he didn't seem to care at all.

"Be that as it may," he began, "you don't have a choice here. Look, all this will be settled by day's end tomorrow. I swear. Just be patient." He raised his voice, and now there was a sharp edge to his tone. "And keep that crazy bitch sister of yours away from me."

"*There's* the real Dennis," I said. "You've come out to play."

"Fuck off," he said matter-of-factly. "Just fuck off and let me handle this. Lois was *my* wife, and there's more to me than you know. I didn't sell medical supplies. Enough said."

He leapt to his feet and opened the front door before I could get up. "Tell your uncle I'm sorry I didn't get to know him."

"Sure."

I found Jan and Brian arguing on the immaculate front lawn. I decided to wait in the car, where I could digest what I'd found out in peace, but I began falling asleep almost immediately. I lay on the back seat, entering that state of mind that mimicked meditation. Jet lag had caught up to me again.

I was grateful when the others piled in, since that would eventually lead me to Jan's guest cottage, where I could rest without a seatbelt embedded in my back. Both my sister and my uncle were silent as we drove to Brian's B and B near the university, which made me wonder if their sharp words outside Mom's house indicated a history I wasn't aware of. After all, there was plenty of room for him to stay at Jan's. Why hadn't he?

For that matter, why hadn't anyone asked me what had happened in Mom's house? Had Jan cut Brian out of the picture for some reason?

"So what did you find out, Ivy?" my sister asked as soon as we'd dropped our uncle off. We sat in her car on a busy street. "Did he do it? Why else would he have Mom cremated so soon? He didn't want an autopsy, did he?"

"I don't think he did it, but he believes her death wasn't natural, and he admitted he might know who did."

"That's great!" Jan bounced up and down in her seat like a four-year-old who couldn't contain her energy. "Who is it?"

"He wouldn't tell me. He said if we were patient and let him take care of things, it would be settled tomorrow."

"You believe him?"

"Actually, I do. I'm not sure why. At any rate, I couldn't make him talk."

"Why don't we call the police and turn him in as a witness or something?" Jan said. "Maybe they could make him talk."

"I'm inclined to see what Dennis does. He might solve the murder on his own. I think that's what he was implying—that he thought he could."

"Dennis could take off for some country without extradition and be gone by tomorrow," Jan pointed out.

"True. So what do you think we should do?" I asked.

"And why did you want to leave Brian out of this?"

"Never mind. I have my reasons." She paused and sighed. "I guess since you were the one who talked to Dennis, and God knows you're thinking about this more clearly than me, we ought to do whatever you decide."

"Okay, I say we wait. If we haven't heard anything by tomorrow evening, I'll call Rick Foster—the policeman I talked to."

"I remember Rick. Rick the Dick, I used to call him."

"Why's that?"

"Well, it rhymed. Can I ask you something?"

"Sure."

Jan had to wait until a slow, noisy truck passed by. "How have you stayed so calm? You just had a conversation with a guy who might've killed our mother. And I haven't seen you crying or grieving about Mom since the hospital. Is this a Buddhist thing? Is it even healthy? Aren't we supposed to feel our feelings? That's what my shrink says."

"You know, I'm surprised by how I'm dealing with this, too. Being sequestered at the sangha didn't give me a chance to field test how my up-to-date self reacts to intense things. But I didn't think it would be like this. It turns out I'm kind of checked-out emotionally. And no, I don't think it's a Buddhist thing or a good thing."

I thought about it more, and Jan let me. What *was* the relationship between my faith and the way I was handling things?

Finally, I spoke. "I guess I'm cherry-picking the parts of Buddhism that make all this easier for me— whatever I can use as a defense mechanism to keep from feeling overwhelmed. Acceptance, equanimity, nonjudgmentalism—I think I've been perverting these to avoid my natural response, which would probably look a lot like yours. You have no idea how extreme everything seems out in the world now, Jan. It's like there was a governor in place back in Asia. Nothing too high and nothing too low could happen. Now I'd be on a crazy rollercoaster if I didn't restrict myself."

"Welcome to my world," Jan said. "It's mostly been a rollercoaster ride for me. And when I took a med years ago that kept me in the normal range of ups and downs, everything felt horribly flat."

"So we've got the same thing—just reversed. I'm staving off the carnival ride, and you're unhappy if you don't have it."

"Yeah. Weird."

Jan started the car, and we headed to Woodside.

Back in the guesthouse, I flopped onto my exquisitely comfortable bed and fell asleep. I'd been sleeping on a straw mat for years, which, after a painful break-in period, was less of a hardship than I would've imagined before joining the temple. Nonetheless, I appreciated the unfamiliar comfort.

Dee came to gather me for dinner. I didn't hear her come in, so she had to roust me from sleep.

"Do you dream like regular people?" she asked as she watched me put my shoes on.

She'd pulled her blonde hair back into a ponytail, which accented her wide jawline and her widow's peak.

"I don't suppose it's any use to remind you I *am* a regular person?"

"Nope."

"Trust me. There are only regular people on this planet. Anyway, I dream like everyone else, as far as I know." I stood. "Shall we?"

"Sure."

Dinner was linguini, a tossed salad, and peach pie. We discussed Jan's latest real estate listing—"a unique quasi-fixer-upper with a ton of exciting and innovative possibilities"—the weather, and local politics. By discuss, I mean Jan spoke at length, and my nieces and I periodically interjected token responses. It wasn't unpleasant, despite the dearth of depth. While we enjoyed our pie—my first real dessert in years—Jan received a phone call.

"I don't usually take calls during meals," she told me, "but I'll just see who it's from." She held up her phone, saw the display, and brought the phone up to her ear.

"Yes?" she said.

Holly spoke up. "So we can't use our phone at the table, but you can?"

Jan listened for a time, her face shifting to display an intense feeling—shock? Her eyes narrowed to slits, and her mouth tightened into a thin, straight line. Yes, shock.

"Thank you," she finally said woodenly and then dropped the phone on top of her unfinished pie.

"Mom! What's going on?" Dee asked.

"Dennis has been shot. He's dead."

Chapter Six

Silence reigned for a long minute. None of us knew what to say.

"We were just there," Jan said. "I guess we were the last ones to see him alive."

"The second to last," Dee pointed out.

Jan gave her daughter a dirty look, her eyes narrowing. Then she abruptly clambered out of her chair, ran across the terra cotta floor, and jerked the sliding patio door open. In a few more seconds, she was out of sight behind the tall hedge beyond the pool.

We all sat and watched her until she was out of sight.

"She's such a drama queen," Holly said. "She doesn't even like the guy."

"I believe your mom is simply doing the best she can under the circumstances," I told her. "Her mother just died, and now there's a murder on top of that."

"Well, whether this is the best she can do or not, it's not good enough," Holly said heatedly. "I'm sick of the way she acts. You never know who she's going to be. I don't even bring friends over anymore. It's embarrassing."

I didn't feel this needed commentary from me. I did catch Holly's eye and nodded. I wanted her to know I'd listened, at least. I looked across the table at Dee. "How are you doing?"

"Weird stuff happens." She shrugged. "Who do you

think did it?"

I could tell the murder didn't seem real to her. It probably would later. Neither of the girls had reacted in a way I would've guessed.

"I have no idea who did it," I told Dee.

"Oh, come on. Use your Buddhist powers."

Holly snorted.

I smiled. "Shall I fly or squeeze a piece of coal until it turns into a diamond?"

"I know who you are, Aunt Ivy. You can't hide from me. You're not like other people."

"Whatever is different about me doesn't make me a detective. If we let the police do their job, we'll find out what happened."

Holly snorted again. "Yeah, right."

"Why do you say that?" I asked.

"Mom dated a fireman once. What a loser."

"Perhaps you're overgeneralizing," I suggested. "That's a sample of one, and he wasn't even a police officer."

This earned yet another snort.

"Holly's a big snorter," Dee told me. "I can't imagine it helps her social life."

"Look who's talking," Holly countered. "At least I have one."

"Stop it," I said. "Both of you." This was my first foray into parenting my nieces. I had no clue if it would help matters.

The two girls glared at one another but stayed silent.

"I'll call my loser friend on the police force to see what I can find out," I told them, smiling.

"You know a cop?" Holly asked.

"I do."

"I'm sorry I said that about cops. I didn't like Mom's guy, but that doesn't mean every macho guy is worthless."

"It's okay," I told her. "We're all dealing with big stuff. That doesn't bring out the best in people."

I rose and strode to another part of the spacious house to make the phone call, ending up in an unfamiliar room. Apparently, it served as Jan's home office, despite not having a desk in it. Papers and folders were strewn onto a long wooden coffee table in front of a black leather couch.

Across the room, a towering walnut armoire was flanked by a tropical landscape print—Kauai?—and an expensive-looking air purifier sported numerous blue LED lights. Matching walnut bookshelves lined a side wall. Instead of books, a parade of small figurines populated the shelves. I took a moment to examine these, discovering they were all ceramic frogs of some kind. A few were cute. Most were odd or creepy, as if the artist had been trying to stir up dark feelings by subtly altering the creature's shape.

I sat down in a modern chrome and brown leather armchair that faced a floor-to-ceiling window, looking onto the tidy English garden in the side yard. Then I pulled out the inexpensive phone I'd bought in the Singapore airport. If it could do more than make calls, I didn't know about it. The small screen covered about a third of the phone's surface.

Rick answered immediately, which surprised me until I remembered he was desk bound.

"Hi, it's Ivy. We just heard about my mother's husband. Can you tell me more about it?"

"There's not much to tell at this point. He was shot

three times in the chest in his living room. A handgun. Nothing seems to be missing, but of course we're not sure what was there in the first place. I was going to call you since you said you were going to see him. What's the story there?"

I paused to consider what might helpful to Rick. "My uncle, Jan, and I talked to Dennis about Mom's memorial—together at first, and then just me."

"Why's that?"

"Dennis said something that angered Jan, so Brian ushered her outside while I finished talking to him. Do you remember how she can be when she's upset?"

"I certainly do. She kicked me once. What was it that Dennis said?"

"He told us he'd had Mom cremated already without talking to us. I think Jan heard that as covering his tracks since she thinks he murdered Mom."

"Yeah, about that. She could be right that your mother was killed. They've opened an investigation based on some new evidence I'm not allowed to tell you about."

"I think Dennis knows what happened, but I don't think he was the one who killed her. And there's more."

I reported the conversation I'd had after my sister and uncle had left.

"Guys like this are really good liars, Ivy," Rick said.

I thought for a moment. I didn't want to press Rick in a way that would be uncomfortable for him, but I was curious about what he'd called "new evidence." "Are you sure you can't tell me why the police have reopened the investigation of my mother's death?" I asked.

"I'd love to tell you more, Ivy. I really would. But I can't. Anyway, I've got to get back to something. I'm going to pass your info on to Art Petrie as soon as we finish. It clearly ties the two deaths together, even if Dennis's statements are now only hearsay. Petrie's the lead detective on the murder—Dennis's, I mean—so he'll call you, I guess."

"Okay. Thank you, Rick."

I sat and pondered what I'd found out. Perhaps I lingered in Jan's office to get more alone time, too. Socializing was tiring for me. After a while, I rose to return to the kitchen to clean up. Detective Petrie called me before I could leave the room. This time, I plopped down on the couch.

"Is this Ivy Lutz?"

"It is."

"Art Petrie. I'm a detective on the Palo Alto police force. I'll need to talk to you, your sister, and your uncle about your stepfather's murder. Can you tell the others?"

"Sure."

"At the station? Tomorrow morning at nine?"

"We'll do it."

"While I've got you, let's go over a few things. Rick tells me you're a reliable person, who probably notices what's going on around you more than most people."

"I'll thank him for that next time I talk to him."

"Actually, it would be better if you didn't talk to him."

"Okay." I was curious, of course, about what that meant.

"So your sister got angry with your stepfather—so much so that she had to be restrained?"

"That's not exactly what I told Rick, but yes, it's true."

"So I should consider her a suspect?"

74

"Of course not. For one thing, I've been with her since we left Dennis's house."

"All the time?"

"I'm sorry. I misspoke. I took a nap once we got back to my sister's house in Woodside. You could ask her daughters for verification."

"So she may have had opportunity?"

"I have no idea, but that's beside the point. I know my sister. She isn't capable of something like this. She gives a lot of money to anti-gun organizations because our cousin was killed in a gun accident. There's no way she'd ever touch one."

"When was that?"

"Let's see…Paul died when I was in my early twenties, so that would be about eighteen years ago."

I heard a keyboard. He was taking notes.

"How did your stepfather seem? Upset? Scared?"

I liked the detective's voice. It was deep, resonant, and it inspired trust. He could've been a spokesman in a TV commercial—maybe for prescription medicine.

"For someone whose partner just died, he was remarkably poised," I told Petrie. "I suspect that's just his personality."

"What kind of personality was that?"

"My take on him—I just met Dennis yesterday for the first time—is that he's a manipulative narcissist."

"Can you tell me what you mean by that?"

I explained my idea of what those terms meant, which satisfied Petrie.

"Now why didn't you meet him before?" he asked. "Are you estranged from your mother?"

"No, I've been living in Asia."

"Why's that?"

"I was a Buddhist nun."

Petrie was silent. He hadn't been expecting that. "Okay," he finally said. "How about what else you talked about with the victim after Jan and your uncle left. Anything helpful to me there?"

"Yes. Very much so."

Once again, I provided a detailed account of my conversation with Dennis. This time, I remembered some additional observations that Petrie seemed to appreciate.

"Are you aware of anything of great value in the home—jewelry, artwork, cash?" he asked me when he'd finished wringing every shred of information out of me about what Dennis had said.

"No, you should ask my sister about that. When I was there, all I saw were my mother's antiques. I'm sure you would've noticed if a table or a breakfront were missing."

"Of course. I won't keep you much longer, but let me ask you this. If you were me, how would you proceed? What do you think happened?"

"I'd look into how the two deaths are connected— my mother's and Dennis's. I think Dennis knew something about my mother's death that got him killed. Originally, I'd guess this was probably all about some money thing. Dennis seemed to be a money-oriented person, and Mom was quite wealthy. Oh, I just remembered one more thing. Dennis said he hadn't actually been a salesman, which was what he'd told the family. He hinted he'd been something more...I don't know...Dangerous? It seemed like the kind of thing someone would say if they'd been a spy."

"You think he was a spy?"

"No, no. I mean it had that flavor—like he was trying to impress me that he could handle himself in a fight or something. Anyway, I'd look into his background if I were you. It might be relevant."

"I will. Who inherits?"

"Unprompted, Dennis told me that Jan, her two daughters, and I will receive most everything. I think the police up in San Francisco looked into that."

"We'll check it out, too. So when you say it's about money, you don't mean the inheritance?"

"Right."

"Do you have plans for your share of the inheritance? Maybe a donation to your organization back in Asia?"

"No, I hadn't thought about it. But I could use a change of clothes."

I could feel him smiling. "Well, technically, you *are* a woman."

I was taken aback and couldn't muster a response.

"Sorry," Petrie said. "I'm a recovering Catholic."

"I was a very different sort of nun."

"Good for you. That's all for now. See you at nine. Thanks."

"Bye."

Before I returned to the kitchen, a piece of paper on the coffee table in front of me caught my eye. The gist of the letter from a mortgage company was that Jan was way behind in her payments. Bright yellow highlighted sections referred to the dire consequences associated with that.

****

After I called Brian and told Jan about our morning appointment at the police station, the evening passed with everyone in the house returning to their prospective corners of the ring. I slept soundly, and then at breakfast I told stories of life in Sri Lanka, prompted by Dee. Jan and Holly had yet to express any interest in the last twelve years of my life.

A little before eight in the morning, we dropped the girls off at their private school, an impressive set of gothic buildings that would not have looked out of place at an Ivy League university. Then Jan and I headed for Brian's B and B to pick him up for our police interview. She engaged in nonstop small talk. Tiny talk, really—how she'd slept, what car she was planning to buy next, and a description of a condo hunter's husband, who looked like a pit bull. She was taking a vacation from thinking about Mom.

For my part, I eschewed watching the scenarios out the car window, remembering growing up with Jan instead. As someone committed to staying in the moment, I rarely indulged in reminiscence.

We'd been close as young children. She was two years younger chronologically and several more developmentally. Jan didn't walk or talk until way past the norm. Our father wasn't patient with her, punishing her harshly for not performing up to his standards. For as long as I can remember, I protected her, taking the blame when possible. I didn't enjoy being hit, but I didn't sob or scream like Jan when our father lost control.

My mother took over the role she should have been fulfilling all along when Jan hit puberty. My sister and mother argued incessantly, with my father stepping in periodically to impose consequences—on both of them. By this time our father was often absent, supposedly needing to spend time in Phoenix to tend to several mobile home parks Mom owned. In reality, he was living with another woman in Palm Springs. Mom discovered this when Jan found a bra in Dad's suitcase. She'd pulled it from the back of a closet to pack for music camp. If the suitcase hadn't been a more attractive color than the others, perhaps my parents might have remained married until my father died.

Brian came to the door of the shingled duplex, ready to roll. My uncle wore khaki pants, a light green button-down shirt, and the hiking boots I'd seen him in earlier. He looked tired.

We piled into Jan's car. I yielded the front seat to my uncle, who immediately expressed his apprehension about the upcoming police interviews.

"I've seen enough TV shows to know how it works," Brian said. "They're going to try to trip us up—find the discrepancies in our stories—pit us against one another. I say we stick together, no matter what."

I was surprised by his attitude. It didn't fit my sense of my uncle.

"We don't have stories," I pointed out. "Just our vantage points on the truth. With nothing to hide, we don't need to worry."

Briam turned in his seat to face me. "I don't think we want them knowing that Jan tried to attack a murder victim shortly before his death, do you?" His bushy eyebrows shot up as if to say, "My argument is persuasive, isn't it?"

"Are you asking me to lie?" I replied.

"I didn't try to attack him," Jan protested. "I was just very emotional. It's perfectly understandable."

"Of course," Brian said. "But the police may not see it that way."

I shook my head. The conversation's wavelength was alien to me.

"Why don't we tell them what there is to tell them and let them sort it out?" I suggested. "That's their job. We'd probably look really suspicious if our stories matched up perfectly, anyway."

"Hmm, maybe you're right," Brian conceded.

Of course, I'd already let the cat out of the bag about Jan's behavior to Detective Petrie. I didn't feel as though my nondisclosure to my sister and uncle represented dishonesty. It certainly wouldn't have worked out well to rile up Jan shortly before her interview. As it was, she was likely to blow up at some police officer while we were at the station, anyway. That's what she did.

****

Art Petri was an attractive, rugged-looking man in his early forties. Darker than most of the African Americans in the area, with even darker, alert eyes, he exuded an impressive presence—that somewhat mysterious sense of solidity and personal magnetism.

His slightly receded hairline was cut straight across, a look I've never favored, but on Petrie it framed his high forehead, while his substantial eyebrows underlined it. They almost met in the middle, just above a wide, somewhat flat nose. Petrie's lips were filled-out, almost plump. A strong, wide jaw kept the lower half of his face from looking androgynous, as did the dark stubble on his cheeks. I've never appreciated Black leading men with Caucasian features, which I think is a subtle form of racism. Petrie was not in that category.

The room we'd been ushered into was clearly not where they interrogated criminals. A row of windows faced us across an oblong conference table. Its polished hardwood surface gleamed in the horizontal streaks of light, and half a dozen plush, green chairs were grouped around it. The walls were light yellow, adorned with black and white historical photos of Palo Alto. One in particular caught my eye. Several artists on scaffolds were painting the mural that still sat above the arched doorways of the Romanesque Stanford Memorial Church.

Ray Petrie ambled to the far side of the table, and we settled in across from him. I sat between my sister and my uncle. The chairs were as comfortable as they looked. Petrie reached forward and started a recorder that sat in the middle of the table.

Brian attempted to take control early. "What can you tell us about what happened? Is there any news since you talked to Ivy?"

The detective held up a hand. His palm was much lighter skinned than the rest of him. "We'll get to that. I need to ask a few things first—starting with Jan. Did your mother ever say anything about her husband's career?"

"Not really. Just that he sold medical supplies before he retired. To hospitals, I think."

I'd forgotten to tell Jan what Dennis had said about this not being so.

"So he never mentioned anything about Ireland?"

"No, never."

"What about exotic animals?" Petrie asked.

"What are you talking about?"

"Bear with me."

"He wasn't a salesman? Is that what you're saying? He was an Irish zookeeper or something?" Jan's voice didn't express surprise, despite the unlikely juxtaposition of Petrie's questions. For her, this news was vindication. Dennis was a liar.

Petrie held a hand up again. This time he extended it farther and moved it from side to side. "What about your stepfather's nationality? Did he tell you he was from Bulgaria?"

"You've got that wrong," Jan responded. "He's Danish. I've seen his passport."

Petrie shook his head in a smooth, even motion. "He's Bulgarian, originally. From Sofia."

Brian spoke up. "Are you telling us this man isn't who he purported to be?"

"Obviously," Jan answered sharply.

Petrie nodded. "His name isn't Dennis Sorenson. It's Anton Todorov. He was able to pass for a Dane because he taught languages at a university in Copenhagen for some years before he moved to Ireland, and then here. Apparently, he was fluent in four languages, which aided him in his smuggling operation. He brought in exotic animals. In Ireland, he's still wanted for that, as well as tax fraud."

I spoke up. "How in the world could you know all this already? It hasn't even been twenty-four hours since the shooting. Surely, Dennis—Anton, I mean—covered his tracks more thoroughly than that. You can't pull off a phony identity for years on end if it's something that could be unraveled in a few hours, right?"

"We got lucky."

Petrie smiled, which started slowly at the corners of his broad mouth. A moment later, his lower lip dropped, revealing his white teeth. Then his upper lip joined the party, along with his dark brown eyes, which crinkled at the outside corners. I'd never seen such a complex smile, or perhaps I'd never watched one develop quite so carefully.

"His other wife stepped forward," Petrie told us. "The Bulgarian one."

"My God!" Jan exclaimed. Now she was as surprised as I was.

"She lives down in San Jose," Petri told us. "I think she has some sort of mental disorder. When Dennis— I'm going to keep calling him that—didn't answer his phone a few times last night, she called us to report a missing person—which is ridiculous. But it paid off in this case."

"Does she know about his marriage to my sister?" Brian asked.

"Yes. That's why she called us up here in Palo Alto. Well, she knew he lived with another woman. She didn't know they were married."

"And she was okay with that?" I asked. Perhaps my naivety about current relationships was in play here, I thought. "Is that what people do now?"

Petrie gazed at me and cocked his head. I guess my question sounded odd, and in detective fashion, he was trying to understand its implications. "No, of course not. She says they've been on a long hiatus."

"Does she sound reliable?" Brian asked.

Petrie shook his head vigorously. "Not at all. Not on the phone. She's my next interview this morning, so I'll check that out soon."

He paused before continuing, as if he wasn't sure if he wanted to say something. "No offense, but in my experience, no one's reliable—and that includes the three of you. Everybody sees things through the lens of their bullshit." He turned to me and bowed his head.

"Sorry about my language, Sister."

Jan immediately replied, with heat. "I don't care what words you use, Detective. I just want to find out what happened to my mother!"

I saw that Petrie had been mildly provocative on purpose to see how we'd react. He was clever. Now he got to see angry Jan in action.

"I understand. Another team is looking at that. We're focused today on your stepfather's murder."

The detective's voice remained calm and solicitous, which impressed me. And I sensed his equanimity was genuine—not just a strategy to handle a difficult witness.

"I'm sure Dennis had it coming." Jan's piercing stare challenged the detective to dispute her.

"Why do you say that?"

My sister had been holding her tongue, but now a barrage of words flowed out of her. "He was a creep—a major creep—even before you told us about his real identity and that he sold beautiful creatures that deserved a better life than the one he gave them. Who buys lions and tigers and whatever? Creepy rich people. That's who. Now it's obvious he's way worse than I thought. Maybe some shady character from his past murdered our mom if it wasn't Dennis. That would still be his fault. I want to know why and how and who's involved, and you'd better tell that other team investigating Mom's murder they're going to be up a creek if they don't get me those answers. My best friend knows the vice-mayor, and I've got money for the best lawyers." She pounded the table for emphasis.

Petrie seemed completely unaffected by Jan's loud diatribe. His features remained studiously neutral, and his relaxed body language didn't shift at all.

"I'll pass on your concerns," he told her. "I'm sure they'll take them seriously."

"Who are these people, anyway?" she asked. "Who are the other cops?"

"They'll be contacting you if it proves necessary. Now, Jan, can you account for your whereabouts after visiting your stepfather?"

"Why should I have to? You think I did this? Really? That's where you're going?"

"It's just routine."

"I don't see you asking my sister or Brian."

"I will. I'm starting with you. Would you prefer to be second or third?" Once again, I was struck by Petrie's poise. None of Jan's antics were getting to him.

"No, that's all right. I get it. You have to rule out everybody."

He nodded.

"I was home—in Woodside."

"Can anyone verify that?"

"Ivy, my kids—and I called a friend. You can check where I make calls from, right?"

Petrie nodded again. Then he asked Brian and me where we were. As it turns out, we were both napping during the estimated time of Dennis's death. I was at Jan's, of course; he was alone in his B and B.

"Any thoughts about the murder?" Petrie asked next, throwing out this open-ended question to all of us. "Just brainstorm if you can. At this early stage, there's no telling what might be helpful."

"I'd look at the other wife," Brian suggested. "A woman scorned and all that."

"We will."

I spoke up. "A man like Dennis will have made

plenty of enemies. It's entirely possible his crimes weren't on the level with the people he dealt with, and if he cheated customers, those kinds of people have access to resources and guns."

"If that were the case, why now?" Petrie asked. "Apparently, he retired when he fled here eight years ago."

"Well, the key word there is 'apparently,' " I said. "That's worth looking at. Other than that, I have no idea."

Brian jumped in. "If the man has been living under a false identity, perhaps it's taken eight years for an enemy to find him. A retired Danish man in Palo Alto? Who would suspect he was a Bulgarian smuggler?"

"It's not retaliation for killing Mom," Jan piped up. "We aren't like that and neither are any of her friends."

Petrie turned his head to solely focus on her, and his tone sharpened just a bit. Was he trying to trigger her again? "You know there's still no hard evidence to support your claim that your mother was murdered, right? Even if we find some, it may not implicate Dennis."

"Goddammit, I'm tired of hearing that. *Of course* she was murdered! *Of course* he had something to do with it!"

Petrie placed his palms on the table and leaned forward. "Can you tell me why you're so upset? I'm not doing anything to antagonize you, am I? This is all routine."

That wasn't how I read the situation, but whatever he'd done, he now put Jan in a position to have to explain herself. I wondered what she'd say.

Jan lowered her voice. "I'm an emotional person,

and my shrink says I have an impulse-control problem. But if you think you're behaving perfectly, you're sadly mistaken. When we walked in here, my uncle asked what was going on at your end and you said you'd tell us later. It's later. I'm still waiting."

"Fine." Now a trace of irritation was in Petrie's tone. "A neighbor called in the shooting at five forty-five. No one saw anything. The back door was forced open, and the victim was shot as he stood in the middle of his living room. No shell casings. Forensics think the perp probably used a revolver, but we'll find that out later."

"He?" Brian asked. "Do you have a reason to think the murderer was a man?"

"I usually go with the odds. Men kill much more often. In this case, the bullets' trajectories suggest the perp was at least six feet tall. Probably taller."

"Got it," my uncle responded.

For some reason, Petrie turned and looked me in the eyes. He was right there, all of him. I wondered if he meditated. I also wondered if he could tell I was just as present in that moment.

"Except for what the other wife provided," he said, looking away quickly, "we don't know a whole lot more—at least not that we're releasing to the public."

"We're not the public," Jan asserted.

Petrie ignored her. Good for him. At some point, it was better not to respond to Jan. Once she became sufficiently worked up, whatever anyone tried backfired. It only provided her with new material to object to.

"You'll keep us apprised as you proceed?" Brian asked.

"We'll see. No promises." He held up a hand again before Jan could react. "That's all for now. Grieve. Live.

Leave all this to us. We know what we're doing."

"Thank you," I said.

Petrie looked directly in my eyes again. His were remarkably alert as he held my gaze, and then he smiled his complex smile again. I felt buoyed by it.

Chapter Seven

Jan had to go to work. She told us she had a "loaded foreign couple" who were itching to "unleash some megabucks on something huge and grotesque."

So she dropped Brian and me at her house and took off to Los Altos, another well-to-do Silicon valley town where the average home was worth well over three million.

I suggested my uncle and I take a walk once Jan had rushed off to meet her clients. He readily agreed, and we set out down the tree-lined street—the opposite way I'd walked with Jan.

April was usually the beginning of the dry season in California, and this year was no different. I didn't mind the sameness of the weather—sunny with a few clouds drifting through every day. Since I'd returned, the temperature had ranged from the high fifties to the low seventies.

Jan's street was narrower than most, with only a plumber's van parked on it. When I glanced up a series of driveways, I saw plenty of cars and SUVs. There were no overhead wires or streetlights on Sylvan Way. Unlike Jan's acreage, most of the other homeowners had opted to leave original copses of live oaks at the front of their property.

"Do you know the area?" I asked. "Are there any trails nearby?"

He whipped out a smartphone. "I'll find out." In a matter of seconds, he found an answer. "Nope."

"That's amazing," I commented.

"Well, it's forested here, but it's essentially a residential neighborhood, isn't it?"

"No, I mean your phone—finding out some random thing so quickly."

"You don't have a smartphone?" He was as incredulous as everyone else about this. His blue eyes widened, and his mouth dropped open a bit. It was as if I'd revealed I'd never seen it rain.

"I've been living on the grounds of an isolated temple for years," I explained. "The nearest village had no internet or wireless phone service. I paid to use an old computer a couple of times a week in the back of a bakery in another village, but I could only afford limited time. And it was a two-mile walk back and forth."

"You need a phone, Ivy."

"I bought an inexpensive one at the Singapore airport, but it doesn't connect to the internet. Have you ever been to that airport? It's a remarkable place— almost like a theme park. Of course, all the money they poured into it could've been used to relieve suffering— for food or medical endeavors such as yours."

"I've never been to Singapore. I find things like that obscene. What sort of priorities run our world, Ivy? Why can't things be more compassion-based?'

"Amen. As a species, we're not as evolved as we'd like to think, are we?"

"War, starvation, crime, greed—they're all still major characteristics of humanity," Brian agreed. "I think that working toward eliminating, or at least minimizing these base elements needs to be humanity's highest priority."

"Of course." I nodded, but my uncle didn't see it. He was busy ogling a teenage girl in tight black yoga pants shooting baskets in her driveway. "Like you," I continued, hoping he was listening, "I do all I can to reduce suffering in the world."

We were past the girl's house now, and Brian returned his full attention to our conversation. When he spoke, his tone was gentle. "I don't mean to be critical, Ivy, but tell me how hanging around a monastery, or whatever it is, reduces other people's suffering. I don't get it. Didn't you abdicate your role as a member of society—as someone who's in a position to enact social justice?"

"Yes. That's one reason I left."

"You left? You're not going back?" He swiveled his head to look at me as we turned a corner by a young redwood tree. His eyebrows elevated and his eyes widened again—not as much this time.

"No, I'm not. It's time to build a life of my own."

"You have plans?" His tone implied that I ought to.

Now he stopped, so I did too.

"Nope. I'm going to play it by ear and see what happens."

"You could join me in Cameroon. We always need more volunteers." Brian nodded his head, priming the pump for me to nod back.

He resumed walking. I scurried to catch up and stay abreast.

"We'll see," I told him. It was certainly an option. If I felt directed by the universe, I'd be willing.

"Let me tell you more about our work," Brian said.

"Sure."

So as we strolled, the remainder of our conversation consisted of a detailed description of the clinic Brian led in a rural area in northwest Cameroon. At first, I sensed he was sugarcoating the facts to entice me. Gradually, the hardships, challenges, and risks emerged. The area was unstable, for one thing, with separatists fighting state troops. My uncle had truly dedicated himself to helping where help was most needed. I told him so as we retraced our steps to Jan's house.

"We all need to play our part if we want this to be a better world," he replied, looking away as if that better world was off to our right somewhere.

Just before we reached the house, a golden retriever charged us. Uncle Brian instinctively covered his crotch with his hands and turned sideways. I leaned down and put my hand out—palm down—so the dog could sniff me. She began barking as she drew closer, but her tail wagged furiously. She was enjoying herself. It was obvious she was friendly.

Pulling up short, she skidded a bit on the asphalt, her nails clacking. After a sniff or two of my knuckles, the dog tilted her head up and watched me with a plaintive expression, so I patted her head and then scratched behind her ears.

I loved dogs, and they loved me. At the sangha, several young monks had called me a dog whisperer, which I didn't understand until they explained they'd seen an American TV show about a man who was gentle with horses.

"Molly!" a woman's voice called from up a nearby driveway.

Molly was enjoying our exchange too much to take off, although she cast a glance at her owner before returning her attention to my ministrations.

"Come!" The woman's voice was strong, with an air of authority. I had an urge to go to her myself.

I pulled my hand away in the spirit of neighborly cooperation, and Molly turned and sprinted away. Uncle Brian's face was red when I straightened and turned to him. A grimace spoke to his embarrassment.

"I hope you don't think I'm a coward," he said. "I had a bad experience with a dog recently."

"No worries."

"Thank you for defusing the situation before any harm was done."

Clearly, Brian didn't understand dogs at all. Molly was excited to meet new friends. She was no more likely than I was to bite him. Maybe less if he kept ogling underaged girls.

The girls were home, which surprised me. I'd lost track of the time, which was unlike me. Holly was visible on the back patio, wearing headphones while she sat up straight in a lawn chair and watched a video on a laptop. I was almost disappointed in her lack of commitment to a wholly slouching lifestyle. Maybe she employed good posture when no one was looking.

Holly could've been a yoga instructor waiting to teach her next class. She was fit enough, and her black leggings and stretch cobalt-blue tank top might've inspired her students to purchase similar outfits in the studio's gift shop. They looked great on her.

Dee joined us in the kitchen when she heard us come in the front door. In contrast to her sister, she wore her customary overalls, over a red flannel shirt this time. Half of her light blonde hair was trapped underneath a strap of her overalls. The other half fell down onto the right side of her chest. Dee had jettisoned her purple ski cap. Perhaps she only wore it for special occasions, such as meeting her wacky aunt.

"Uncle Brian!" She rushed into his arms. "Did you bring me anything? I love the mask you brought last time. It's on the wall above my bed."

"Be careful, Dee. It's a fertility mask. I think it's a bit premature for you to start a family."

"Really? A fertility mask?"

"Well, more or less." He paused for a moment. "Was what I said inappropriate? How old are you now?"

"I'm fourteen, and I'd say it was."

"Me too," I added.

"Sorry. Anyway, no. No gifts this time. I hurried here when I heard about Lois."

The three of us settled in around the kitchen table. From that vantage point, I could see the LED clock on the oven. It was 1:10.

"Why aren't you at school?" I asked Dee.

"It's a half day today," Dee told me. "The teachers need to get together now and then to plot against us—to figure out how to trick us into learning." She grinned. "It's in short supply at my school."

"Why's that?" Brian asked. "My understanding is that you attend a highly rated institution."

"It's the whole Western educational system. It's completely obsolete."

"In what ways?" Brian asked.

"Oh, lots of ways. I don't want to talk about that. I want to talk about the murder. Do they have any suspects?"

"No, not yet," I responded. "But they have found out some surprising things already." Brian and I filled her in on Dennis's real identity and background.

"Wow," she responded when we were through. "I've never liked the guy, but Grandma definitely loved him. That's so weird. What's this other wife like?"

"We don't know anything," Brian answered.

"She's from Bulgaria, like Dennis," I offered.

Dee lowered her head and researched Bulgaria on her phone, announcing tidbits of information every few seconds.

Brain excused himself after a few minutes of this. "I'm going to lie down in one of the spare bedrooms," he told us.

"Consider your audience," I suggested once he'd departed.

Dee looked up. "What?"

"Your uncle isn't quite as interested in Bulgaria as you are."

"Oh, gotcha. I need to keep better track of that, I guess." She put down her phone and faced me.

"Let's talk about your mom for a minute," I suggested. "Is that okay?"

"Sure." She shoved her phone across the table to where she couldn't easily reach it. "Go ahead."

"You know she wants me to play detective about our mom—she thinks Dennis is responsible for her death—and he might well be."

"Yeah, I know. I overheard her on the phone. Aunt Ivy, I haven't seen her like she's been lately in a long time. She's really fixated."

She stared out the sliding door at Holly, who seemed mesmerized by what she was watching on her laptop—a band dancing around a construction site.

"You think Dennis did it?" Dee asked. "I mean,

somebody definitely killed *him*, right? So there's a killer out there who *isn't* him."

"Right. It seems unlikely to me for that reason."

"Poor Grandma. She was the best. Did you know she bought me a trombone once just because I said I liked the sound of it when we listened to one of her old records?"

"Do you play it?"

"No, I couldn't make enough wind when I was eight—that's what the music teacher said, anyway. So I traded it in for a violin."

"I didn't know you played the violin."

"I don't. It's a long story. Let's get back to something more interesting."

"You know, Dee, most girls your age love to talk about themselves."

She rolled her eyes. "Tell me about it. I'm at school with them all day long. They're so self-absorbed, you could light their shoes on fire, and they'd tell you all about the cool new ones they were going to buy."

I laughed. "Okay, here's something with more substance. I think you're mature enough to hear this. Actually, I think you need to hear it, based on what you said about your mom. And share it with Holly if you think it's a good idea. I'll leave it up to you."

"That's kinda ominous, Aunt Ivy."

"Sorry." I smiled to diffuse the vibe I'd put out. "Let me start with a question. I wonder if you noticed anything in particular I need to know about Jan. You mentioned she hasn't been herself lately. Did that start before Mom's stroke?"

"Yeah, but it's worse since." Dee shook her head slowly, the way an old man would.

"Anything you'd call a symptom?"

"You mean like a mental health thing?" Her surprise was evident in her eyes.

"Yes. I don't know what she's told you about her history, but I think you're old enough to know she's always going to be at risk."

"At risk of what?" Dee stared at me intently.

"Jan takes meds for bipolar disorder. Years ago, there were some incidents." I felt a frown creep in, and I dispelled it with some effort. The memories were intense.

Dee was silent. I wondered if I'd erred in confiding in her. Was it an aunt's job to out her sister to anyone, let alone one of her children?

"I appreciate your telling me this," Dee finally said. "It makes sense."

"It's an atypical version," I told her.

"What does that mean?" She searched my face for an answer this time.

"If you look up the diagnostic criteria, Jan doesn't fit the profile perfectly. Some people don't. But her poor impulse control, emotional dysregulation, unstable moods, and bouts of disrupted sleep certainly fit. Plus she sometimes cycles into hypomania or mania. By that, I mean, she speeds up even more and makes poor choices."

"I know what those terms mean," Dee told me.

"Sorry. Of course you do. What I'm trying to say is that not everyone's like the TV movie version—acting crazy and out of control all the time."

"Why are you telling me this? I'm only fourteen."

"Fourteen going on forty, Dee. I see who you are, like you always say about me. I think I know what you can take in and use in a helpful way."

"That's kinda arrogant, isn't it?"

I nodded. "I suppose it is. I have a problem with arrogance."

"That's all right. I forgive you." She smiled wanly.

Then she looked down at her feet for a while, displaying the ragged middle part in her hair, and the pinkish scalp under it.

"I'm sorry if knowing about your mom is creating problems for you," I said, interpreting her body language as distress.

Dee looked up immediately. "No, I'm glad I know now. Like I said, it explains a lot. But it's weird you're telling me. No one else talks to me like I'm an adult."

"Do you think you are one?"

"In some ways, but I still act like a stupid kid sometimes."

"Don't we all?"

She looked at me for a moment, but her attention was inward. "So what am I supposed to do about this?"

"Keep an eye on Jan. You know her better than I do—at least in recent years—so you're likely to notice things I might not catch. Then let me know what's going on, and I'll take it from there."

"Okay." Dee nodded.

"And in my experience, when she gets an idea in her head—like your grandma being murdered—it's best to proceed as though it's so, and then gradually disprove the idea if it isn't. No amount of reasoning will get through at first."

"She *is* incredibly stubborn," Dee agreed.

"It's more than that. It's a symptom."

We both paused. Through the sliding patio doors, I watched Holly rock her head in time to the music pumping through her headphones while she watched another music video. I hoped she wasn't destroying her hearing.

"So are you're going to play detective like Mom wants?" Dee said. "If you are, can I help?"

"The police are investigating. If that doesn't go anywhere, I know Jan won't let go of the idea unless I intervene and explore things more thoroughly. So I'm prepared to do that. I can bring certain skills to the table that the police lack."

"Like what?"

"They're short on intuition, I think, and I suspect they miss the big picture element."

"Okay, fine, but you haven't answered my other question." Dee's youthful impatience was there in her tone.

"I'm sorry. What was it again?"

"Can I help? I want to help. This is so exciting."

"Sure—if it turns out we need to pursue this. I'm hopeless with tech and computers, and I imagine you're a whiz compared to me."

"Compared to most everyone," she replied proudly.

"That could really help."

"Great. Is it wrong for me to hope the police don't make progress?"

"No, I understand."

Chapter Eight

I called Rick early the following morning. "Is there anything you can share about the ongoing cases? Ray Petrie told me not to bother you, so let me know if this call is a bother."

"No bother. I've been keeping an eye on both cases. It turns out the so-called other wife is full of it. Oops. Sorry, Ivy."

"I'm fine with off-color language, Rick. You can even fart and tell dirty jokes if you want."

He laughed. I'd always liked his laugh, a low rumble.

"I think I'll pass. Anyway, Dennis was separated from Maria and had been for years, and they were never married, except by some friend when they were all drunk. There's no paperwork. The thing is, she's a nut job all the way around, and the way Dennis dealt with her was to always take her phone calls so she wouldn't freak out and show up at the house or something. Apparently, your mom knew about her."

"She did freak out and call the police when he didn't answer," I pointed out.

"Yes, which was handy. She about drove Petrie nuts in his interview, though. They were in there for an hour and a half, and mostly I think she talked about her cats."

"So she doesn't know anything about his murder?"

"Who knows? She said Dennis used to deal with

100

some nasty types in the past, but he'd been out of the business for years."

"Nasty types? Criminals?"

"Maybe. I don't know."

"What about my mother's death?"

"They're still investigating up in the city."

"Can you tell me more about that?" I needed to find out all I could before Rick clammed up.

"I shouldn't, but what the hell. The nurse on duty— the guy who was supposed to keep an eye on her—got a phone call and disappeared for twenty minutes shortly before you arrived at the hospital. Pretty convenient, right?"

"Absolutely. Oh, and I just remembered something," I said hurriedly. "My sister said Dennis's sister was an administrator at the hospital. That might figure into things."

"I'll pass it on, but I'm sure the force up there already knows that. I'm sorry, Ivy, but I shouldn't even be on the phone right now. You need to deal with Art Petrie on the murder down here. He's a great cop."

"Can't you put me in touch with whoever's looking into Mom's death? I think I have some insights gained from talking to Dennis that might help."

"No, I can't do that. Sorry."

"I understand. Are you comfortable telling me a little more about Detective Petrie?"

"Why?"

"He intrigues me."

"Intrigues you, huh? Is that Buddhist code for wondering if he's single?"

"We don't use codes. We just speak pig latin around Christians. Sometimes we surreptitiously pass notes in the back of classrooms."

Rick laughed again. "Like us in high school."

"Exactly. That was proto-Buddhist behavior. I stuck with it and you didn't."

"So is that what you want to know, Ivy—whether he's single?"

"You detectives are relentless, aren't you? Yes, I'm interested in his life circumstance. It's a little embarrassing to admit it."

"No, I get it. If I were a woman, I'd go for him. He's a great guy, as well as a great detective. The thing is, he doesn't hang out in bars with the rest of us or gossip at the water cooler, so I don't know him all that well."

"That's a real thing? Water cooler talk?"

"Absolutely. Water and coffee are the only free perks we get, so we all end up in the break room. I can tell you this about Art. He lost his wife to breast cancer about six years ago, and he doesn't have any kids. Originally, he's from somewhere like Chicago or Milwaukee. I don't remember exactly."

"Thanks, Rick."

"I'm surprised you're interested. Isn't being a nun all about not hooking up with men?"

"My future is full of possibilities."

"Well, there's a vague answer if I ever heard one."

"Thank you. That's what I was shooting for."

"In other words, it's none of my business?"

"Thanks for your help."

"I get it. Bye, Ivy."

I sat and pondered my side of the conversation. Had I been rude to cut Rick off? Had it been inappropriate to ask about Petrie? For that matter, had I taken advantage of Rick's good nature to get the information I wanted?

I checked in with my gut. How did it feel? What could it tell me? All was well down there—no tension, no sourness, no churning. My body adjudicated my behavior as passing muster, regardless of my conscious doubts.

Asking about Petrie was simply expressing a normal human need to explore connection with an attractive man. Whether anybody found it odd I'd transitioned to someone with active hormones so quickly was beside the point. Truth be known, I was probably more surprised than anyone else.

I was definitely using my history with Rick to gather information from the police I would otherwise have no access to. But Rick was an adult who could decide not to talk to me if he didn't want to. In fact, that was what he planned to do, it sounded like, at the request of his boss.

Satisfied with my assessments, I headed to Dee's room, where she was playing an alarmingly violent computer game. I watched over her shoulder as she vaporized several multi-armed aliens with a huge ray gun. Her victims resembled statues of Shiva I'd seen in Varanasi—if someone had painted them purple and injected them with steroids.

"Don't you have to get ready for school?"

"Crap. What time is it?"

I told her and she ran to her backpack, stuffing it with schoolbooks. She suddenly looked up at me. "What's the story with the police? Do you know anything new?"

"I've thought it over. We're on," I announced. "They're investigating, but they don't seem to be taking in my input with the weight it deserves. I know what Dennis told me, and I have ideas about what that might mean. The police are just thinking of me as some schmo expressing an opinion—worse yet, a schmo with an ax to grind because the victim is her mother."

"That's great! What should I do first?"

"Go to school. Pay attention. Don't let your mom know what we're up to."

"You know what I mean, Aunt Ivy."

"When you get time, see what you can find out about an administrator at the hospital Mom was in up in San Francisco. I don't remember her name, but she's supposed to be Dennis's sister. His real last name was Todorov, so that's a start. Then research who the nurse on duty was on Mom's floor and what his background is. That'll get us started. Can you remember all that?"

"Of course." Dee nodded several times to emphasize her capabilities. "What are you going to do?"

"I'll go talk to some people, assuming your mom will lend me her other car."

"The Jaguar? No one's driven that for weeks. Mom only took it in the divorce so Brad couldn't have it. He loves that car."

"I wish your mom wasn't so spiteful. It's not doing her any good."

"It sure doesn't do Dad any good, either," she replied. "I mean, he's a crap father, but still. He's angry all the time now, and he's drinking a lot. He didn't used to be like that."

Then Dee sprinted out of the room without another word.

"Sorry I kept you!" I called after her.

Jan slept in—the mother of a friend of Holly's was driving the girls that day. When she finally woke up at nine, she willingly lent me her extra car.

"I only drive it every now and then past Brad's work. He's got a window facing the street."

"Jan, how does it feel to take the low road about the divorce?"

She grinned. "Delicious. I love it."

I sighed and shook my head.

After a shower, I headed to the Palo Alto police station. Or tried to, anyway. Driving a car for the first time in over a decade proved to be an adventure. For starters, I couldn't find where to put the key into the ignition after I figured out how to extract a strange-looking key from the electronic fob that unlocked the door. Finally finding a button to push, I backed out of Jan's driveway, faced the wrong way, and drove a mile or two before I realized I was heading away from my destination. After that, each iteration of merging, changing lanes, and coming to a dead stop in the middle of Highway 280 when traffic backed up was like learning to drive all over again.

The silver sedan itself rode beautifully and smelled of expensive leather. Just a few knobs and buttons were scattered around the dash and center console. There must've been other ways to control the Jaguar's features, but I didn't try to find out. My familiarity with high-end English cars was limited to James Bond movies. I knew I wasn't likely to launch an ejector seat, but who knew what else the car might do if I pushed the wrong button.

Parallel parking proved to be another challenge. A space almost in front of the police station tempted me, and I tried my hand at the maneuver. I gave up after holding up a line of cars for much longer than they were happy about. Unlike Asia, no one leaned on their horn, but as several drivers passed me when the oncoming lane opened up, they shot me withering looks. I ended up in a public lot two blocks away, parked next to another Jaguar—this one a sports car.

"How can I help you?" a chubby, very young officer asked at the now-familiar front counter when my turn to approach him finally came.

There had been four people ahead of me, and the line had moved slowly, especially when a heavy-set woman in a pink muumuu refused to leave until her son was released. Two officers had to escort her out as she shouted epithets.

"I'm worried about my sister," I told the man behind the glass divider. Even this first lie felt awful. I told myself it was for a good cause and continued. "She was supposed to be in here yesterday afternoon for an interview, and she has a serious mental health problem."

"Name?"

His tone was stentorian. Perhaps weathering so much abuse a few minutes earlier had exhausted his goodwill. The woman had called his rosacea disgusting, and had belittled his fledgling beard and shaggy hair—"You look like a drunk hobo, you waste of space!" Before she'd been ejected, she'd even backhanded his baseball cap askew, and he hadn't fixed it.

"First of all, thank you for your service," I said. "You shouldn't have to deal with people like that woman. Your job is hard enough."

"I appreciate your saying that, ma'am."

This was the first "ma'am" in my life, an unwelcome milestone in aging. I'd been a father figure in Jan's eyes, and now a stranger believed I was middle-aged. I mollified my reaction to this latest insult by reasoning that the officer might have simply been employing military-style courtesy. A lot of ex-soldiers became policemen.

"Well, the thing about my sister," I continued, "is that she uses all sorts of names because she thinks she's a lot of different people. It's really crazy. Can you just tell me if someone crazy was here yesterday? She might have used Maria as her first name. She does that a lot."

Just then, another male officer—older and even heftier—emerged from a door to our left. His white hair and neatly trimmed white beard lent him a kindly, grandfather-like air, but his eyes belied that. The dark circles under them and his downturned mouth further indicated his depression.

"Hey, Bill," my guy called, his voice friendlier now. "Any crazy women in here yesterday?"

"Yeah, Maria Kostova. If you see her coming, run." Then the sad cop hurried out the front door.

The front counter officer turned to me. "Is that her?"

I nodded. That sounded like a Bulgarian last name.

"There you go. Anything else?"

"No, I guess I just wanted to make sure she got here okay. Thanks." I turned to leave.

"Hold it," the officer said.

I felt a surge of fear race up into my throat as I pivoted to face him.

"You have a nice day, ma'am." He smiled and I could see he was trying to make up for his earlier sharp tone.

I smiled back. I appreciated his gesture even as my heart pounded. "Oh, sure. You, too."

Being an investigator could be harrowing, I realized. And my deception wasn't passing the gut test. My stomach churned, and I felt muscular tension in my jaw and neck. Even though I believed it was for the greater good, lying was scarcely aligned with my value system.

New consequences reared their head a few minutes later as I returned to Jan's car. It was as though I'd swallowed something spoiled that wasn't dissolving in my stomach. And my arms felt as though they were coated with toxic sweat, a prickly layer that refused to evaporate into the air. My body had found new ways to punish me for lying.

I was shocked by the intensity of all this. I knew there would be consequences, and I could've guessed some of them would be somatic, but this? Lesson learned, I told myself. No more lying unless it was absolutely necessary.

I drove to the public library where I could use a computer to try to find Maria Kostova—Dennis's ex-partner. I probably wouldn't get anywhere since all I knew how to do was google her name, but it wouldn't hurt to try.

I'd spent a lot of time in the previous library building as a child. A refuge from my father and sister, the Spanish-style interior afforded me an assortment of nooks to curl up in. I probably read three books a week, expanding my world exponentially. For some reason, despite our wealth, our family never traveled far. If I wanted to understand people in other countries, I needed to read about them.

The new library building—well, new to me—was a work of art. Unlike the minimal, modern design of the police station, this architect had created a multi-level, multi-surfaced exterior with a glass-faced main structure. Inside, an atrium, curved walls and counters, and well-lit rows of books charmed me. I wondered if they'd brought in a feng shui consultant to create the feeling of harmony.

A generous row of computer terminals—hidden behind the reference section—meant that I didn't have to wait to try to find Dennis's ex.

A news article popped up immediately. One of her cats had won a major cat show down in Los Angeles. Maria raised and sold exotic purebred cats. The photo of the winner looked like a cross between a raccoon and a skunk. I almost shuddered when I saw it. The article mentioned that Maria's business was called Rose Garden Cats, which was a district in San Jose, twenty-five minutes south.

I googled the business, found her website, and discovered she operated out of her home, part of which had been converted to cat-friendly quarters. In her gallery of photos, instead of kennel pens, the digs were more akin to a cat playground, with all sorts of apparatus, toys, and fuzzy, brown walls to scratch. I counted sixteen of the weird-looking breed in one of the photos.

From the library, I headed to Maria's. I try not to have too many expectations, which I've learned are a precursor to all sorts of negative attitudes and feelings. Nonetheless, when I met Dennis's ex, my surprise tipped me off that I had unknowingly harbored inaccurate ones.

I knocked on the red door to her ranch-style home, and she greeted me with a wide smile spread across her pleasant, fair-skinned face. Her naturally blonde hair cascaded onto her broad shoulders, which also supported the straps of stained, rust-colored corduroy overalls, which were coated with cat hair. Under this, she wore a dark green T-shirt. She was probably in her early fifties. I would've guessed she was some sort of artist if I didn't know better.

"Good morning," she said with only a trace of a Slavic accent.

"Hi. I hope it's okay that I just dropped by."

"Sure, sure. Come in. Have some coffee. Meet my cats."

Her voice was strong and high-pitched, like an opera singer.

"Thank you."

Maria ushered me into a spacious living room, with pieces of Scandinavian-looking furniture scattered on figured maple 'flooring. There was no evidence that a cat had ever set foot in the room. She saw me notice that.

"This is my refuge from the horde."

"I see."

"I'll just go get the coffee."

"Thanks." It didn't feel appropriate to tell her I preferred tea.

She bustled out of the room, and I looked around more closely. Perhaps a real detective could've discerned clues from the spare furnishings and the photos of European cathedrals on the walls. It was beyond me.

I seated myself on a quite uncomfortable light-colored wood and brown leather couch that had looked wonderfully comfortable. Maria came back and settled into an even more comfortable-looking chair across the simple wooden table on which she set our plain white mugs. I suspected her perch really was comfortable, but, after all, you never know. Clearly, if I could be tricked by the likes of a couch, I was no maestra about chairs.

"So you're interested in a cat," Maria said, leaning forward.

"Actually, no. I'm Anton's stepdaughter. I'm trying

to find out what happened to him."

She stood abruptly, and her hands went to her hips. "I don't appreciate your lying. First you want a cat. Now you want to interrogate me. You're not the police. I don't care about you."

Her eyes blazed, and her lips squeezed shut.

I showed her my palms and softened my voice. "I'm sorry for the confusion. I never mentioned a cat, and I'm not here to give you a hard time. Like you, I'm grieving—for my mother, Anton's wife—and like you, I want to know what happened to him as well. That's all. If you don't want to help me, that's fine."

Maria sat down as suddenly as she'd stood, and then stared at the two squat coffee mugs neither of us had touched. "I don't trust the police," she finally said wearily. "I told them nothing. I pretended I was crazy. Where I come from, they are always your enemy, and Anton was not always a good boy."

"What do you mean?"

"He sold things to bad people. This very house was bought with that money."

"He sold animals, you mean?'

She nodded. "And some other things."

"And you feel guilty about that money financing your home?"

She laughed. "That's a three-thousand-dollar sofa. Should I feel bad about that? About having a new roof over my head? No, I'm just telling you to watch out. You can't trust the police. Never trust the police. And if you stir things up, you may meet some other people you don't want to meet."

"Tell me more about them."

"When Anton had meetings with his customers in

Ireland—in his own office—he had two bodyguards in there with him. When he went overseas—all over the world—I prayed he'd come back. I worried and I prayed."

"Did he always come back safely?"

"No. Once he was in jail in Africa for two months. And once he came back from South America with both arms broken. After a while, I couldn't take it anymore and I left him. Because Anton bought papers for us with new names when he got indicted, I could come here when he did, but we weren't a couple anymore. Now I have my cats. My beautiful cats."

"I appreciate you sharing this with me."

"You, I trust—now that we're talking. I have second sight. My family has always had it. I see that you are a good person. Naive, but good. Are you a social worker? Or maybe a minister?"

"Something like that."

"And you have not had sex in many years," she pronounced.

I blinked several times involuntarily, but didn't reply.

"That's all right," Maria said, grinning. "I'm just showing off."

I felt uncomfortable being the focus of our conversation. "Can you tell me more about Anton?"

"Well, besides his work, he was a bad person to be with for other reasons. He lied, he cheated. He was mean sometimes. In Bulgaria, this is normal. The men there are pigs. Eventually, I found out I didn't have to have this. I didn't have to have anyone. And Anton was generous when we split up. He had so much money when we got here, it was easy for him to give me the house and an allowance."

"That seems out of character."

"Well, it was important for him to keep me happy because of what I knew about him."

"Ah, I see. And you don't want to tell me any details about what you know?"

"No, it wouldn't be safe. It's better you don't know. Someone may come to my door with a gun someday. I don't want that for you."

"I understand."

"Everything he did was because it was good for him. My therapist says he was a narcissist—like Trump, but not so bad."

"Why were you with him in the first place if he was such an awful partner?"

"I was young and foolish, and I needed to get away from my father, plus he was a wonderful lover—very manly. His family had money, too. They owned a mill."

"Was it hard to adjust to coming here?"

"First we went to Copenhagen—after Anton graduated with his languages. So I got used to being somewhere different before I had to do it again. It wasn't so bad moving here from Dublin, except I couldn't make friends for a long time. People in San Jose act friendly and they wave and say hello, but they don't let you into their hearts. They don't even sit and talk like we're doing."

I reached out, grabbed my mug, and took a sip. Maria made wonderful coffee, and I told her so.

"Thank you. Coffee is important to me. It's the only way I can keep up with my cats."

"I can't imagine how hard it must be to have so many cats."

Maria talked about cats for twenty minutes before I excused myself.

At the door, she asked if we could meet for coffee again. I told her yes. She was lonely and needed a friend who didn't hunt rodents.

Chapter Nine

Dee called while I was driving north in heavy traffic. I pulled off onto the shoulder and asked what she'd found out.

"Dennis's sister Agnes is the number-two person at the hospital. She's in charge of the day-to-day stuff. She's about as ugly as anyone you ever saw. Her head is giant, and even so, her nose is about three-quarters of her face. She's got a married name now. Murphy. I can't imagine why anyone would marry her. Ugh. She's got an old name from when she was a Catholic nun, too. Sister Agatha. Before that, she was in the military back in Bulgaria."

"Where did you find out all this?"

"Everything's online somewhere, Aunt Ivy. That part was easy. To find out about Grandma's nurse, I had to get sneaky."

"Do I want to know what you mean? Are you talking about subterfuge on the phone or illegal hacking?"

"You're right. You don't want to know. But don't worry. I know what I'm doing."

"I hope so, Dee. So maybe Agnes's background makes her a viable suspect?"

"That's what I'm thinking. She'd definitely know how to use a gun, and maybe she killed people when she was in the army. I can't remember if they had any wars in Bulgaria when she was there."

"What about her motive?"

"I can't think of one, but she was there in the hospital right before Grandma died, and she must know about medical stuff."

"Would she kill her own brother?"

"I guess not. Hey, maybe they weren't really related. Maybe that's a scam or something."

"We'll see."

"Anyway. Grandma's nurse is named Paul Forbes, and he just got married to another guy. He lives in Daly City near the freeway. He seems okay. He goes to a non-evil church, and he's never been arrested or anything."

"How would you know all that?" Dee was silent. "Okay. Anything else?" I asked.

"The police left a voicemail. They want to talk to Holly and me—with Mom there, of course. Should I be worried?"

"No, not at all. They're just trying to find out all they can about Dennis. He kept a lot of secrets. Maybe he said something significant to you two." I paused a moment. "Aren't you at school, Dee?"

"It's lunch."

"You did all this during lunch?"

Once again, Dee was silent.

"Fine. Just don't make me regret asking for your help."

"I won't."

After we hung up and I returned to the freeway in harrowing fashion—no one wanted to let me merge—my stomach rumbled, so I took the next exit and prowled for an interesting restaurant. Jan had lent me enough money to splurge, but that felt wrong. On the other hand, fast food restaurants didn't cater to vegetarians.

I ended up at a colorful taqueria, where I ordered a burrito with beans, rice, and every peripheral ingredient available. Then I heaped on their hottest salsa before each bite. After spending time in India, spiciness inflation demanded fire.

****

Jan was busy showing houses that afternoon, so she asked me to accompany her daughters to the police station, which felt inappropriate to me, but who was I to decide her priorities for her?

When it was time to leave, while I waited in the driveway, Dee ran out of the house and clambered into the front seat of the Jaguar in her personal uniform— voluminous denim overalls, a T-shirt, and a ski cap. This time the cap was black, and the T-shirt was bright orange. Her honey-blonde hair cascaded down from the sides of the cap. One ear was covered. One wasn't.

I leaned against the steeply sloped hood and waited for Holly. When she finally emerged, I thought about directly challenging her clothing choices. Jan would've. Holly had decided to visit a police station in cut-off jeans and a midriff-baring top that proclaimed "I'm worth the wait."

I looked at her as she approached and said, "Really?"

She knew exactly what I meant.

"You're not my mother," she retorted.

"Okay, then. Hop in. But don't complain to me when you draw unwanted attention at the station."

"I won't." She looked away, up into the trees across the street.

"I forgot something," I told the girls, and then I returned to the guesthouse and collected the blue work shirt I'd bought in Sri Lanka.

The minute we walked into the lobby, an unshaved young man with dead eyes pretended to tie his shoes so he could try to see up Holly's shirt. She noticed.

Wordlessly, I handed her my extra shirt. She hurriedly put it on and folded her arms across her chest.

Dee spoke to her sister while we waited our turn to step up to the front counter. "You should listen to Aunt Ivy," she said. "She knows stuff. You don't have to rebel against her. Like you said, she's not Mom."

"I own my body," Holly answered sullenly, looking down at her blue running shoes.

"That wasn't very convincing," Dee told her. "When you say things like that, don't look down. Look people right in the eye."

"I don't need advice from you." Her tone was scornful now.

"Fine. Excuse me for trying to help."

The "howdy" guy was back, patiently dealing with an elderly man who'd lost his wallet. I was glad I wasn't going to have to explain to the rosacea guy why I'd returned.

"Aloha," the Asian officer greeted when it was our turn.

"Is that a keeper?" I asked. "I like it even better than howdy."

"It's just for you. The chief has me saying 'how may I help you?' to everyone now."

"That makes it sound like you work in a store," Dee said from beside me.

"Indeed," he answered.

Holly lagged behind me.

"No hiding," the officer told her.

She sidled up to the other side of me. "You're kind of weird for a cop," she told him.

"Thank you." He turned his attention back to me. "Have you managed to fence that bridge yet?" he asked.

For moment, I was confused. I pictured constructing a picket fence alongside a wooden bridge in the country. Then I remembered our first encounter.

"You bet. There's a Saudi prince who has the Golden Gate in his backyard now. Well, his back sand dune. The one you still see in the bay is a clever imitation my two nieces here cobbled together."

"Very good. Congratulations, girls. Now, how can I help you?"

Dee wanted in on the repartee. "I'm looking for a size ten in something casual. Maybe in green?"

"Oy, that stings. You cut me to the quick."

"Shakespeare," she told him.

"Shakespeare right back at you. Unfortunately, there are people waiting, so…"

"Art Petrie is going to interview us—about the Anton Todorov murder case," I told him. "He was my stepfather."

"Ah, let me get him out here. I'm sorry for your loss. You can take a seat over there by those scary men, or stand over this way, which I recommend."

"Right," I said. "And thank you for the fun interchange."

"You bet. Don't forget to tip your waitress."

"What did he mean by that?" Dee asked once we'd retreated to the safe half of the lobby.

Holly answered. "Comedians work in nightclubs, and they supposedly say that at the end of their acts. If they really do, I think it's to get on the good side of the servers so they can sleep with them. A lot of these guys are really funny-looking, so they have to do extra stuff to get laid."

"Oh, that makes sense. Thanks."

Dee looked at me and winked. She'd taken a one-down position on purpose. I winked back. We'd launched a benign conspiracy to help Holly feel better about herself.

Art Petrie's face brightened when he saw me instead of Jan. I was charmed by the combination of his remarkable smile and his alert brown eyes.

"Ivy! It's good to see you. And this must be Dee and Holly."

"Yeah, we must be," Holly said.

I could see this was bravado. Her voice gave away her nervousness.

Dee proffered her hand and shook the detective's. "I've been looking forward to meeting you," she told him.

"Why's that?" he asked as he ushered us through a door that led to a large, noisy room with about twenty desks arrayed in ragged rows.

"I think we have something important in common," Dee told him. "We both think Ivy is someone special."

"Dee!" I admonished.

I guess she'd inferred that from my report about meeting him the day before. I was still surprised by how astute she could be. In this case, I was also annoyed.

Holly laughed. "Welcome to my world, Aunt Ivy. That's what I put up with every day."

"It's obvious she's special, isn't it?" Petrie answered. "I wish we had your aunt on the force. She's a great detective."

"No, that's not what—"

I cut her off. "That's enough, Dee. Let the man do his job."

Petrie wanted to interview each girl separately, with me present. He asked Dee to be first, so Holly shoved ear buds into her ears and climbed into his office chair, an elegant-looking black model with a half a dozen levers under its seat. I watched her try in vain to slouch in it before following Petrie and Dee out of the room.

In an almost bare interview room, four stools surrounded a high metal table. They wouldn't have been out of place in a seedy bar. Chrome legs snaked down from worn, red vinyl seats that looked as though they were the top of poorly designed snare drums. The walls were light green cinderblock with no decoration. I glanced around for the two-way mirror I expected to see. There wasn't one.

A single light fixture dangled over the table—a large globe with a strong LED bulb placed asymmetrically within it. Was that on purpose to subtly disorient suspects? It shed an unnaturally white hue with no warmth to it. Dee looked horrible illuminated by it. Petrie weathered it much better. It lent a gleam to his rich skin color—a delightful shade of dark brown.

"I'm sorry about having to be in this room," he said. "The conference room is being used today."

"That's okay," I told him. "I'm just glad I'm not a criminal."

"I think it's fascinating," Dee told him. Since we'd begun walking toward the back of the building, Dee's head had swiveled from one scenario to another. "The whole station is modern, but then they made this room look like the old ones on TV. Only on TV, they always use chairs."

She and I climbed onto the quite uncomfortable stools across the table from Petrie. I tried shifting my weight, leaning back, and taking weight off my posterior by placing my feet on the bar connecting the legs. Nothing helped.

"My boss thinks that if perps can't lean back against something, it'll encourage them to open up." Petrie told us, noticing my efforts.

"How's that work?" Dee leaned forward. "That sounds stupid."

"Well, TV is right that we leave people in here a long time to stew before we get going, and we want them as uncomfortable as possible by the time we talk to them. Did you notice how the seat of your stool wobbles so it's always tilted forward? You have to work to keep from sliding off, right? Some of us heat the room up so perps literally sweat, too. I think that's going too far."

"But why make you use a stool, too?"

"Believe it or not, our lieutenant spent a half hour covering this at a roll call after several officers complained. He's taking psych classes at community college, so now he thinks he's cornered the market on procedures."

"You didn't answer my question."

"Okay, one more answer and then I start asking you what we're here for. Deal?"

Dee nodded. "Sure."

"For one thing, while we're out of the room, anyone could switch seats and use one of our chairs. As far as I was concerned, that's all Cline needed to say. Satisfied?"

"Yes, thank you."

"So what can you tell me about Dennis that I don't

already know?" Petrie asked Dee.

I admired Petrie's open-ended question. In my experience, most people lead with overly specific questions that impede the other person them from telling what *they* thought mattered. Dee, on the other hand, didn't like his question.

"How would I know what you already know?" she responded.

"Guess. I'll bet you're a good guesser, Dee."

Despite his irritation, he'd complimented her and used her name, two good ways to establish a positive connection. I realized that police work and psychotherapy overlapped more than I thought.

"I *am* a great guesser," Dee said. "Okay, I'll give this a try, but I still think you ought to ask me specific questions."

"We'll get to that."

"So Dennis was pretty fake. I don't mean because he turned out to be someone else. I just mean about little stuff when you talked to him." She took off her ski cap and shook her head to settle her hair. "It *is* warm in here. Are you sure you're not trying to get us to sweat?"

She tossed her cap onto the table and wriggled on her stool.

"I'm not. Can you give me an example?"

"Like if I said I was in a school play, he'd say how proud of me he was."

"What's wrong with that?" Petrie's head tilted to the side as though he was puzzling this out on his own while he waited for her answer.

"I found out later he thought it was a bad idea—that I'd screw up and get humiliated. Another time I said I liked his shirt—you know, just to have something to say.

It makes people feel good when you say things like that, right? So Dennis said that Grandma picked it out for him, but she didn't."

"Why would he lie about that?" Petrie asked.

"I don't know, but you couldn't believe him about anything. After a while, I started counting how much he did it. I mean, the guy was an idiot. You could check out what he said easy enough—at least a lot of the time. Once we were at Holly's birthday party, and he made up things three times. Three times!"

She picked up her cap and waved it in the air emphatically before tossing it onto the table again.

"Why do you think your grandmother chose to be with him if he was like that?"

Dee paused before continuing. I think she was out of breath just from waving her cap.

"I asked her once years ago. She said he was fun and he loved her to pieces. Those are her exact words."

"You remember exactly what people say?"

"Yeah. I remember almost everything—not literally, but if it matters to me, yeah, I do."

"What else can you tell me about Dennis? Did he ever drop any hints about his past?"

"No. He had me fooled about that. Let me think what might be important. I guess you probably don't know he used to sneak away to go to this dive bar downtown."

"Which one?"

"The Rusty Snake, which doesn't make any sense at all. What kind of name is that? How could a reptile rust?"

"The owner's name is actually Rusty. I don't know about the snake part," Petrie told her. "That place is a hub for drug dealing. Did Dennis ever seem like he was on drugs?"

Dee shook her head. "I don't know what drug users are like, so I can't tell you about that. I figured he was hiding an alcohol problem and maybe he had creepy friends down there."

"How did you find out about this bar?"

"I'd rather not say."

Petrie stared at her. Dee didn't budge. He realized he was engaged in a staring match he was going to lose. I felt absurdly proud of my niece; she'd stood up to an authority figure and made him back down. A moment later, I felt empathy for Detective Petrie. He was trying to do his job, and now two of my family members had made that harder for him.

"Okay, fine," he said. "We'll look into that bar. Any ideas about who might want to kill Dennis? Did you know about any enemies?"

"No. I have ideas now, based on what I found out since he died, though." She leaned forward, eager to tell him what they were.

"So do we, Dee. What are yours?"

"Dennis's sister seems pretty evil."

"Why do you say that?"

"Just look at her. I saw her photo on the hospital website. And she was in the army."

Petrie wasn't sure how to respond to that. "Who else are you looking at?" he finally asked.

"That Maria person. If she has that many weird cats, who knows what else she might be capable of. That's not normal."

Petrie nodded. He was giving her a long leash.

"But mostly I think someone Dennis screwed with in his business caught up to him," Dee told him. "I don't know how you'd find out who that is."

"Right now, I don't either," Petrie responded. "We've got an officer working on it."

"That's good."

Petrie smiled at me. He was amused that a fourteen-year-old was giving her stamp of approval to what the police were doing. I felt my face heating up—flushing. That smile…

Dee caught the detective's look and misunderstood.

"Hey, no flirting with my aunt in here," she said, narrowing her eyes. "This is a serious investigation."

"Yes, ma'am. I'll watch myself."

He paused, glanced at me again, and then said, "I think that's all for now, Dee. Could you go wait with your sister until I come out to get her? Grab a chair from an empty desk."

"Okay."

When she'd left, Petrie turned to me. "Your niece is quite something. She talks like a thirty-year-old."

"Yes, she's the most precocious teenager I've ever met. And she pays attention to everything. Now and then, she acts her age, of course."

"I gather you pay attention, too."

"Yes. I have years of training."

"At a Hindu temple? Is that what you said on the phone?"

"Buddhist."

"What's the difference? You worship Buddha and they worship cows?"

He was being provocative to draw me out, and perhaps to induce me to underestimate him. He certainly remembered I was a Buddhist, and I'm sure he knew his characterization of the two religions was wildly inaccurate.

"That's not how it works, as I'm sure you know. And you don't have to play dumb or manipulate me to get straightforward answers."

"I'm sorry. Force of habit." He paused for a moment. "The thing is, I'm trying to get a better feel for you. You're no more typical than Dee is—in a different way. You're perfectly calm in here, and I think you would be anywhere. Whatever was going to happen with your niece was all fine with you. You track everything, and I'm guessing that nothing knocks you off center."

"Some drastic things certainly do. But generally, yes, it's true that ordinary life events are just that to me—ordinary."

I paused to look Petrie in the eyes, struck again by *his* poise and alertness. "You're good at your job, aren't you?" I said. "Not many people can read me that way."

"Thank you."

"And I saw you handle Jan in here—well, in that conference room yesterday. You never lost your cool for an instant. I've seen how her energy affects people. I think you're at least as poised as I am."

"Fair enough."

We caught eyes again. This time, it was an intense, almost intimate experience. I would never have imagined a policeman could be so real—so connective. It was remarkable. Petrie hadn't journeyed to Asia to learn how to do this. It was simply who he was—or so I theorized.

"What do you make of Dee's interview?" the detective asked, breaking the connection with his words.

"It was engrossing." I made sure I didn't look him in the eye. That was way too distracting.

"I mean the things she said. Is she reliable about

what she says?"

"As far as it goes. She's much more sure of herself than her life experience warrants. But she's honest, smart, and if there were things about Dennis for her to notice, she would've noticed. Of course, her comments on possible suspects are another thing altogether."

"They might turn out to be as useful as anyone else's. What about her knowing about that bar?"

"I have no idea how she might've known that. I know she's a whiz on the computer, but I can't see how that would help."

"Okay, let me go get the other one—Holly, is it?"

I nodded.

"If you wouldn't mind, let's talk after that interview, too."

"Sure."

Not surprisingly, Holly couldn't find a way to get comfortable on her bar stool. "This stool sucks," she declared. "I want a chair."

Petrie fetched one and then gave her a moment to settle in and slouch. She crossed her arms and waited for whatever came next. I could tell by her quivering lips she was scared.

"What can you tell me about your stepgrandfather?"

The detective's tone was studiously neutral—the way he'd been with Jan. With Dee, he'd stepped away from his formal role and just chatted.

"He was an asshole." Holly said this with no heat. She meant it as a descriptor, not an insult.

"Why do you say that?"

"The way he looked at me—at my body. I wouldn't be surprised if he was a pedophile. And then he was nasty to my mom all the time."

"Like?"

Petrie was employing another technique I'd learned in a clinical psych class—matching the other person's speech pattern.

"Once he hid her purse—I saw him do it. Then when she couldn't find it, he moved it into plain sight so when she came back into the room, she'd feel like an idiot. Nasty."

"Were you in the room? Did he know you were watching?"

"Yeah. Afterward, when Grandma was in the bathroom, he laughed and acted like we'd pulled some cool prank together. Creepy." Holly snorted.

"What else can you tell me?"

"Recently, I caught him spying on the neighbors."

"Tell me about that."

"He had binoculars, and he said he was checking out who was in a car that was parked down the street, but I saw a woman in a window past that. It'd be just like a pervert like Dennis to peep like that." She treated us to another explosive snort.

"When was this?"

"Um, a few days before he got killed, I guess."

"Can you tell me anything about the car?" Petrie asked.

"It was just a car—a white one."

"You don't know cars?"

She shrugged melodramatically. "Who cares about cars?"

"Right now, I do," Petrie told her.

"Oh, I get it." Holly's eyes widened. "It might have something to do with the murder, right?'

"Right. So what else can you tell me? Did Dennis

seem worried? Did you get a look at who was in the car?"

"I don't remember if he looked worried, and I think there were two guys in the car. Sorry. If Dee had been in the living room, she'd tell you all about it for half an hour."

"She wasn't with you at the house?" Art asked.

"Yeah, she was. We always went together to visit Grandma, but this time we were going to get some things to bring to her in the hospital. Dee was in Grandma's bedroom when I came back to the living room because I'd dropped something on the way in. So Dee didn't see the car. After that, we headed up to the city. Our mom was waiting out on the street. She hated being around Dennis."

"Wasn't your grandmother in a coma?" Petrie softened his voice. "What things did she need?"

"Mom said people in comas still notice what's going on, and when she woke up, Mom wanted her to have familiar things in the room."

That was interesting. I hadn't seen any of her things in her hospital room. Was that a clue? Maybe the hospital had simply removed them to keep the room sterile.

"She believed your grandmother would wake up?"

"Definitely," Holly told him, nodding vigorously. "And when Mom makes up her mind, that's it. I'll bet she was no fun for you to interview, was she?"

Petrie ignored that. "What did the doctors say when you visited your grandmother that day?"

"They didn't let Dee and me into the ICU because we weren't eighteen yet, which is ridiculous. What were we going to do—pull out crayons and write on the walls? So we had to hand the box of Grandma's stuff to this guy who said he'd bring it down to her nurse's station. Mom was in the car because she wanted us to have a chance to spend time with Grandma by ourselves. When we got back, Mom was ready to go in and tear them a new one— sorry, Aunt Ivy. But she didn't want to leave us alone because she said there were still too many crazy hippies in the area."

Petrie asked a lot more questions—nearly twice as many as he had with Dee. Clearly, he didn't trust Holly to just volunteer useful information. The only other relevant tidbit she revealed was that once she walked by Dennis on the back patio while he was on his phone. He immediately hung up without a word to whoever he was talking to. "It was probably some skank he was banging," she added. As the interview progressed, Holly's hostility toward Dennis increased. Clearly, she had hated him as much as Jan.

When Petrie finished with her, she begrudgingly agreed to go back and wait again while he talked to me.

He stood once Holly sauntered out. "I'm not spending one extra minute on this damned stool," he told me. "Any thoughts about the case now that you heard what I heard in here?"

I stood as well. Petrie was about six inches taller than me. In high school, I'd fantasized that six inches was the perfect differential for slow dancing.

"If I were you," I answered, "I'd check out that bar and look into the suspicious car—I don't buy the Peeping Tom deal. Maybe a neighbor saw the car or who was in it. I'd also check Dennis's phone records, which you're probably doing anyway."

"We are. And I'm with you on the other stuff. Anything else I might've missed?"

"On the one hand, like Dee, I think the murder could

be connected with Dennis's past. Maybe something caught up to him. Maybe there was an obituary about Mom that helped the murderer find him even though he'd changed his name. I don't know. But on the other hand, it seems like her dying right before he did is unlikely to be a coincidence. Have you found out much about his career as a smuggler?"

"Not so far. We're waiting on the Dublin police to get back to us, and he covered his tracks well here. If Maria—the ex—hadn't told us about his real business, I don't think we'd know he was involved in anything. Sometimes you get lucky early in an investigation, sometimes it's later."

"Or sometimes not at all, I imagine."

"Yeah, that's true."

"Maybe it depends on how you define luck," I said. I didn't actually believe in luck; in my world, everything that happened was due to other factors.

"Maybe. This one guy from Santa Cruz says I'm lucky because it's my karma, but I don't buy that—no offense. Still, some people are lucky, and some aren't."

"True." I smiled. We were almost talking about spirituality. "I'd better get back to the girls before Dee shows everyone up by solving all your cases."

Petrie laughed. "I wouldn't put it past her."

Chapter Ten

"I'm glad Mom wasn't there," Dee said in the car on the way home. She'd been too slow to grab the front seat this time.

"Yeah," Holly echoed from the passenger seat. "It was great that you just sat there and listened, Aunt Ivy. Mom can't shut up. She's always getting set off by every little thing."

When I dropped off my nieces at their house, I headed to my mother's neighborhood. I wanted to talk to her neighbors about the white car before the police did. I reasoned that if anyone had seen it, getting to hear about it firsthand before they told anyone else would be advantageous. I knew I might get in trouble, but I also knew I could get out of it. Both Rick Foster and Art Petrie liked and trusted me, at least so far.

I picked a direction based on where Mom's living room picture window faced, and drove three houses down the street, parking in front of a peculiar, burgundy home straight out of an architecture magazine. It looked as if the two-story steel structure might tip over any minute as half of it was cantilevered over a wading pool. The other half slanted up and away to a severely peaked roofline.

I closed my eyes and meditated in the driver's seat to center myself. Recent events, including my encounter with Detective Petrie, had pulled me away from who I wanted to be in the world. The contrast between Ivy at the sangha and the woman playing detective in the Jaguar was discouraging.

I must've lost track of the time because I was startled back to full consciousness by a rapping on my window.

"Open up!" a shrill woman's voice demanded.

A slim Caucasian in her forties sporting a burgundy spiral perm and a red sundress glared at me. I fumbled to find the button on the Jaguar that rolled down the window.

"Yes?" I ventured. I was only slowly coming back on line.

"This isn't a parking lot. I'm sick and tired of chasing off you people. Why do I want to look out my window and see feds littering my view?"

The woman's face was pinched, as if her baseline setting was anxiety. Her intense brown eyes reminded me of Jan's.

"Feds?" I asked.

"FBI, if you like. And don't bullshit me. I know who you are." She stepped up close to the car window, intentionally invading my personal space.

"My mother and my stepfather just died three doors down," I told her softly. "I'm not an FBI agent."

"Oh, God. I'm so sorry. I just assumed."

"Can I get out of the car? Can we talk?"

"Sure, sure."

She invited me in, and we sat in a huge living room with soaring river stone fireplaces at each end. The walls and wooden floor had been painted in various earth tones, the shade subtly changing every ten feet or so. There were no carpets or rugs. As much as I disliked the home's exterior, I liked the interior even less. Both were disorienting—challenging for me to make sense out of without working at it. I felt as though I were sitting in the middle of an atonal symphony.

I recovered a bit as I examined the brightly colored plastic furniture, abstract marble statues, and large tapestries around me. Most of the latter featured horse motifs. A row of tall trophies sat on each mantel—more horses, without riders. Some of them were two feet tall.

"What can I do for you?" the woman asked solicitously. I could tell by the tightened lines beside her eyes that this was an effort.

"I'm looking into the two deaths—as a private citizen—and I was told that men had been parked in a white car on the street a few days before Dennis' murder. They're suspects. Did you see them or anyone else suspicious?"

She clutched her hands to her chest. "How do I know you weren't sent by those men to kill me because I can identify them?"

"You can? That's great. Do I look like a murderer?"

"Well, no. But I don't know you, do I?" She leaned back. My response had calmed her.

"My name is Ivy Lutz. What else would you like to know?"

"Are you a Christian? Have you taken Jesus into your heart?"

"Buddha."

"Really?" She hadn't expected that.

"Yes. Very much so. I believe in loving kindness— just like Jesus."

"Well, that's not ideal, but I suppose if you're not Christian, it's better than some of the others. All right, here's what happened. I went out to talk to these two men who kept sitting in their car in front of my house. It's not okay to do that. I told them I was calling our security company if they didn't leave. Those guys get here in six minutes, and they don't fool around. I've called them before.

"So the tall one—there was a very tall one driving and a short one in the passenger seat—and you could tell even when they were sitting because the difference was so big—pulls out a badge and says, 'FBI, ma'am. I'm Agent Foster and this is Special Agent so and so.' I don't know what FBI badges look like, but it looked real, so I asked them what they were doing here, and the short one said it was an ongoing investigation and they couldn't talk about it. So I brought them some coffee and said they were welcome to stay another half hour, but that was it. I expected them to say they'd stay as long as they wanted, but they took off right at half an hour and didn't come back." She paused, stared off into space and grimaced. "You're saying they weren't feds?"

"They may have been. I don't know. The police haven't had a chance to look into it yet. I've just started playing amateur detective myself. I don't know much."

"What should I do? This is very alarming." The woman wrung her hands. I'd never seen that outside of books and films.

"Am I safe?" she continued. "I don't mean from you. I mean from whoever knows I know what I know." She struggled to get through all the "knows." Her fear manifested on her face, as well. Her upper eyelids pulled up, revealing the whites of her eyes. Her hand wringing morphed into clenched fists, which hovered above her lap.

"I think it would be a good idea to contact Detective Petrie at the Palo Alto police department," I told her. "Tell him more about the men. Let him know you approached me and we talked, if you want. If he checks it out and discovers the men aren't FBI agents, ask him if you're in danger. If you are, I'm sure he'll advise you about what steps to take. He's a good man."

"Okay, I'll do that. Now I'd like you to leave. This is all very disturbing. I need to take a pill and chill."

"Sure. Thank you for your help."

She waved this away and led me to the door.

I headed back to Woodside after a brief stop down the street to leave a voicemail for Detective Petrie, suggesting he check with the FBI about the possible agents. I also steered him to the woman's house. I'd never gotten her name, so the address was all I could tell him.

I was late for dinner, and Jan let me know she wasn't happy about that. Since Dee had ordered in pizza, at least I hadn't squandered any efforts anyone had made to prepare a meal.

Jan's outfit consisted of stiff black jeans and a Mexican peasant blouse with light blue embroidery along its scoop neck.

"You must've gotten home early if you had time to change out of your work clothes," I commented.

"I was showing a house to a guy from Venezuela who said he won the lottery. I think he's probably a criminal. Anyway, he wore jeans and a T-shirt when he walked into the office, so I tried to match him when I showed him this great place not too far from here."

"I think you look terrific, Mom," Dee told her.

"Thank you, hon."

The interchange warmed me. My family actually appreciated and supported one another occasionally. I'd only seen hints of this before.

Holly tore into her slice of pizza, folding it East Coast style first.

"Where's Uncle Brian? I asked.

"God knows," Jan answered. "I asked him if he wanted to stay for dinner—this was hours ago—and he said yes. Then he disappeared."

"He took an Uber," Dee said. "He said he had some business in the city. I forgot to tell you."

"That's an expensive ride," Jan said. "He should've rented a car if he wanted to gallivant around instead of being with his family."

"We don't know the back story here, Jan," I said. "It may be that what he's doing makes sense and we just aren't aware of it."

"What is that? What kind of condescending thing is that to say? You're accusing me of judging Brian while you're judging me yourself. Judge not, lest ye be judged, Ivy."

"I'm sorry, Jan. You're right."

"Where does Uncle Brian get his money?" Dee asked. "I looked up the organization he's working for, and everyone's a volunteer there—even the doctors."

"His wife was loaded," Jan told us. "And you can save a lot of money on a doctor's salary."

"Whatever happened to her?" Dee asked. "Did they get divorced?"

"I don't know. She was here for Christmas one year, then when we had a family reunion a couple of months later—it was your grandmother's sixty-fifth birthday— she wasn't there. I asked him about her, of course, and

Brian just shook his head. That was the end of it. I guess she got tired of him."

"Why do you say that?" I asked. She knew our uncle far better than I did.

"He's quite the ladies' man, Ivy. He always has been. You know that."

"Who cares?" Holly added with her mouth full.

I was exhausted by the meal's end, so I retreated to the guest cottage to read a mystery I'd bought in the Honolulu airport, thinking I'd be bored waiting for the next leg of my journey home. As it turned out, I couldn't tear my eyes away from my fellow travelers. The variety of people had fascinated me, although their behaviors had been puzzling sometimes. I liked trying to solve puzzles.

I fell asleep after a chapter and a half. And I dreamt.

I was in a poorly lit cave, and I somehow understood that I was in the highlands of Peru. I knew I needed to find a way out of the cave, so I began treading carefully over the uneven, rocky ground toward a light in the distance ahead of me. When I turned a corner, I saw that the light wasn't originating from outdoors. An old man in an orange robe balanced in a lotus position at the apex of a pyramid-shaped rock. He was glowing—a bright white light. I felt a strong sense of awe. I knew he was someone special. He opened his eyes and said, "Hello, Ivy. I've been expecting you," in an unaccented, deep voice. I studied his face; he looked like my paternal uncle Phil, who had been a mean drunk before dying in a car accident. But this man's face radiated love—his eyes, especially. I sat down in a matching posture and waited. "Don't be impatient. If you are, you'll get lies," he told me. Then I woke up.

Sometimes I received messages from wherever such things come from. My subconscious? An actual holy man in a cave? It didn't matter. I just needed to pay attention and heed the advice. Dreams along these lines had always proven helpful in the past.

So was I being impatient or moving too fast? Was that interfering with my efforts to discover the truth? Perhaps the man in the dream had meant to warn me about some future untoward action. I'd need to keep an eye on that.

It was three thirty. I couldn't get back to sleep, so I meditated for two hours, read a bit more, and then took a long walk around the neighborhood as dawn began to illuminate the upscale homes.

I pondered how I was coping with what I'd come back to in the States, and I realized I was being influenced by my need to grasp onto a new life focus— a purpose beyond simply being somewhere else. If I hadn't been playing detective, it's likely I would've seized on whatever else was at hand. I wasn't proud of this inability to tolerate a purposeless interlude. Unfortunately, having this insight didn't change anything. I wanted to keep investigating, regardless of the reasons why.

****

Back at the house, I joined my family where they were gathered in the living room. Other than the kitchen, this was my favorite part of the house. Most of the furniture was what Jan and I knew from our childhood— our mother's old household. I don't know how my sister had gotten hold of it. My nieces sat on a navy-blue L-shaped sectional in one corner of the rectangular room. Beside them, the sturdy stalks of a tall, mature fern in a terra cotta pot soared over their heads, parting at the top as though each frond was trying to escape the others.

"That's Zeus," Dee told me, looking up from a book in her lap. "He's planning a coup. He's going to take over the Mom regime."

Jan stretched on a red yoga mat facing the sofa, her legs corkscrewed in what looked like a very uncomfortable pose. She wore tight black clothes that resembled a wetsuit.

"Over my dead body," Jan responded, as though a plant represented a legitimate threat to her rule.

"Mom said we could have breakfast without you," Holly informed me.

"That's fine. I had a little something before I went out walking."

As I clambered into a familiar, too-soft brown armchair, I felt an even stronger sense of resolve about Mom's death. I would see this through, and I told Jan so.

She clapped her hands together and raised her voice. "Wonderful! I knew I could count on you! The police are idiots. We need an enlightened detective. And now we've got one!"

Holly chimed in. "Yeah, right. Enlightened." She grimaced as though the very idea that someone could be fully awake disgusted her.

"I'm helping," Dee told her mom.

"No, you're not. Absolutely not."

Dee rose and balled up her fists.

"She's just finding things online for me," I told Jan.

"Oh, that's okay then."

Dee sat down again, fully mollified. As always, I was amazed at how quickly a strong emotion could arise and dissipate in some people.

Jan turned to me and smirked. "I guess you don't know how to do much, do you, Ivy? Even finding things online is beyond you."

I nodded. An insult is only an insult if you react to it as though it were about you, not the insulter.

"I didn't have a computer or a smartphone even before I left for Asia," I told her. "I was committed to a low-tech lifestyle. Now I can google and email. That's about it. But I'm a whiz at Scrabble, and I can meditate like nobody's business." I smiled.

"They should have a meditation Olympics," Dee said.

"Yeah, right," Holly said. "Anyway, how is that possible—not having a phone or anything? I mean, how do you get around? How do you find out things?"

"Maps. Books. The computer at the public library if it's necessary. The way everybody did before you were born, Holly."

"That was back in medieval times, right?" Dee said. "And you had to do all that while you fought off all those Visigoths and Vikings."

"Exactly," I agreed, "along with all the European invaders whose names didn't start with V."

"You mean Magyars, Saxons, and Huns," Dee said, beaming.

"That's impressive," I told her.

"That's all wrong," Holly informed us. "It was the Muslims and the Ottomans. We just studied that at school."

"Nope. Wrong era," Dee corrected.

"Just give it a rest, Dee," Holly said heatedly. "Who cares if you know everything? God, you are such a pain sometimes."

"*You* give it a rest, you big jerk!" Dee jumped to her feet and sprinted out of the room.

"Well," I finally said, pushing back my chair. "I have some things to do."

In yet another hitherto undiscovered room with a TV and dark wood furniture, I found Dee on a loveseat facing the blank screen, holding herself perfectly still.

"Are you okay?" I asked, sliding in next to her.

"I was just trying to help. Holly should know those things for college. How's she going to look in her European History class when she says the Ottoman Empire expanded in the Middle Ages?"

"Is that really why you said it? Are you being honest with yourself?

Dee looked down. "Maybe not." Then she turned and faced me, eager to change the subject. "What did you find out today?"

She'd varied her clothing. A tie-dyed T-shirt with a swirling pattern of yellow and orange were matched with forest green corduroy jeans she'd mostly outgrown. The hem was several inches up her ankle and the weathered fabric looked uncomfortably tight around her thighs.

I was struck by Dee's efforts to be her own person. Perhaps injecting her prodigious knowledge into conversations wasn't just showing off. It could also be her way of demonstrating her individuality. I'd have bet that what Dee truly wanted out of life was to be *significant*. To be that, you had to find a way to set yourself apart from everyone else.

I filled Dee in on what Maria and the woman who'd seen the so-called FBI agents had told me. Every time I thought of the latter, I struggled to remember her name, and then belatedly remembered she hadn't told me.

"I'll bet those guys were the killers," Dee said. "Real FBI guys don't act like that."

"Do you know any agents?"

"Well, no, but I've seen them a lot on very realistic TV shows."

"You hear yourself, right?"

"Yeah. I guess we have to wait for the police to check into them. Will they tell you what they find out?"

"I'm not sure. I think Art Petrie likes me, and I was the one to steer him to that, so maybe. Rick can't talk to me anymore—orders from above."

"*Likes you* likes you?"

"What do you mean?"

"Like is he interested in you because you're so good-looking? You know—that way. I got that impression before—from what you said and then down at the station."

"Oh, I see. To tell you the truth, I have no idea, but it seems unlikely. And I think you're overestimating my attractiveness. Men don't swoon over me. They never have."

"Nobody really knows what they look like."

"That's an interesting perspective, Dee. What about when we look in a mirror?"

"Mirrors lie." She nodded vigorously. She was sure of this.

"Okay. Let's stay on topic here."

"Sure."

"I'm going to go to the Rusty Snake tonight—the bar that Dennis frequently visited, according to you," I told her. "I can't imagine how you know that, but it's fine not to tell me if you'd rather not."

"Are you sure you should do that? It might be

dangerous."

"I'll see what it's like when I get there. If I don't feel safe, I'll leave."

"What should *I* do?"

"Go to school and pay attention."

"It's Saturday!"

That reminded me we had to organize a memorial service for my mother in a week's time. I hoped Jan was working on that because I sure wasn't.

"So it is," I said. "Sorry. What would you do to help if I didn't direct you?"

"Let me think." Dee scrunched up her face, bringing furrows on her pale forehead down near the bridge of her snub nose. "I guess I'd try to find out more about Dennis's past—you know, his business and who he sold animals to—all that. I'll bet he sold some creepier stuff than just animals, too."

"Yes, that's what his ex implied."

"My theory is that the hitmen in the car were working for someone he sold stuff to—maybe terrorists or drug lords. Remember that guy who had a private zoo in Colombia? There are still hippos all over the place down there. Anyway, maybe whoever it is needed to eliminate people who knew about them."

"We don't know yet if those men in the car were agents or suspects, Dee."

She nodded begrudgingly.

I softened my words. "I guess we'll find out what makes sense for us to do when we get a little further along."

Dee abruptly changed the subject again. "Let's watch TV," she suggested.

So we did—a funny sitcom about uptight teachers

having to attend a seminar taught by a free-spirited poet. Laughing with my niece turned out to be one of the highlights of the visit so far. At one point we were both in tears, shaking uncontrollably with laughter—I don't remember why. I guess we both needed to release whatever energy we'd stored up from recent events.

I put my arm around Dee's shoulder, and she snuggled up with her head on my shoulder. This was what I'd missed when I was overseas. This was what I'd traded for self-improvement. Love.

Brian showed up at the house as the show ended, announcing loudly from the vestibule that he'd brought strudel from a German bakery up in San Francisco. When Dee and I met him and Jan in the kitchen, I helped myself to more of it than I should've.

My uncle wore a tailored, unwrinkled gray suit, with an open-collar white shirt. Why would someone tote a suit to tropical Africa, and then tote it back here, for that matter? And how could it look so perfect after a long journey in a suitcase? Perhaps he had a storage unit in town he could draw from. He certainly hadn't had time to buy a suit and get it so perfectly fitted to his long, slim frame since he'd arrived.

"So where have you been?" Jan asked in a challenging tone, as if our uncle needed to prove his absence at dinner the evening before had been justified.

She'd been sitting at the table reading a fashion magazine, which she'd closed when we arrived. I didn't know where Holly was. An impossibly skinny, wasp-waisted model lounged on the cover of Jan's magazine in a one-piece bathing suit and a hijab, her legs open suggestively.

"I've just been taking care of some details for

work," Brian answered, waving his hand airily as though the details didn't matter.

"Like what?" Dee asked. "Medical supplies?"

He turned his head to look at her, irritation on his face. She hadn't respected his cue to drop the subject.

"I took the opportunity of being in the area to interview nurses."

"How did that go?" I asked.

"It was not fruitful. I believe in candor—full disclosure. When I explain what it's like in Cameroon these days—out on the plateau where our clinic is situated—candidates usually decide they'd be better off volunteering somewhere else."

"Bummer," Dee said. "Why do you do it if it's so bad?"

"They need me. And once you're anywhere, you make friends—and lovers. Then you especially care."

"Uncle Brian!" Jan protested. "We don't need to hear about your love life again. I thought we talked about that."

"Sorry." He didn't look sorry as he grinned and shook his head.

When Dee retreated to her room to continue researching Dennis's past, and Jan returned her attention to an article about Milan's contribution to haute couture, my uncle and I moved to the back patio.

A light breeze wafted in from the woods behind the house, bringing the fragrance of pine. I was a bit cool, but after living in Sri Lanka, it was a welcome sensation. At the sangha, you perspired continuously, and only some of your sweat could evaporate into the humid air. We weren't far from the equator. Only being on a ridge in hill country kept the climate tolerable for most of us.

Brian leaned forward in his chaise. "Listen, Ivy, what do you make of Dennis's murder at this point? Jan won't talk to me about it. She says I'm insensitive and I say things that set her off."

"From her perspective, that characterization fits pretty much everyone," I commented.

"You seem to do all right with her," Brian said. "What's your secret?"

"It's just been trial and error through the years. Believe me, I'm not exempt from triggering Jan."

"So what's the story with Dennis?"

"I'm looking into it—investigating."

His eyebrows shot up and his eyes widened, which seemed like an overreaction. "How's that?"

"Well, you know there may be foul play with Mom's death, as well," I told him.

"I do not. That's Jan's fantasy. Now that the target of her rage is dead, I think we can drop that notion."

"Actually, I think it's probable that Dennis's murder is connected to Mom passing. I'll tell you why."

I proceeded to lay out what I knew, unfolding my story in chronological order.

"It's best to leave such things to professionals, Ivy," Brian told me when I'd finished. "It's too dangerous to investigate murders. What if you make progress and the killer finds out? Will you be safe? I think not."

"I'll be careful," I told him.

Brian frowned. "Your idea of careful might be insufficient. Let's face it. You're naive and inexperienced in such things. You're not like me. You've been locked away from the world for a long time, haven't you?"

"You're taking a strong one-up position here, aren't

you, Brian? Are you saying that someone like you—a physician—is familiar with murders?"

"Sadly, yes. You have no idea what it's like where I've been. Soldiers torture and kill civilians. Rebels storm into villages and take hostages. We treat many patients with gun wounds. I've seen things I would never tell anyone about, Ivy."

"I'm sorry. You're right. Compared to you, I'm a babe in the woods. How have you managed to stay alive in the midst of all that. Wouldn't you be a valuable hostage?"

"We treat everyone—both sides of the conflict—and I've learned to protect myself. We're all armed at the clinic."

"Wow, I had no idea."

"I didn't want to worry the family. But now you can see I know a lot about villainy—what our base instincts make us capable of."

"As I said, I'll be careful. If need be, I'll consult you about any shady characters I meet. Tonight, for example, I'll be visiting a dive bar that Dennis visited regularly—the Rusty Snake. It would be helpful if I could debrief with you afterward."

He stared at me intently. His eyes reflected a complex mix of feelings. "I'm going with you. You shouldn't go alone."

"No offense, Uncle Brian, but you're a bit old to be a bodyguard."

"A woman alone in a bar will be harassed—at the least. Trust me on this. Dive bars are the worst."

"Okay. Maybe you're right. I was thinking I'd leave around nine. A place like that doesn't get busy until later in the evening, right?"

"Right. I'll drive. I obtained a rental car in the city. Bring a photo of Dennis and wear what you're wearing. I think it's sufficiently unattractive to stave off would-be suitors."

I smiled. "Thanks a lot." My thrift store outfit—cheap jeans, a black T-shirt, and a blue overshirt—purchased before my trip back—was still all I owned. Well, that and a change of uncomfortable underwear.

Brian continued. "If we weren't related, even *I* wouldn't approach you in those wrinkled, cheap clothes."

"Eww. You really need to self-censor more, Brian. You're not a college student anymore."

"People tell me that. Sorry."

Chapter Eleven

Uncle Brian bustled off to visit with Jan. Holly reappeared momentarily and then sauntered off to meet a friend down the street. I read, meditated, and napped in my room until it was time to go to the bar.

On the way to the Rusty Snake, as a voice from the rental car's dashboard directed us, Brian quizzed me about Buddhism and day-to-day life on the temple grounds.

I studied his face in profile. He really could've been a film star—based on his looks, anyway. His nose was absurdly straight, and his chin jutted out just enough to take charge of the lower part of his face. He held himself erect as though he were a chiropractor role-modeling good posture.

"How did you get involved with Buddhism, anyway?" he asked after a few miles. "You were raised an atheist, right? Lois left the church when she was twelve and never looked back. I can't believe she ever let you and Jan set foot in one."

"In graduate school, I took a class called Transpersonal Therapy. That opened the door for me."

"What's transpersonal therapy?"

"It posits that we're more than screwed-up individual people—who we usually think we are. So it addresses spiritual elements, as well as all the rest. It takes people past 'getting fixed' to a more harmonious state—when it works, of course. It's not for everyone. Anyway, what really nudged me out of my life paradigm was the man who taught the course. He was both a psychologist and a Buddhist teacher—at a retreat center up in Marin county. I realized I wanted to be like him."

Brian nodded and I continued.

"One weekend at a workshop at the center and I was sold. These people were the community I'd always yearned for. In hindsight, I think growing up with no spiritual background at all left a void. When something came along that fit into that empty space, I felt whole— or at least en route to wholeness. I dropped out of school, moved to San Anselmo—down the road from the center—and after a while, I took off to find my teacher's teacher in India."

"What was that like?"

"Much more challenging than I thought it would be. He'd retired and moved away from Ladakh to parts unknown."

Memories flooded in, including enduring a literal flood from the Adyar river overflowing its banks near Madras. I'd climbed a sturdy tree, and I was there for seven hours.

"What did you do?"

"I found him. It took me eight months."

Now I remembered my disappointment when I met Sadhguru Devi. He was living in a converted school bus outside Ahmednagar. A teenaged girl waited on him hand and foot. He spent his days watching TV. Fortunately, he passed me on to who I needed to meet next.

"I admire that kind of commitment, Ivy, but wasn't it dangerous traveling through India as a single woman?

And I thought you were living in Sri Lanka."

"I was blessed to remain safe, or at least stay alive. It wasn't always what anyone would call safe." I shook my head, remembering a particularly harrowing incident with a drunk policeman in Pune. "I'd never tell any woman to do what I did," I continued. "It was amazingly naive—even stupid. And how I ended up in Sri Lanka is a long story."

The car's disembodied voice told us we'd arrived, interrupting me.

Brian parked the car down the street from the bar's gravel parking lot, which was packed with pickup trucks and older American cars.

"Never park in a bar parking lot if you value your vehicle," he told me. "How do you want to do this?" he asked as he climbed out of the rental car.

"Just stand near me while I do whatever seems to make sense to me."

"You don't have a plan?"

His disapproval of this approach was obvious from his tone.

"I'm going to start by talking to the bartender. That's it. We'll see where that leads."

"Okay." Clearly, he wasn't happy with this.

When we walked into the Rusty Snake, we stopped just inside the heavy wooden door to let our eyes adjust to the dim lighting. The wall of noise and the barrage of odors overwhelmed my senses, blocking me from seeing much even as my eyes adjusted.

Music that seemed to be nothing but repetitive bass notes competed with the babble of voices, some of them quite loud. Billiard balls clacked against one another from somewhere to the side of us, and from the other side of the room, glasses clinked against one another. I smelled beer, sweat, and cigarette smoke—a thoroughly unpleasant combination. It was supposed to be illegal to smoke in public spaces.

"Oh shit," Brian said. "That's Skip Hofstadter behind the bar."

"You know him?"

"Yes, I do. Actually, I've been here before."

"Why didn't you tell me that?"

"It's a little embarrassing. Look around."

I did. Many of the bar's denizens—an older, working-class demographic—appeared to be quite drunk. Competing arguments rang out from opposite ends of the bar itself, and a Latino man in a power company uniform knocked his beer over, the glass crashing to the worn, wooden floor as he gazed into space.

Several men at a nearby table clapped. Another one—younger than the others—shouted, "Pete's here!"

This guy wore winter clothes, including a ski cap pulled down over his ears, despite the warmth the crowd of bar-goers generated.

Otherwise, everything was fairly shabby. At one time, the Rusty Snake must've been upscale. Elegant light fixtures resembling deer antlers lined the walls, but most had burnt-out bulbs. The ceiling was plated with embossed tin. In the crevices of this geometric pattern, dark grime spoiled the impression of bygone grandeur. The wooden tables and beige vinyl booths were scarred and worn.

"Well, we're here," I said. "Let's go talk to Skip the bartender."

Quite a few heads turned to watch us as we strode

forward. We must've looked like an odd pair—a dapper man in his seventies—still wearing a suit—with a much younger woman by his side.

"Brian!" the bartender called. "You're back!"

"Hello, Skip. It's been too long, hasn't it?"

Skip paused, and then said brightly, "Oh, right. Too long. And who's this pretty lady?"

He turned to look at me. Skip's face was out of place in the bar. His eyes demonstrated intelligence, and his smile was warm and sincere. He resembled a character actor who played friendly neighbors in films.

I introduced myself and told him I was Brian's niece. "Can I ask you some questions about my stepfather—Dennis Sorenson?"

I had to shout to be heard. The music was louder at the bar.

"Hold it. Let me shut off the stereo."

He turned and fiddled with something that didn't look anything like any stereo I'd ever seen. It was square black box with only one knob.

"There. Never heard of him. Sorry." He glanced at Brian as if he were checking if it was all right for him to say that.

"You might know him by another name. Let me show you a photo." I pulled out the photo that Dee had found online and laid it on the slick wooden bar.

"Oh, you mean Anton. He comes in all the time."

"He won't be coming in anymore," I told him as gently as I could.

"Why's that?"

"He's been murdered." I watched Skip's face closely. His expression didn't change.

"Really?" he responded matter-of-factly.

"Really. You don't seem surprised."

"I'm not. If you lie down with dogs, you get fleas."

"Meaning?"

"Look, I'm talking to you because you're with Brian. We go way back. But you don't want to know who Anton used to meet in here."

"Yes, I do."

"Trust me. You think you do, but you don't. Brian'll back me on this."

I turned and looked at my uncle, who was in the act of trying to erase a grimace.

"Why's that, Brian?" I asked. "Why can you back him?"

"Regrettably, I've seen some illegal activity in here," he told me. "Ruthless types."

"We need to talk about that later."

I returned my gaze to Skip. Now he was frowning and slowly shaking his head, as if to emphasize what he'd said before.

"Is there anyone else in here who knew Anton?" I asked him.

His gaze shifted to a booth in the back of the room, but he quickly dragged it back. "No," he then said vehemently. "There's no one."

"Okay, thanks."

I headed toward the back booth, which was occupied by a hard-looking giant and a slim older man in a gleaming blue sharkskin sport coat over a cream-colored silk turtleneck. He looked even more out of place than Brian and I did. In fact, I couldn't imagine where he'd be *in* place.

"Hold it!" Brian said, grabbing my arm. "You can't do this. I think that guy's a drug dealer."

"Brian, how do you know that?" I felt my face heat up.

He didn't answer.

"Let's sit down right here," I said.

We hunkered down onto two rickety wooden chairs at a nearby table. I glared at my uncle.

"What's the story?" I asked. "I need to know what's going on."

"It's hard to explain," Brian prevaricated, looking down and to his left.

"Let me guess. It's something to do with a woman." I knew my scorn had leaked out, but I couldn't control it.

"That's right." He looked up, pleased that I'd named it so he hadn't needed to.

"And she was mixed up in some unsavory things?" I was able to ask this more neutrally.

"Exactly. She grew up around the corner." He pointed toward the door. "It's a rough neighborhood."

"Brian, this is Palo Alto. There are no rough neighborhoods, unless you count fraternity row at Stanford."

He looked away toward the door again. "Anyway, we spent time in here, and I noticed things."

"When was this? I thought you've been in Africa for years." I wondered if he was still lying.

"I was back and forth for a while. You were away. How would you know?" His tone was slightly aggressive now. Defensiveness had replaced his hesitancy.

"Okay, I understand. So you think that man back there is dangerous—even just to talk to."

"That's right. We shouldn't go talk to him," he asserted energetically.

"You stay here if you want. I don't think anyone's

going to hurt me in a public place for asking a few questions."

"Maybe not here, but you might be tipping someone off that you're investigating. What comes later?"

"You think this man is connected to Dennis's murder?"

"No, no. That's not what I mean."

"You think villains are scared by the likes of me?" I smiled demurely.

"Fine. I give up. Do what you want. But I'm coming with you if you're going to do this."

"Okay."

The giant looked up as we approached. His gaze was studiously blank. Close-up, even sitting, he scared me simply because of his size, but his face was also intimidating. He didn't have the dead eyes that assassins did in movies, but his deep-set blue ones still seemed to be profoundly disinterested in what happened around him. Whatever it might be, it was all the same to him. Upon closer examination, I thought he might be someone who'd been wounded and had adopted this attitude in response to trauma—to protect himself emotionally.

The older man kept his eyes glued to a tablet he'd propped up on the table in front of him. His face was lined, with several small dents in his temple and forehead, probably from skin cancer removals. My mother had exhibited similar scars.

His jet-black hair, which was mostly what I saw because of his slightly bowed head, was thick and lustrous.

"Excuse me," I said. "Do you have a minute?"

"I have many minutes," the man said without looking up. "Who wants to know about these minutes?"

He had a thick Eastern European accent and spoke in a low-pitched growl. On the other hand, his tone wasn't unpleasant in the way I usually associated with that timbre. It was almost playful.

"My name is Ivy. I was Anton Todorov's stepdaughter."

At that, he looked up and surveyed me with interest. "Ah, the poor man. So he had a stepdaughter? What can I do for you? And why are you here with Brian?"

He knew my uncle? I was thrown off-balance for a moment. Brian and I were going to have another little chat soon.

Now I could see a complexity to the man. If he was a criminal, he wasn't a garden-variety one. His dark, alert eyes sat above a hawk nose. A bushy, stiff-haired mustache below that drooped onto his upper lip, which was a thin slash mismatched to his generous lower lip. His teeth were yellow and jumbled as if his parents had never brought him to a dentist.

I couldn't read him at all, which was anomalous. Right or wrong, I usually got a sense of who someone was, at least in general terms. Even the man's energy— his chi—was a mixture of indecipherable elements.

"You know my uncle?" I asked.

"Your uncle, eh? Interesting. Brian and I are old friends."

I turned and stared at my uncle for a moment. He smiled a shaky smile, seemingly aware of my thoughts. Then I returned my attention to the man at the table.

"I'm looking into my mother and Anton's death, and—"

"Why? Why are you doing this?" The man held his hands up, palms facing me.

159

"I want to find out what happened."

He shook his head and muttered, "It's better not to know these things."

"I disagree. In my world, it's all about knowing."

"What world is that? Are you a librarian? No, don't answer. I think maybe a tech person who answers me when I google."

"I'm a Buddhist."

"So? Is that supposed to impress me?" He leaned back, apparently pleased with himself. I couldn't see why.

"Can we get back to the deaths? Is there anything you know that I should know?"

"Should? No. But I know many things about many people. Perhaps some of that could come your way. But what do I get from this?"

"What do you want?" I couldn't imagine what I could offer from my side of a deal.

"A date." He smiled a wicked smile—almost a smirk.

"You're serious? You want a date with me?" My eyebrows shot up, and I felt my mouth form an O.

"Yes. One date and I tell you who to go talk to about Anton. If you want to go on more dates, that's up to you."

"What's your definition of a date?"

"Dinner. Talking. That's it. I am an interesting man. You are an interesting woman. And a very pretty one. We may have many things in common."

"I'm told you're a criminal." I wanted to see how he'd would react to this.

"Who told you that?" He'd raised his voice, and his head bobbed forward on his neck.

I tilted my head at my uncle. "Brian."

Brian raised his hands in front of his chest. "Dimitri, I only said that to dissuade her from coming over here and bothering you."

"I see." He turned his attention back to me. "What do you say? A date?"

"If you're not a criminal, then who are you? Why would you know anything about a murder if you're just an ordinary citizen?"

I hadn't gotten much of a read from calling him a criminal. After all, anyone would be defensive when accused of something like that. I was hoping this follow-up question would serve my purpose better.

"I don't know anything about the murder. I know someone who might know. We run in the same circles because we're all from Sofia in Bulgaria—me, Anton, and this other man's wife."

"What do you do for a living?"

"Import-export."

"What does that mean?" I knew the answer, but I wanted to hear how Dimitri characterized his version of it.

"What it sounds like. I bring things in, and I ship things out. It's simple."

"What things?"

"That's enough. If you don't want to take my deal, that's fine."

"Don't do it," Brian blurted out.

Dimitri spoke up. "Jerry, why don't you buy a nice drink for Brian at the bar?"

The giant arose, unfolding himself as though he'd been a huge origami sculpture. He wore a voluminous gray sweatshirt, jeans, and black cowboy boots. Now a frown stretched across his wide face. He'd been dragged back into caring about something in order to fulfill Dimitri's request.

Without a word, he gestured to my uncle, who dutifully followed him.

"Sit," Dimitri said. "Do you think I'm too old for you? Is that it?"

I sat where his bodyguard had been. The seat was quite warm. "I haven't been on a date in fifteen years. I don't think I'd be very good company. Isn't there some other deal we could make?"

"What do you have that I might want? Are you rich? I don't think so. Not in those clothes." He gestured at my midsection as though the problem was the lower part of my shirt.

I smiled. "Nobody likes my clothes. I think they're fine."

"In two weeks, they'll fall apart. I know about this. I moved pallets of those pants from India to the Middle East. Never again."

"You're right about me. I'm not rich. I've been a Buddhist nun until recently."

"See? I knew you were interesting. I want to hear all about that over dinner."

He certainly was persistent.

"Where would you take me?" I had no plan to agree to his ridiculous proposal, but I was curious.

"Wherever you like. My treat, of course. You like Thai? I like Thai."

"Let me think about it. Do you have a card or something?"

"Give me your phone. I'll put my number in." He held out his hand, as if he were accustomed to—no, entitled to—instant compliance. A la Jan.

I handed him my phone.

He studied it, turning it over and then back again. It looked tiny in his incongruously meaty hands. They were the only part of him that weren't slim—even elegant.

"What is this? I can't put a number into this piece of shit. I'll bring a real phone to dinner. You need a real phone."

"No, thank you. Maybe you have a card you could give me."

"Sure, sure."

He handed me a black card with yellow script. As promised, it stated that Dimitri Nicolov was CEO of Nicolov Export-Import Enterprises.

"You should buy some nice clothes," he told me. "Do you need money? I can give you money."

"No, thank you. Are you sure you can't tell me anything helpful right now?"

"All right. Here you go. Look at Anton's dealings in Africa. That's your big clue. I give you that because I like you. It won't do you any good, though. Trust me."

Chapter Twelve

On the way home, Brian told me his Croatian girlfriend had been the daughter of Dimitri's former business partner, and that he'd met Skip the bartender in a pottery class.

"These are not my kind of people, Ivy, as you can imagine. But I was smitten with Ana. I couldn't help myself."

"I understand. But don't you think it's quite a coincidence that Dennis's bar is the same one you used to frequent? And that you know at least two people there."

"Yes, I was struck by that, too." He paused for quite a while, squinting in concentration. "What the hell. Here's the real story. I met Dennis at the bar quite a few years ago—he said his name was Dennis, anyway—and I was the one who introduced him to your mother. I think they were happy together, and I felt good about it. It was only after Dennis died that I found out who he really was."

"And why would you hold that back?"

"I told you. I don't think it's a good idea for you to pursue this. The more I tell you, the more you're going to be drawn in. You're my favorite niece, Ivy. I want you to stick around."

"Jan can disappear and you'd be fine?" I regretted saying this as soon as it was out of my mouth. I needed to stay more mindful.

"That's not what I meant, Ivy. You know how difficult Jan can be."

"I'm sorry. I shouldn't have said that. I'm just miffed that you lied to me."

"By omission only. It's not lying when you decide not to divulge something for the good of the other person."

"Arguing about semantics won't get us anywhere. Did you find out anything from that Jerry character?"

"He only wanted to talk about how smart his Bulgarian girlfriend is. She's got some important job up in the city. What did you and Dimitri talk about?"

"How interesting I am. Whether we should go to a Thai restaurant on our date."

"You're not seriously considering doing that, are you? He really is a criminal, or at least that's what Ana told me."

"If I can't get anywhere without him, I'll revisit his offer. For now, no, I have no interest in spending time with someone like that."

****

I slept deeply—I'd stayed up way past my bedtime. I awoke at six to a predictably sunny Sunday morning.

Everyone seemed to be in a good mood out on the patio as we ate two hours later. The early morning sun cast long shadows that draped across the brickwork beneath our feet, mingling with oak leaves and the reddish dirt caught in the cracks between bricks.

I wondered why I was looking down instead of up, and realized my neck was sore from using a pillow. Several nights of the unfamiliar angle had taken a toll. With an effort, and a few tweaks from a pesky cervical vertebra, I held my head up and surveyed my family.

Holly's flannel pajama pants sported a forest camouflage pattern. A black hoodie extended down over her hips. Her pixie haircut was off kilter, canting toward to the high side of her tilted head, seemingly defying physics. I remembered Jan's hair doing something similar. Like mother, like daughter.

Dee was back in her overalls, this time with a white waffle-knit thermal shirt underneath the bib. A black baseball cap roosted uneasily on top of her tangled hair, threatening to slip down and plop into her oatmeal if she leaned forward too far.

Jan told us she didn't have to work, although she usually did on the weekends. Her outfit reflected that. Perhaps to compensate for having to strategize what to wear with her clients, the old jeans she'd chosen displayed white paint smears, and her purple turtleneck sweater had seen better days. The front was littered with pills, and a stray strand of yarn hung down from one of its elbows.

"How did you sleep?" Holly asked me. I was pleased she was initiating contact. Perhaps I was beginning to win her over.

"Quite well, actually. You?"

"Me too. Do you dream about Buddha?"

I think she'd saved up this question. I was struck that both girls had asked me about my dreams.

"I wish. Sometimes my dreams have a spiritual element, but no Buddha so far. Maybe you'll prime the pump by bringing this up."

"What's priming the pump?" Dee asked.

"You don't know that?" Holly said. "Everyone knows that."

166

Dee's face turned red. Before she could respond to her sister, I answered her question. "A pump mechanism doesn't work unless there's already water in it, so when it's dry, you have to add water to get it going. That's called priming it."

"I get it. So in this case, priming the pump would be Holly mentioning dreams and Buddha together?"

"Duh," said Holly.

Jan had been disengaged—staring off into space—but now she intervened. "Holly, be nice to your sister."

Holly shrugged. "When a know-it-all doesn't know something, I think—"

"That's enough!" Jan blurted out fiercely. "I'm sick of all this bickering. Everyone bickers at work, and then there's you two. I need peace and quiet when I'm home. Is that too much to ask?"

Her intense stare darted back and forth between my nieces. It was as if they'd poisoned the family pet or something else of that magnitude. God knows why I thought of that.

"I didn't bicker," Dee said. "It was just Holly being mean to me."

"You're bickering with me right now," Jan told her with heat. "And I said I was sick of it!"

After that, everyone was silent for a while, and, I hope, thoughtful.

I suggested to Dee that we go to her room so she could show me what she'd found on her computer the previous evening. I trailed her to the other end of the house.

Posters associated with interests from an earlier age faced me from Dee's pale blue walls. Surely, she no longer wanted to be an NFL cheerleader or a pop singer, and I doubt she still revered a rugged-looking race car driver.

She spotted me examining the posters. "They're ironic," she told me. "I don't like it when people know about you from what you put up."

"Ah."

Then I spied the mask Brian had given her. Dull brown, the long face with exaggerated African features wasn't anything I'd hang on my wall. In fact, it looked like an offensive caricature.

"Here's the main thing," Dee began when she settled behind her desk. "Dennis owned at least a couple of companies—one here and one in the Caribbean."

I sidled over to my niece's desk and stood behind her. The opening page of Bulldog Outfitters pictured an array of camping gear and safari clothes. Underneath them was a caption: *Wholesale only: Currently Available At Competitive Prices.*

"This is the American company?"

"Yes, it was incorporated in Delaware."

"Who were his customers? Is it a legitimate company?"

"I haven't found out anything about that. Yet."

I studied the website more closely, which yielded me nothing.

"Look at this," Dee directed as she hit a button that took us to another site. It was an article in a French newspaper. In French.

"I can't read that."

"Oh yeah, wait a minute. It's about Dennis's other company." She typed briefly at amazing speed, and a translated version appeared.

The headline read *Cayman Islands Corporation*

Accused Of Massive Fraud Has French Roots.

"Should I read the whole article?" I asked.

I didn't want to if I didn't have to. Real life stories about crime depressed me. I was fine with fictional fraud, murder, and the like. But true crime stories and media reports of misdeeds...I guess they reminded me too much about the sorry state of humanity.

"You don't need to," Dee said. "I'll tell you the good parts. Majestic Consultants was like a clearinghouse for companies that wanted to avoid paying taxes wherever they were. This was mostly European countries, especially in former Soviet republics. The main backer of Majestic was this French guy from Marseille who was a major criminal."

"So Dennis had a partner."

"Sort of. Dennis ran things, but this other guy financed the whole company to start with. And he's the one who got caught when things went wrong. Back then—it was like nine years ago—there wasn't any way to trace things back to Dennis."

"Now there is?"

"Well, I did, so I guess so."

"Do you think the police know all this?" Obviously, it was important they did.

"I don't know. Maybe."

"What happened to the French guy? Is he in prison?"

"He was. He got out. They only got him on a couple of white-collar fraud charges, which pissed off a lot of people."

"Great work."

"Here's my theory," Dee said excitedly. "Jacques Morin—the French guy—came over here and found Dennis, who'd changed his name and everything, but it didn't work. So Morin killed him because he had to go to jail and Dennis got off. What do you think?"

She swiveled her desk chair and studied my face.

"That sounds like a strong possibility. I'll definitely tell the police about this." I thought about things for a moment. "Let me ask you this. Did you find out anything about Dennis and Africa?"

"No, why do you ask? Is that where he got his exotic animals from?"

"A scary man at the Rusty Snake told me to look into that. That's all I know." I filled Dee in on what had happened at the bar. She listened intently, asking an occasional question.

"You should go out with him—find out about this other guy who knows about Dennis," she told me when I'd finished. "Plus it's a free dinner somewhere nice."

"I might. We'll see. Did you discover anything about Dennis that ties in with your grandmother's death?"

"No, I got caught up in all this business stuff. But if I were evil and I wanted revenge, maybe I'd kill someone's wife first to make the husband suffer extra."

"Dee!"

"Well, it's true. That's how evil people do things."

"And you know this how?"

"Okay, maybe I don't know something like that for sure. Here's another idea. Grandma could've seen this French guy—he could've been one of the men in the car down the street. Maybe they wanted to eliminate a witness."

"Before they even committed a crime? Mom died first—remember?"

"Oh, yeah. I guess I'll look deeper into the hospital

stuff today. I've got no plans besides my riding lesson this afternoon."

"You ride horses?"

"Yeah. It was Mom's idea, and I didn't think I'd like it, but it turns out I do. What are you going to do?"

"I think I need to buy some clothes and other items. Maybe your mom could help me with that. It'll be good to take a break from the case, too."

"She'd love to help. She loves to shop, and she loves to get other people to do what she wants. You'll probably come back in stiletto heels and a big designer handbag."

I laughed. "That'll be the day."

****

As promised, Jan was eager to shop with me. She chattered away about her own clothes on the ride to the Stanford Shopping Center, an upscale outdoor mall. I would never have picked this as our destination, but Jan insisted.

"I'll pay for everything," she told me, "so pick out whatever you like, and then I'll tell you if you look like you're Amish or a pioneer woman from the 1870s."

I laughed. "You remember what I wore in college, I guess."

"I certainly do."

"I didn't want men to see me as a sexual object."

"Mission accomplished. And then some. How did that work out for you?"

"As you know, not so well." My social life had been a disaster at UC Berkeley. Apparently, a woman hiding her body in modest clothes served as a lure for aggressive men to try to find out was under all the layers. Lust and curiosity were not the traits I'd hoped to attract.

The parking lot next to the shopping center was

relatively empty, which suited me. I'd never cared for shopping, especially in crowded stores. So many people were caught up in believing clothes and products were the remedy to all their problems. It lent an air of desperation, or at least neediness, to their behavior in stores. A gaggle of these folks crowding around me wasn't my idea of a good time.

In the first store, a small boutique full of brightly colored clothes, the salesperson took one look at me and exclaimed, "Oh, my God! Jan, who is this delightful creature, and where in the world did she find those horrid clothes?"

"Hi, Samantha. This is my sister Ivy—you know, the Buddhist. She's back."

Samantha's long black hair snaked down her shoulder in a tight braid, the end of which rested on her sternum, visible because she wore a low-cut yellow tank top. She looked unhealthily slim, as if she had worked hard to defy her body's natural programming to be mid-sized. This left slightly hollowed cheeks, and I could see several ribs outlined against the cotton top.

She formed her hands into a prayer position and bowed to me. "Namaste, Ivy. It's a privilege to meet you. Our shop is honored by your presence. I apologize for my unkind remark about your clothes."

I looked at Jan and she shrugged.

"Are you a Buddhist?" I asked.

"Oh yes. For six months now. I meditate every day, and my teacher says I've reached the fifth level already."

"That's great."

This business of levels was strictly an Americanized version of what Buddha had offered. He wouldn't have turned over in his grave if he knew about such hierarchal

172

thinking. I think he would've laughed.

"Can I ask a question?" Samantha asked. "My teacher was very unclear when he tried to answer this."

"Sure."

Jan wandered off to the other side of the store to browse through clothes racks.

"Why are Buddhists supposed to accept everything—you know, be okay with the way things are?" Her voice was a bit whiny, as though having to think about the concept was an imposition.

"Good question. Would you like a long answer, or are we just having a conversation about this?" I didn't want to revert to teacher mode if it wasn't called for.

"The long answer. Please." She smiled and nodded her head. Her teeth were absolutely straight and uniformly white.

"Radical acceptance means being as directly connected with reality as we can manage," I began. "In other words, acceptance includes striving not to distort what we perceive based on ego, or desire, or delusion. Another way to talk about acceptance is to say don't play games with the way things are. Don't kid yourself. Get real."

As I listened to myself, I felt dissatisfied with what I'd told Samantha. It was so dry, so academic. Where was the heart in it?

"You mentioned delusions. Do you mean crazy people? Do they have a harder time with this?"

"No, I mean that most people have ideas about life and themselves that are inaccurate. Perhaps it's a bad idea to use the word delusion since in this country it generally indicates pathology, but as Buddha used it, it means having false ideas that one believes are true."

"Okay, I get it." She suddenly looked around and saw she was ignoring several new customers. "Listen, I've got to go. Would you consider becoming my teacher? I have a lot of friends who are unhappy with Rinpoche Moskowitz, too. We could start a new meditation center." As she turned to go, she added, "Think it over. I'll get in touch with you through Jan."

Jan strolled over. "I found some things I think will look great on you. Do you like blue? I think blue's your color."

"Sure, blue is great."

She pulled my arm toward the back of the store and said, "What was all that about? Samantha looked like she was really listening. That's not her thing. I don't think I've ever seen her shut up for more than thirty seconds."

"She wanted to know what I thought about acceptance. And she wants me to be her teacher."

"Just like that? After you answer one question? That's just like her. She took piano lessons for a month, switched to clarinet, and then joined one of those Up With Jesus choirs—you know, they go around and recruit kids using glitzy shows? This was when we were freshmen in high school. Anyway, what do you think? You want to go back to your Buddhist career here? If it gives you a reason to stick around, then I'm all for it. Dee adores you, and she needs a father figure."

"A father figure? You said that before. Are you aware of how that sounds to a woman?"

"You know what I mean—a sensible role model. She's crossed me off her list, I think. I guess I've given the girls reason to sometimes—when my meds stopped working, or sometimes stress can set me off. Anyway, the way you think is more like a man. Here you are in a

174

fabulous store. I've dragged you over to these amazing tops, and you haven't looked at one of them."

"I'm sorry. I appreciate your help. Let me get to it."

Every item in that first store screamed, "Look at me!" If it wasn't an odd combination of bright colors, it was a plunging neckline or a cut-out at the midriff.

"Really, Jan? You thought I'd find these suitable?"

"No. I wanted to start with these so you'd be willing to wear something normal later in another store. You know, the others wouldn't look so bad after this. Plus, I wanted to show you off to Samantha. She's always crowing about her sister who's an actress, and that loser can't hold a candle to you."

All I could do was shake my head at that. "Let's keep it casual today," I suggested. "Maybe a better pair of jeans, a simple long-sleeved top, and underwear that doesn't itch like crazy. If I see a dress I like, maybe that would be a good idea, too."

"You'd look great in leggings, Ivy. Those are casual."

"I saw them at the airport. They pretty much reveal the exact shape and jiggliness of your butt."

"Well, yeah. That's the whole idea. Plus, they're really comfortable. Just try on a pair. You'll see."

"Okay, but I'm telling you right now, I jiggle more than I want the world to see."

Five stores and dozens of debates later, we finally settled on a compromise. Jan remained heavily invested in my looks for some reason, so I let her pick out a dress and a pair of uncomfortable shoes, and I chose the rest. No leggings. My favorite item was a black fleece pullover. When I put it on, I felt safe. Maybe it mimicked the way my security blanket had felt when I'd been a toddler.

In the parking lot, chi-chi shopping bags in hand, a male voice called out my name. It was Detective Petrie. He strode up to us just as we reached Jan's car.

"Ivy, I'm sorry to intrude, and by the way, I like that pullover on you, but you weren't answering your phone, and your niece said you were here."

"No worries." I pulled my phone from the pocket of my new jeans. The battery was dead.

"Can we talk?" Petrie asked. "How about Jan and your packages head home and I drive you somewhere? Afterward, I'll take you wherever you want to go."

I turned to my sister. "Is that okay with you?"

"I guess so. I need to get to the grocery store anyway, and you probably wouldn't be any use there." Her tone was unexpectedly scornful. Perhaps she hadn't appreciated my resistance to her wardrobe selections—or Detective Petrie's interest in me.

After piling my bags in the back seat of my sister's car, and parting with my new fleecy friend—it was too warm to wear for long on a sunny day—I climbed into Petrie's unmarked police car.

"Is your sister always like that?" he asked.

"Jan runs hot and cold. She's a work in progress—the same as us, Detective."

"Please, call me Art. Personally, I wouldn't put up with that kind of insulting language."

"I try to accommodate what others do as best I can. They're not likely to change just because I have a problem with their behavior, which I don't in this case. Jan is Jan. Who am I to say she should be different? And she's probably right. I haven't been in a real grocery store in a long time."

"We live in a civil society," Art asserted. "We all need to treat each other well."

"You can be a policeman and say that? Don't you encounter an uncivil demographic all day long?"

"They're the exception. And that's my job, not my take on humanity. Don't you think that at heart, people are good?"

"I do. I'd go beyond that. I'd say our default setting is kindness."

"That's interesting. You're thinking that kindness trumps goodness in some sort of virtue hierarchy. I'd put them the other way around. I like the default setting idea, though. I'd love to talk to you more about this sometime, but I guess we better get back to the case."

"Sure."

"First of all, I don't appreciate your interference in our investigation. Yes, you saved us some time by finding June Vormelker—the witness who saw the white car. But you don't know what you're doing. We need to see people's initial reactions to our questions. We need to hear their unvarnished stories before they have time to polish them. It's much harder to get to the truth when someone has a chance to prepare themselves for an interview. There's more to it than that, but I think I've made my case. Do *not* do something like that again." Art turned and glanced at me. His eyebrows danced down and up.

"I'm sorry. I didn't consider all that."

"No, you didn't. Enough said."

"I can see I put you in an uncomfortable position. I'm sure you don't like having to say things like that."

"No, I don't. But I forgive you. I know your motives are good. You just need to slow down. You can't trust things to turn out well when you rush things."

Here was the message in my dream. I felt a chill snaking up my spine, and my mind shut down for a moment.

"I've heard that," I finally managed to say.

Art maneuvered around a moving truck.

"Anyway, Ms. Vormelker was able to pick out one of the men she talked to from our photo array of violent arrestees. There are only so many in a town this size."

"So you checked with the FBI?"

"Yes. The men in the car weren't agents. This guy she identified—Bruce Peralto—was picked up a few years ago for aggravated assault, but the victim recanted her testimony, so we couldn't get too far. Anyway, he and the taller man keeping an eye on Anton's home makes them the prime suspects in his murder, of course.

"Now here's where you come in. Here's why I went looking for you. Maria Kostova—Anton's ex—knows a lot of his old associates, but she won't talk to me or look at our photo arrays. She says she'll only talk if you're there. I wish you hadn't gone down to see her on your own. Do you see how that's tied our hands? I should've read you the riot act after you pulled that one."

"I'm sorry you feel that way. I see it differently. I think she shared information with me she would've continued to withhold otherwise. And now she's prepared to share again."

"Why do you think that is? Should we have sent a woman to question her?"

"No, she simply distrusts police, and probably any authorities. It goes back to communist Bulgaria. And people tend to trust me—confide in me."

"Why's that?"

"You tell me. Do you trust me?"

"Yeah, I do. I did right from the start for some reason."

"There you go."

"Anyway, are you willing to help?"

"Of course."

Art wore more formal clothes than I'd seen him in before—a blue sport coat over gray pants and a white shirt.

"Do you have to be in court today?" I asked.

"No, why do you say that?"

"The jacket."

"I wear it when I'm out and about to hide the gun I have holstered on my hip."

"Ah, I didn't think of that."

"Around here, people get alarmed when they see a weapon. And I don't look like a typical Palo Alto policeman. I've had citizens call the station when I'm just walking down the sidewalk in an upscale neighborhood. Imagine if I strolled around with a visible pistol."

"I'd rather not. Racism nauseates me. I actually get sick to my stomach."

"That's interesting. I've never heard that," Art responded.

"Are we headed to Maria's home?"

"She's not at her cat-infested house today, thank God. She looks after a sick sister in Santa Clara, and she's agreed to meet us in a coffeehouse near there."

"Okay. What do you have against cats?"

"I'm allergic. I get hives in the corner of my eyes."

"That's no fun."

I almost told him about Maria's cat-free living room

but realized it didn't matter.

"It certainly isn't," Art said. "I asked her to wear something that wasn't covered with cat fur. I had a hard time when she came into the station."

"Listen, I need to tell you some things I found out," I said.

"Go ahead."

I filled Art in about Dennis's corporations and the French gangster who'd taken the fall for their fraud.

"How in the world did you come by that information? How could you be so far ahead of us on this?"

"A consultant did research for me online."

"Forensic accountants don't come cheap. I appreciate how you're spending some bucks trying to help. But Ivy—can I call you Ivy?"

"Of course."

"Ivy, like I said, you've got to stay out of our way. We'll look into this Morin guy, maybe contact the police in Marseille. I don't know. And we'll certainly keep sorting through Dennis's companies. What I'm saying is, once you tell me something, we'll take it from there. Okay?"

"Sure. One more thing. Apparently, Dennis's African activities might be important to look into."

"Why's that?"

"I don't know. It's just something I was told."

"Well, I'm certainly not going to ignore anything you say. And to be honest, nothing you've done so far has actually done any damage to the investigation. It might've, but it didn't."

He glanced at me again. This time, his face looked thoughtful. We hadn't exchanged any super-connective glances since back at the police station, and we didn't now. I wondered why. Perhaps I was blocking them from happening. Some part of me may not have been ready for whatever might follow.

"Actually," Art said. "You seem to be a crackerjack amateur detective."

"Thank you. This is my first case, you know. I haven't even bought a fedora yet."

"A what?"

"You know, the hat that private eyes wear in old movies."

"Oh, sure. Sorry." Art smiled. "Maybe I'll get one."

"You'd look great in a gray one, maybe with a little red feather."

He smiled again. I loved his slow-developing smile. Each step toward completing it was warm and connective in and of itself. We were back in business as far as heart-centered significant expressions went.

For the rest of the twenty-minute drive south, Art made small talk about how much his job had changed over the years, especially the last decade while I'd been gone. His insights about the root causes of this were insightful. He could've chosen to continue our earlier discussion about kindness and civility, but apparently, like many people, he needed to limit his dosage of Buddhist perspective.

As Art talked, I realized more fully how much I liked him. I even imagined kissing him, which shocked me. Where had that come from? Was sitting in close quarters, conversing with a good-looking, intelligent man all it took to catalyze a fantasy? Perhaps celibacy created a rebound effect once temptation appeared. At any rate, we arrived at Perk Up without my attacking him.

The coffeehouse was quite small, with more wrought iron tables outside than in. The decor was minimal—just old movie posters in budget frames on the white walls. I'd never seen any of the films, which made more sense as we walked farther into the room. The writing on them was in Cyrillic.

Maria sat in a corner, watching for us. A smile lit up her face when she saw me. Art noticed.

"She's a fan. How do you charm people this way?" he asked as we wove our way through crowded tables.

"Sometimes it's an energy thing."

Maria stood and I hugged her.

"Thank you for coming, Ivy. I was telling the detective here that I feel less crazy when you're around."

We all sat down. I picked a chair next to Maria—facing Art.

He spoke up. "There's no need to keep up the crazy act, Maria. We know you're not mentally ill or any odder than the rest of us, unless you count the cat thing."

"I think cats should count," she asserted. "Do you have twenty-two cats in your house?"

"It's your business, isn't it? Let's just be straight with one another. We all want the same thing—Anton's killer. Now that Ivy's here, can I show you some suspects? Can you see if you recognize any of them from Anton's past?"

"Okay, sure. Ivy, you're a witness if he tries any tricks."

I nodded. I expected Art to whip out an actual mug book, but of course he had photos preloaded on his phone. Maria scrolled through these while Art and I strolled to the counter to order tea and croissants. I was surprised Art opted for herbal tea.

"Caffeine makes me crazy," he told me. "One cup of coffee, and next thing you know, I'd be filling up my house with weird cats like Maria, hives or no hives."

I laughed. "Oh, you've seen those?"

"In photos on her website."

"Me, too. They really are ghastly, aren't they?"

"That's the perfect word for them."

We shook our heads simultaneously at the exact same speed, and we both noticed. He quickly looked away. I smiled at the back of his head.

Once again, my black tea didn't come close to meeting Sri Lankan standards. The pastry was similarly disappointing. As I finished scarfing it down anyway, back at the table, Maria exclaimed, "Bingo!" and handed Art his phone.

"What can you tell me about this man?" he asked Maria, showing me the photo.

In his early thirties, completely bald, with a pointy chin, and a sallow look to his skin, he could've been a patient in an oncology waiting room. There was something off about him psychologically, as well. I imagined that people instinctively avoided him. I would.

"He worked for Anton years ago," Maria said. "His name is Bruce Something. Something Mexican, maybe. I can't remember. Anyway, he married a girl from the neighborhood and beat her, so some of his neighbors framed him for an assault, but he didn't do any time for it. We take care of our own."

"What neighborhood is this?"

"Little Sofia—in south San Jose. Around Alvarez and Curtis—you know, by the old bus station."

"So if I looked at a list of people we've arrested, and

I saw a guy named Bruce with an address down there, he'd be our man? We might find him that way?"

"I suppose so."

"Could this be Bruce Peralto?"

"Yes, that's him."

So June Somebody—the woman who saw the pseudo-FBI officers—and Maria both identified the same guy. This was a real breakthrough. Excitement built inside me. And fear. Now that I could match a face to a killer, it all seemed much more real. And more deadly if I made a misstep.

"Who was Peralto married to?" Art asked.

Maria looked away. "She moved back home. America wasn't for her."

"Could we contact her in Bulgaria? Maybe she knows where we can find this guy." Art leaned forward, closing the gap between them. "We're talking about murder here."

"I'm sure she doesn't know, and I'm not giving you her name. She's been through enough." She glanced at me. "Ivy, tell the detective to leave me alone. I'm speaking the truth. You can tell, right? He doesn't need to bother a nice lady in Bulgaria."

"She's being honest," I pronounced. I was fairly sure of it, but I also wanted to support Maria to encourage her to keep talking.

Art spoke softly. "We'll see."

"Am I a suspect?" Maria asked. "Is Ivy? On TV, everyone's a suspect."

Art shook his head. "I can't get into that." He looked at me, raised his eyebrows, and said, "I think I'll get a refill," as he rose from our small, round table with his mug. I watched his backside as he strode away.

"You like him," Maria said once he was out of earshot.

"Why do you say that?"

"I know things—remember? Our family once told fortunes for King Ferdinand. Anyway, it's obvious from the way you look at him."

"It's true. What do you think his feelings are about me?" I asked.

"He finds you interesting. He likes you, too. But he's not sure if you're sincere."

"Sincere?"

"If you're who you seem to be. Most people who say they're spiritual are just full of themselves, especially around here. In my country, we have real holy men."

"How did you know I'm spiritually oriented?"

Maria just smiled. She'd already answered that question, I realized—second sight.

"What do *you* think?" I asked. "Am I sincere or just full of myself?"

"Sincere. Your energy is 88% pure."

"That's a very specific number," I said.

"Okay, round it up to ninety if you want."

I glanced toward the coffeehouse counter. Art caught my eye and waved to me as he chatted with the young man taking orders. He'd left so we could talk without him.

"What do you really think about Anton and my mother?" I asked.

"Your mother? She's gone, yes? I don't speak of the dead."

"Yes, she's gone. Suppose she wasn't, what would you say about her?"

"I never met her. Anton was happy. That was good

enough for me."

"Could she have been murdered, too?"

"How would I know?" She threw her hands in the air.

"Forgive me. I don't know enough to ask the right questions."

"That's all right." She looked around and smiled at an older woman across the room. "Oh, I remembered one thing since you came to see me."

"What's that?"

"A man named Dimitri came to see me a few months before you did. I know him from before. He wanted me to tell him where Anton had been last year when he was gone for a month. I told him I didn't know, and that was that."

"I met Dimitri. What do you know about him?"

"Not much. He came in a nice car, and he was polite. Back in the day, he beat people up and you wouldn't want to owe him money. Now he seems more like a businessman. He was nice to my cats. He said his son had two—Flim and Flam. Siamese, or so he said. From their pictures, I could see they aren't purebred."

We didn't learn anything else of consequence once Art returned. I could tell Maria was holding back and knew more. After we climbed into Art's car and I hooked my phone up to charge with a cord Art produced from the glove compartment, we set off and began debriefing.

"So what do you think?" I asked.

"She knows more than she's saying. I'm not just interested in what that might be. I also care about *why* she isn't telling us everything."

"Perhaps that would implicate her in some crimes. After all, she was with Dennis when he was active in his business."

"You know, that raises a question." Art turned to look at me, and I worried he wasn't watching the road. "When exactly did Anton stop? Do we know for sure he was fully retired? Maybe the murder is associated with a recent or a current deal."

"That could be. I've been meaning to ask you about Mom's nurse, too—the one who went missing at a key time. What's the story there?"

"It turns out his sister was giving birth down in the maternity ward. That was the phone call he got that pulled him away. He'll be disciplined by the hospital, but he's clean—no priors, no reason to suspect anything criminal."

"It still establishes opportunity for someone else," I pointed out.

"There was no way for anyone to predict if or when he would be away. That was dependent on the sister's labor, right? And besides opportunity, we still don't have a motive. For that matter, the doc who signed off on the death certificate didn't find anything suspicious. I know what you told me Dennis said, but basically the other team working on what happened at the hospital isn't making much progress. Without progress, a case loses steam—becomes a lower priority. You've got to realize that up in the city, they get a fair number of major cases to investigate, and due to budget cuts, they only have so many officers on hand."

"That's a shame." I paused and thought about what else I wanted to discuss with Art. "Can we go through the list of suspects?" I asked. "I'm finding it hard to keep them all straight."

"Sure. You want to start?"

"Okay. There's Peralto."

"Who was probably paid to kill Dennis," Art commented.

"Why do you say that?"

"That's what he does. That's his history. You pay him and he gets violent. The question is: who paid him?"

"Right. Do you think you'll find Peralto?"

"Probably. We're good at finding people."

"Then there's the tall man who was in the car with Peralto," I continued. "I guess he's another hired killer—not the person who ordered the killing."

"That's my assumption at this point," Art said. "Why hire someone and then put yourself in a car with him in the victim's neighborhood? It defeats the purpose of staying anonymous."

"Okay. There's also Dennis's sister Agnes, and I suppose Maria—although I don't think she did it. And …who else? I feel like I'm leaving someone out."

"We might as well put any of Dennis's associates from his criminal career on the list—once we find them, that is."

"Oh, yes. That reminds me," I said. "There's the Frenchman who went to prison—Morin. He'd been Dennis's partner in their Caribbean company."

"Right. We're still checking him out, and I need to meet Agnes Murphy. She's definitely in the running."

"Can I ask you something a little sideways?"

"Sure." He tilted his head. "Like this?"

I laughed. "I'll give it a try." I slanted my head at the same angle as I spoke, which was more disorienting than I would've thought. "Why are you including me in your investigation? I get why you needed me to be with you when you talked to Maria, but why collaborate on the rest? Why are you willing to have the conversation we're having now? In books and movies, the police always freeze out civilians."

"I'm not sure. Maybe it's because you've done good work on this case and people talk to you—people like you." He paused and then softly added, "I know this is unprofessional, but I do, too. I think I've been looking for an excuse to spend time with you." He kept his eyes on the road now. "You're a straight shooter, so I want to be straight with you. I don't know what it is about you. I mean, you're very attractive—don't get me wrong. But I've met plenty of good-looking women on the job. It's something more."

"Maybe it's chemistry—pheromones."

Art nodded as though he were agreeing, but then said, "I don't know. I think it's more. You talked about energy before. Do you think something's going on with that, too? Tell me more about that."

"First of all, thank you for sharing your feelings about me. I like you too, Art. And you've jumpstarted my lower chakras."

"That one I know. I know the chakra thing."

"To answer your question about energy, I think that when we meet someone and they immediately seem creepy or wonderful, what are we going by? I think we're sensing their energy. And what about when we know someone out of sight is watching us? For most people, sensing energy is an unconscious thing."

"Not for you?"

"Once you sit long enough, things change."

"By sitting, you mean meditating?"

I nodded.

"You know, some people would say this energy idea

is crazy."

"Would you?"

"No, not at all. I'm just saying you have to be careful who you talk to about this."

"Oh, I don't think so. In a conversation, my job is to say things, and the other person's job is to make of it what they will. What anyone thinks about me is none of my business."

"Surely, there are situations where that doesn't hold true."

"Of course, and don't call me Shirley."

Art laughed. "I love that movie."

"Me too." My phone rang. "It works while it's charging?"

"Sure. Go ahead and answer it. I don't mind."

"Hello?"

"Hello, Ivy. This is your new friend Dimitri."

"How did you get this number, Dimitri?" I emphasized his name for Art's benefit. He caught my eye and nodded.

"I have my ways."

"Only the police and my family know this number."

"There's your answer. Either I have a spy in your family or the police. So? What does it matter? Here we are on the phone. Have you considered my offer?"

"Yes. I'm still not sure what I want to do. Can I call you back later?"

"Okay."

"Give me your number. I don't have your card with me."

"Even a crap phone like yours knows my number now. You go find it on there. Learn how things work."

"Okay." I hung up.

At some point, I'd told Art most of what had happened at the Rusty Snake, but not the date proposal. I'm not sure why I'd left that out. So I told him. I wanted to know what he thought about the idea.

We were driving north on I-85 past an enormous tech facility. You could've fit a couple of college campuses on its grounds. All the buildings were long, one-story white rectangles, like hangars for rockets on their sides. I imagined that if I had an aerial view, these might form a crop circle-style pattern—or maybe spell out the company logo.

"You should meet with Dimitri," Art told me. "We'll plant a couple of undercover police at the restaurant, you can wear a wire, and maybe he'll let something slip besides the name he says he'll give you. We need help on this case. I'm sure you know that the longer we have to investigate, the lower the odds are that we find the perp."

"That's asking a lot. You don't know what this guy is like."

"Yes, I do. He's been on our radar for some time. And I've interrogated suspects like him hundreds of times. Well, maybe dozens. It can be like getting slimed. I'll grant you that. Will you do it anyway?"

I paused and thought it over.

"I'll take you to dinner myself if you do it," Art added. "Maybe that'll counterbalance the creepiness."

"You're asking me out on a date?"

"It's more like an inducement. You know, a police technique we use." He grinned, a more sheepish version of his baseline smile.

"Uh-huh. Well, we'll see." I smiled back to reduce his obvious discomfort. "It's just that I don't know if I'm ready for that, Art. But I'll wear your wire and help out."

He arched his eyebrows and smiled—the real deal this time. "What? You'll go out with a thug, but not me?"

I laughed. "That's right. I dig the bad boys."

"So where should we set this up? Where do you want to have dinner with Dimitri?"

"I'm so far out of the loop, I don't even know the names of any restaurants. Where would you take me?"

"Herb's Grill."

"Okay, then let's make it someplace else. I don't want to ruin that one."

"So you really might go out with me sometime?"

"Well, it does seem to be part of an important police procedure. Let's leave the door open and see how things go. So where should I tell him?"

"There's a place that's set up well for monitoring a wire. We've used it before. The Palace. It's near the post office downtown."

"Sounds good."

Art dropped me off at Jan's, getting out of the car to give me a hug but bailing out at the last minute. So I hugged him. You can tell a lot from a hug. Art was a very good hugger. Our energies merged briefly and then reluctantly parted company. I felt a tingling warmth in my chest.

Chapter Thirteen

I called Dimitri from the front porch after puzzling out how to find his number. It only took seven tries.

"Okay, let's do it," I told him.

"Excellent! You won't regret it. I am wonderful company. I have stories. Many interesting stories."

"I'll bet you do. Do you like the Palace restaurant?"

"Oh, yes. A fine choice."

"Can I meet you there?"

"Tonight? Eight o'clock?"

"I can do tonight. Let's make it seven. I'm still weaning myself off of Sri Lankan time."

"What is this weaning? And why were you in Sri Lanka? We have nice beaches here. That's very far to go for a beach."

"Let's save all that for dinner, Dimitri. Have a great afternoon."

"I will do that."

Dee accosted me the minute I walked into the main house. I wondered if she'd eavesdropped on my phone conversation from behind the front door.

"Aunt Ivy, I found out some important stuff about Grandma. Come on up to my room."

She ran ahead of me up the staircase, looking back once to make sure I was following. Her oversized overalls hurried to keep up with who was in them.

As I entered her room, Dee plopped onto her desk

chair and fired up her laptop. A bit out of breath, I joined her in the far corner of the room, where I sat on her unmade bed.

"I made notes. Let me read them to you." Her words tumbled out. "Here goes. I got access to Grandma's medical records, and there's some interesting stuff in there. When she came in to the ER, they thought her stroke wasn't too bad even though she'd passed out, and they did all the stuff you're supposed to do right away. After that, they sent her up to intensive care, expecting her to wake up. Maybe she'd have to do a lot of rehab, maybe she wouldn't talk the same, but everyone was pretty hopeful."

"That's what your mom told me, Dee. So what happened? Were they just wrong?"

"She had another stroke—a bigger one—even after all the medicine and everything. I looked it up. It happens sometimes. And you can make it happen."

"How in the world did you find all that out?"

I was worried about what I might hear in answer to my question.

"I talked to a nurse who was there in the ER when Grandma came in. I said I was a cop."

"Dee!"

"It's okay. She didn't believe me, so I told her who I really was and she was nice to me, even though she said she could get in a lot of trouble. She has a daughter about my age. Anyway, my point is that if someone knew how to induce a stroke, and they had the opportunity, they could've murdered Grandma by giving her that second stroke up in ICU."

"Have you wondered why anyone would want to do that?"

"Something to do with Dennis, I guess. I don't know what."

"Did you find out how to induce a stroke?" Uncle Brian had said he would look into that, but he hadn't gotten back to me. In the past, he'd broken plenty of other promises, including taking me to Disneyland on my ninth birthday. That one had been really rough.

Dee grinned. "Of course I found that out. There are two main ways. Giving somebody really high blood pressure or giving them too high a dosage of blood thinners. Sometimes that second one happens in hospitals by mistake."

"How do you give someone high blood pressure?"

"There's all kinds of ways, including giving them too much salt or caffeine—I mean a lot too much. There's also thyroid pills, or a whole lot of nicotine patches, or migraine medicine. I guess the blood thinners is how I'd do it. It's more guaranteed."

"So someone could've given her extra blood thinners and killed her?"

"Sure."

"Pills or intravenous?" I asked.

"I'm not sure she could swallow pills. According to the nurse on the phone, she was pretty out of it." Dee shook her head.

I think she was picturing her grandmother lying inert in her bed. I was, too.

After a while, I spoke, as much to escape the sadness that had welled up as to move the conversation along. "So we've narrowed this down to someone with a medical background—someone who had access to Mom and knows how to administer intravenous meds."

"Like Dennis?" Dee asked. "Once he told me he

sold medical equipment."

"That was just his cover story, remember? He was actually a smuggler and a fraud."

"Oh yeah. Well, there's his sister. And any nurse or doctor could've been bribed to do it."

"You can't bribe people to kill someone. That's asking too much." I very much wanted this to be true. "But I think we need to take a closer look at the sister."

"Right."

Dee fully swiveled her chair to face me, and I was struck by how young her face was. With her back to me, while she spoke as if she were a peer, I'd forgotten she was only fourteen—and not for the first time.

She continued. "I still think Grandma was murdered—more than I did before."

"I heard there was no autopsy or toxicology report?"

"Right. Nobody besides Mom was suspicious, and you know how she gets. It's easy to ignore what she says when she gets upset. I mean, she sounds so hysterical and all. Then Dennis cremated Grandma right away."

"Great work, Dee. Just be careful about breaking the law. You may be a minor, but hacking into computers is still a serious crime. They might not go easy on you."

I hoped this warning would be sufficient to keep her out of trouble. Part of me knew my willingness to allow her to continue "researching" was self-serving—that I needed her help.

"Yeah, I know. There's a forum online where kids talk about that. Some of them have gotten caught—dumber ones than me. You can be smart about computers and really dumb about everything else. Me? I'm well-rounded. My test scores are always pretty even whether its math, or science, or English."

"Think about how handy those scores will be in prison."

She made a face as though she'd eaten sour fruit. "Oh, Aunt Ivy. Don't be so dramatic. What should I do next?"

"I don't know. Whatever you think might help, I guess. I need to find out more before I can aim you at anything in particular."

"Okay."

****

As per instructions from Art, I drove to the police station an hour before meeting Dimitri, and a very chatty woman named Deborah rigged up a tiny transmitter in the ladies' room that perched on the top of my bra. She and a younger male officer would precede me to the restaurant and pose as a couple. Art and another man I didn't meet would be parked down the street in a commercial van with the electronics they needed.

"Who are we this week?" Art asked the woman officer when we'd returned to the upscale conference room. He turned to me. "We repaint the van periodically."

"Jeb's Blinds and Shades. Hudson likes the *Beverly Hillbillies* reruns."

"And *Leave it to Beaver* and *Gunsmoke*. Ward and June's Gutter Cleaning? Miss Kitty's Pet Grooming? Criminals watch reruns too, don't they?"

"Talk to Lieutenant Cline if you want, but it won't do any good. I complained about this last year. One of these days, it's gonna matter, and we're going to be the ones out there on the street."

I spoke up. "Tell me what I should say to Dimitri to get him to incriminate himself." Butterflies fluttered in my gut. Suddenly, I wasn't sure I really wanted to do this. Could I really pull this off? What if Dimitri discovered the microphone? What would he do?

Art answered. "Don't worry about that. Just chat with him and get the name of his contact. We'll sort through whatever else he says to see if it's helpful to us. If you try to work him, he'll know. I've looked into this guy a little further. He's savvy and you're not a professional actress, are you?"

"Far from it." I shook my head and couldn't stop until Deborah spoke. Her delicate Asian features defied my ability to discern her heritage, which, of course, didn't matter at all at that moment. It was just something to focus on instead of tuning into my fear.

"He's probably suspicious of you already," she said. "The most important thing is to stay safe."

"Absolutely," Art agreed. "Flirt if you want, but don't engage with him on a deep level. Don't upset him."

None of this reassured me.

"I'm a bit rusty at flirting," I told them.

"Let's practice," Art said. "Hey, you've got beautiful, soulful eyes, Ivy."

"Well, thank you."

"No, no. You go next. Flirt back."

"Uh, I like your nose, Art. It reminds of a statue of the Buddha I saw once in a cave in north India."

The woman officer made a loud buzzer noise. "Nope. That's not even bad flirting. And Art's nose looks like a potato."

"The hell it does," he protested.

"What's wrong with what I said?" I asked.

"Noses aren't sexy. Caves aren't sexy. India is semi-sexy, maybe," Deborah told me.

"So what would *you* say?"

"I'd smile and say, 'You really know how to compliment a girl, don't you? Your English is terrific.' "

"This is Art?"

"No, I mean with Dimitri. I heard the guy speak on a wiretap once. His English stinks. So *that's* what you compliment."

"So I should lie, basically."

"Exactly. Everything that happens early on between men and women is a lie," she asserted.

"Deborah, that's a little cynical, don't you think?" Art said.

"Nope." She turned to me and gestured. "Flirt with me, Ivy. Let's see what you can come up with now."

I thought about it and decided to take a different approach.

"Deborah, I think we could fly to the moon together on the wings of a giant swan, much like the one mentioned in ancient Greek literature."

She sighed.

Art spoke. "Okay, let's forget about flirting. Just be yourself. That's what attracted him to you in the first place. Well, that and those amazing eyes."

Deborah glanced at him. "Still role-modeling how to flirt, Art?"

"Nope," he answered, smiling at me.

****

I entered the Palace wearing my new dress, my new shoes, and a horrible jacket of Jan's that she insisted I wear. The puffy white sleeves made it look as though my arms were swollen from an allergic reaction, and bright red embroidery decorated the black body of the jacket in an abstract pattern that reminded me of intersecting spiderwebs. I'd wanted to wear my black fleece top, but Jan wouldn't hear of it. I was successful at warding off her attempts to make me wear makeup, thank God.

The restaurant's decor couldn't have been much more pretentious. I immediately felt wildly out of place. I suspect my jacket didn't. The palace the restaurant designers had emulated seemed to be Versailles, but their budget hadn't allowed for anything beyond garish murals. Two dimensions just couldn't do justice to Baroque architecture. And the huge chandelier looming over the center of the vast dining room was obviously not crystal. The glass pieces only murkily reflected the flame-shaped bulbs above them.

I didn't see Dimitri at first. Like in the bar, he'd taken a table along the rear wall, with his back against it. He stood and waved his arm as if I were out at sea and he was on the shore.

When I reached his table, he took my arm.

"Come. I want to show you something," he said, pulling me toward a door to the side of the table. Before I could protest, we were through it and into a dimly lit hallway.

"Hold it!" I tried to dig my heels in. My new shoes slid on the slick linoleum floor as Dimitri pushed me in my lower back.

"Where are we going? What are you doing?"

"A change of plans. I know a better restaurant. My car is out back."

"I want to eat here!"

He ignored me. In a moment, I was ushered into an alley next to a low-slung sports car.

"Here we go. It's all good. You're going to love it."

He stood blocking the door. If I wanted to get away,

I'd have to run. In my new shoes, a sloth could've caught me.

"I'm not getting in that thing," I said. "I don't know you, Dimitri. I'm not getting a car with someone I just met. And what a ridiculous car. I don't know I could even climb into it. Its roof is at knee level, isn't it?"

"No, you are mistaken. Everyone fits in in. Jerry fits in. You remember Jerry?"

"Yes, I do. I certainly don't believe your giant colleague could fit. You're damaging your credibility here, Dimitri."

"Okay, maybe not Jerry, but you're not Jerry. Get in the car, Ivy."

I hesitated.

"This is a wonderful car. It's the fastest one you can buy. It is a treat to be in my car. And do you think if I wished you harm, I'd meet you in a restaurant? That I'd be standing here talking to you? That would be very foolish."

I made up my mind. "I said no, and I mean no."

"Then I won't help you with Anton."

The Asian police officer—Deborah—popped her head out the door. "Is everything all right? I saw this man grab you. Are you all right?"

"Mind your own business, lady," Dimitri growled.

"I'm fine, I said. "My date wants to take me to another restaurant. That's all."

"Well, okay." She closed the door.

"Americans are so nosy," Dimitri said.

"All right, I'll go," I told him, "but we'll take my car—well, my sister's car."

"Okay. I can compromise. I can bend to make you happy, Ivy."

I made a point of walking with Dimitri the long way to the car to give my police escorts a chance to scramble. I didn't know if the wire I wore could transmit from behind the restaurant to the van, and I guessed the couple in the Palace were no use now that Deborah had revealed herself, albeit as a nosy bystander. Perhaps Art and his partner could follow us and set up near the next eatery.

As we approached the car, I saw no sign of any police.

"You sister has a Jaguar? Very nice."

"It was her husband's. She won it in a divorce."

We climbed in. He immediately adjusted the seat to its farthest back and most upright position. Then he flipped down the visor and checked his hair in the mirror.

In profile, Dimitri's hawk-like nose was more prominent, and a skin cancer removal scar I hadn't noticed before slanted up to the corner of his nostril. An older dark red line on his temple sat in a dent—they'd had to dig deep for that one.

It occurred to me that my theory about the origins of the wear and tear on his face might be too benign. Maria had said Dimitri used to beat people up. Maybe these were knife scars or something along those lines.

The thought didn't cheer me up. Here I was in a car with someone who might be a violent criminal. My protectors could probably follow us, but from this point forward they'd be winging it. Would they be able to monitor me wherever we were going?

The fear was deep in my gut and chest—a tightness that was almost painful.

"Very nice," Dimitri said again after he'd flipped the visor back up and glanced around the car. "What leather is this? Napa? Calfskin?"

"I have no idea. Where to?"

"Go straight ahead and take the next right."

"Okay."

As I turned the corner, a semitruck pulled out of a driveway behind us and blocked the road. I decided to pretend I hadn't noticed. I was on my own now.

A stronger surge of fear twisted in my gut, and the adrenaline in my system amped up my nervous system. On the plus side, I felt fully alive—on high alert, with enhanced senses. Alternatively, my heart pounded—painfully—a tremor rippled down my arm to my hand, and my head vibrated as if to loosen its perch on my neck. It was all I could do not to betray myself by crying.

The new restaurant—and there *was* one instead of an abandoned quarry, thank God—was an Italian bistro on Camino Real south of Stanford.

Dimitri had reserved a table for two in the back of the modest dining area. The cherubic maître d' greeted him by name, and clearly, they had taken away what would've been two nearby tables. Otherwise, the restaurant was packed with well-dressed diners.

"Here we are," Dimitri said.

He'd been silent on the ride over, which surprised me. Perhaps he feared I was wearing a wire. After all, he'd already gone to quite a bit of trouble to separate me from any police. Maybe he'd set up some sort of signal blocker at the restaurant, letting him go ahead once we were inside. I didn't have any confidence in these notions. They just floated into my mind and then drifted away.

We sat across from one another after I took off my horrible jacket and slung it onto the back of my chair.

Dimitri's conservatively cut charcoal gray suit

competed with his pale blue seersucker shirt to set a tone. The suit belonged in a corporate boardroom. The shirt was straight out of an L.L. Bean catalogue—geared toward preppie beachgoers on Nantucket Island. Or maybe wannabe preppies who'd been forced to ruin their lives at non-Ivy League schools. Ah, the horror.

I recognized my reverse snobbery, once again disappointed by my inability to remain nonjudgmental.

Dimitri's face was more triangular than I remembered, tapering down sharply below his dark eyes. His prominent mustache had been tamed since we last meet. Each stiff hair now marched in unison down to his thin upper lip.

An elderly man sidled up and introduced himself as Giovanni as he handed each of us brown leather-bound menus. He was probably five feet tall if you didn't count his towering pompadour. Other than a rockabilly revival singer I'd seen in my teens, who also wore high-heeled boots, Giovanni's hair was the most impressive height-enhancing strategy I'd run across.

"This is my restaurant, and I'm honored to have you both here," he told us in a slight Italian accent. "You are a beautiful couple. Miss, that is a lovely dress."

"Thank you." I looked down to make sure I was wearing the one I thought I was. I wouldn't have described it as lovely. I'd have gone with adequate, or maybe suitable for the occasion.

"You drink wine?" Dimitri asked me without taking his eyes off our host.

For a moment, I thought he was asking him. Then Dimitri swiveled his gaze to me when I didn't immediately answer.

"I haven't in many years, but I'll try it," I told him.

"Good for you. Wine is elixir from the gods. Everyone should drink wine. Giovanni, once we pick our food, you bring what you think is the best wine for us. And turn up the fucking heat." His swearing was casual. He hadn't raised his voice.

"Of course, Dimitri." Our host bustled off.

"Now then," Dimitri said. "You see if I'm right."

"About what?"

"This restaurant. Giovanni's. It's much better."

"I thought you liked the Palace?"

He smiled a creepy smile. "Okay, you caught me. I always change plans at the last minute. I have many enemies."

"Why is that?"

"It's the business I'm in. Ruthless men do what I do. And they want to be like me—to take my place."

"That sounds hard." I couldn't put myself in his shoes, but maybe I could empathize with his feelings.

"Oh, I'm used to it. Nothing is hard for me. I think we are alike this way, no?" He tilted his head and raised his bushy eyebrows.

"You think I breeze through my life?"

"Yes, I like that. Breeze. Don't you?"

"Compared to most people, I guess I do, but I'm sure it's for different reasons than you."

"What do you mean?"

"It's not because I've established a secure position in life. I don't have a job or possessions that other people want. I can handle what comes my way because I've learned to live with uncertainty."

"Maybe that works for you," he said. "It sounds crazy to me. Let's talk about something else. Tell me about Sri Lanka. You had a nice vacation there?"

"I lived there—on the grounds of a Buddhist temple."

"No men for you?"

"No sex, if that's what you mean. Lots of monks."

"Sounds pretty bad. You have TV?"

"No."

"Internet?"

"No."

"You sit and pray to Buddha all day? This is your life? Why did you come here if that's so great?"

"My mother had a stroke and died."

"I'm sorry for your loss," Dimitri said woodenly, as if by rote. Perhaps he'd had to say it more than most people.

"Thank you."

He thought about what to say next. "It's hard to go from one thing to another? So different."

"Yes. But enough about me. Tell me more about yourself. Why did you say you're interesting?"

"You can't tell already? You hurt me. Look at how I listen—how I care what you say. Do men do that? No. They just want sex. And here we are where they know me. Did you hear Giovanni say he was honored? Do you think he says that to everyone? No, he doesn't. Usually, he hides in the kitchen."

"Perhaps he's scared of you."

"Are *you*? Are you okay here with me like you say you always are with uncertain things? I can see you're scared. And you said you were nervous. You haven't been with a man like me, have you?"

"I'm okay feeling fear. It's not something going wrong."

"You like the roller coaster? You jump out of

planes?"

"Yes to the roller coaster. No to skydiving." I paused to consider what I felt like saying next and decided to go ahead. "Dimitri, have you noticed that almost everything you say is phrased as a question?"

"No. So what?"

"I'm just pointing out something you might not be aware of."

"Why do that? Don't do that. If I'm not aware of it, it's because I don't want to be."

Giovanni crept up. "Are we ready?"

"You pick for us. Okay, Ivy?"

I decided to plunge into mainstream eating. "Okay," I agreed.

Our host departed, and Dimitri spoke. "Small people?"

I felt confused again. Was this a reference to Giovanni. "I beg your pardon?"

"Sri Lanka. Small people?"

"Yes."

"Like Indians?"

"Yes. Very similar. But in my experience, they're warmer, at least with foreigners like me. We're still not talking about you, are we?"

"What do you want to know?"

"How and why did you get from Bulgaria to here?"

Dimitri pursed his lips and looked up and to his left. "My uncle, my sister, and I stole a boat and crossed the Maritsa at night into Greece. In Sofia, life was very hard with the Russians. We stayed in Athens for a year, but the people there didn't like us, so another uncle in Philadelphia paid money so we could come to the States."

"What brought you from Philadelphia to California?"

"Love, of course. Why did *you* go to this other country of yours?"

"A deep yearning for wholeness."

"What kind of reason is that? Why not be whole here?"

I looked across the room as I pondered how to answer that. Art winked at me from a plush loveseat by the maître d' stand.

My gut relaxed a bit. "If you can't find what you're looking for nearby," I told Dimitri, "then you go somewhere else—like you did. Do you have any children?"

"Of course. Three boys. One is in a very good college. Very expensive. One helps in my business. And one, I don't know where he is. He doesn't like me."

"Do you still have a relationship with their mother?"

"Of course. We are married."

"You're currently married?" I was shocked, which reminded me what a sheltered life I'd led.

"Sure."

"How does she feel about your having dinner with another woman?"

He laughed. "You think I tell her such things. Do I look like a fool?"

A slim, tough-looking woman served us antipasto.

"Who are you? Where is Giovanni?"

"I'm sorry, sir. He was needed elsewhere." Her tone didn't imply an authentic apology, and she looked quite out of place. She wore more casual clothes than the other servers—tight jeans and a somewhat ratty black V-neck sweater. It was hard to imagine her smiling.

"What is more important than me?"

"I'm sure I don't know, sir."

"Make sure he brings us the next course. I don't trust strangers. You are a stranger."

Dimitri glanced around the room in a vain effort to locate our host. The server winked at me. My remaining fear dissipated. There were at least two sets of police officers' eyes on me.

When we were alone again, I asked Dimitri if he was ready to help me about Dennis. I called him Anton, but I still thought of him as Dennis.

"I can tell you this. Many people were not happy with him. He owed a lot of money to people you don't want to owe money to."

"Loan sharks?"

"No, no. Politicians, police, taxmen. Not here. In Ireland. He thought he was safe here as this Dennis person."

"You knew he was pretending to be Dennis?"

"Of course. He paid me for protection."

That sounded like Dimitri was admitting to being a gangster.

"Which you evidently failed to provide."

"Yes, it's true. If a man really wants to kill you, he'll do it, as long as he can find you."

"If you were me, what would you do?"

"Go home. Forget about this. Go out with me again. I'm having a great time. Next date, wear something sexier."

"I'm going to pursue this, Dimitri. Who's the man I need to talk to?"

He sighed as our tossed salads arrived, accompanied by Giovanni, who apologized profusely for his earlier absence.

When we were alone again, Dimitri answered me. "Okay. A deal's a deal. You need to talk to Joseph Hamadou. He lives in East Palo Alto somewhere—near the Ikea, I think."

"Why does he know about this?"

"He's a broker for deals—smuggling deals. He partnered with Anton many times."

I suddenly thought of something. "Was Anton really retired?"

"No. He had a deal in the works when he died."

"What about my Uncle Brian?"

"What about him? What do you mean?"

"How does he fit in? He knows you and Anton from hanging out at the Rusty Snake."

"Isn't your uncle a doctor?"

"Yes. He could still be mixed up in this, couldn't he?"

"You suspect your own uncle? A doctor? What's wrong with you?"

I shrugged. "I'm just trying to cover all the bases."

"Brian is a pussycat," Dimitri asserted. "We take care of him in the bar because he buys drinks. I think he likes the kind of women who go there. They are very friendly."

"That sounds like him."

Our fish, when it finally arrived, was wonderful, and a lot more palatable than red meat would've been. The rich sauce provided another reason not to jiggle in a pair of leggings. The wine made me shudder, so I only took a few sips.

"Drink, drink," Dimitri implored. "Everything will seem better after some wine."

"For me, everything would be less clear, and I'd have stepped sideways from myself."

"You say many odd things, Ivy. I'd love to screw you, but maybe we're not so alike after all. I think I'd get tired of you and all these ideas of yours."

"That's fine. As far as I'm concerned, this is the last time we'll ever see each other. I wish you well, but we live in different worlds. I may have left the temple, and I may be experimenting with new behaviors, but I will always see things differently from you."

"Okay, okay." He threw his hands in the air. "Did you like your food?"

"Very much."

"I told you! I told you it was worth a ride."

"Yes, you were right." I tossed my napkin from my lap to the tabletop beside my plate, stood, and retrieved Jan's jacket. "I think I'll be going. Do you have a way to get home?"

"Yes, don't worry about me. No dessert?"

"No, thank you. I'm stuffed."

"Why don't we have a nice hug good-bye, Ivy," he said as he rose and stepped away from the table.

"I think not. Thank you for the dinner, and thank you for keeping your side of the deal."

"I am a man of my word. Call me if you need anything. You still have my card?"

"Yes."

"If I can help you more, I will. I don't want some killer loose in my town. And there are only so many Bulgarians here. We can't spare too many."

"Okay. Thank you."

Chapter Fourteen

When I passed Art, reached the sidewalk, and headed toward my car, I also passed the server/police officer who'd winked at me. She leaned against the brick wall of the hardware store next door to the restaurant, smoking.

"Drive to the station," she whispered. "We'll meet you there."

I nodded.

We gathered to discuss the fruits of the evening in the now-familiar conference room down the hall from Art's desk. Art, the server—Kay—and an older detective—introduced as Lieutenant Cline—sat across the polished, wooden table from me. Cline explained crankily that he'd been called away from home to help man the monitoring van.

Art looked tired. He slouched, albeit only half as much as Holly. There were lines at the corners of his eyes I hadn't seen before.

Kay's expression was mostly neutral, with minor irritation in her eyes. I imagined she was an intimidating interrogator. A fierceness sat just below the surface—I sensed it energetically.

Cline did not make a good first impression. He'd tilted his large, wide head back so he was literally looking down at me. His smug mouth seemed to say he knew so much more than me about everything that I was hardly worth talking to. To my eyes, he embodied the worst of our patriarchal culture. We rewarded arrogance by promoting men like Cline to positions of responsibility and power—as long as they were White, of course. Arrogant minorities—men and women—could find their own way.

The only thing I liked about Cline—and I worked to find something—was his reddish brush-cut hair. That was mostly because I pictured how it would feel to rub his head. A fellow nun had shaved her head upon entering our sangha. As it grew out, she convinced some of us that rubbing her new bristles brought good luck. I think she just enjoyed the sensation as much as we did. After all, after taking our vows, we were all starved for human contact. In hindsight, this felt like an unnecessary hardship.

Art spoke first. "Good job, Ivy. We caught most of it through your mic. I had an earpiece in while I kept an eye on you. Was there anything Dimitri said early on before we got there? Anything relevant to the case?"

"No, I don't think so. How did you find me?"

"We attached a tracer to your wire—that little pod thing that dangled down. I didn't want to worry you about some of the ways this could turn out, but I did want to be prepared."

"I thought that was a battery. Thank you for that. I felt immensely better once I saw you at the restaurant."

Art nodded. "So now we know several new, important things. There's a man in East Palo Alto we need to talk to. Dennis may still have been engaging in illegal activities, and putting together what Dimitri told you at the bar and tonight, maybe there's a current deal that's connected to Africa somehow."

"You believe what that slimeball said?" the lieutenant asked scornfully. "Saying Anton was under his protection is a giveaway, isn't it? That's crime boss talk there, Petrie. Why should we take his word for any of this?"

"I think I do believe what I heard, but let's check and see what Ivy thinks. She's sharp about people."

They all looked at me. Cline frowned. I think Art's eyes strayed to my dress.

"I'm fairly sure Dimitri was telling the truth." I told them. "If he wasn't, if I were you, I'd still follow up on what he said. Why not?"

Kay muttered, "Thanks for telling us how to do our job."

"Here's the why not," Cline said scornfully. "Sending us off on a wild goose chase pulls us away from what we'd otherwise be doing that might actually get us somewhere."

"And what would *that* be?" Art asked. "What other leads have we got at this point?"

"It's your job to generate them, Petrie. If you don't have any leads, whose fault is that?"

Art nodded but didn't reply. It was distressing to watch him endure this. It reminded me of when he'd told me I shouldn't tolerate Jan's insults. I think I felt the way he had—protective.

Cline continued in the same deprecatory tone. "I just don't like this—getting a civilian involved with a suspect—and now she's at our meeting, too. Who is Ivy, anyway?" He turned and glared at me. "A relative of the deceased. That's who. She shows up from out of nowhere, and all of a sudden we're trusting her? No offense, lady, but I don't know you from Adam. Just because Art's vouching for you doesn't mean you oughta be here."

"I understand your point of view," I answered.

His words hadn't stung me. They indicated far more about him than me. "Consider the source," Bhante had always told me when I was unduly affected by someone's words. "Are they credible—someone you respect? Do their words have weight?"

"I'd probably feel the same way if I were in your shoes, Lieutenant Cline," I continued. "And I sense you're Art's boss?" He nodded. "The thing is, I'll be investigating this whether it's on my own or as a collaborator because I believe my mother's death may be tied in with Dennis's murder. From what I can gather, the police haven't gotten too far in that investigation."

Now I was fulfilling my mother's advice—standing up to a bully.

"If I say so," Cline responded, "your so-called investigation is going to turn into tampering with witnesses, obstructing justice, and whatever else I can think of."

"I'll abide by whatever you decide about that, but I know I can help, and I'll keep trying as long as I'm not behind bars."

"She's been a big help so far, Lieutenant," Art told him. "You've seen my reports."

Cline turned to me and glared again. This time, he narrowed his eyes down to slits and jutted his face forward on his neck, closing the distance between us.

"I've got my eye on you. Watch your step."

"I will. Thank you," I said as sweetly as I could, pretending he'd offered solicitous advice.

Cline leapt to his feet and strode out of the room.

"Do you still need me?" Kay asked Art. "My babysitter will kill me if I'm late."

"No, go ahead. Ivy and I will chat a bit more."

"Okay. Goodnight. And Ivy? Don't worry about Cline. He's like that with everyone he doesn't know."

When she'd gone, Art switched seats to be right across from me. "I need to ask you about your uncle. Is that okay?"

"Sure. However I can help."

He'd become more animated, and he sat up straighter as he began to talk.

"When I questioned him, Brian told me he flew back from Africa once he heard about your mother, but we checked with the airlines and he actually flew in two weeks earlier, accompanied by a Cameroonian woman— or whatever you call someone from there."

"That's news to me." I thought about whether I wanted to share more information about my uncle. "I did find out some other troubling things about Brian," I continued. "I'm sure he's not a murderer—I've known him all my life, of course—but he was the one who introduced Mom and Dennis. And when we visited the Rusty Nail, he knew the bartender and Dimitri, who described him as 'an old friend.' "

"That's interesting, Ivy. Thank you for that." He paused to consider the implications, and then asked, "Why would your uncle be traveling with a thirty-year-old African woman?"

"He's a womanizer. He always has been. She could be a girlfriend."

"What is he? In his sixties?"

"Seventies, actually. This wouldn't be the first time he was with a much younger woman."

"Why lie? To me or to you?"

"I don't know. Do you think he's involved in the conflict over there? Maybe that's his connection to all this."

"I didn't know there was a conflict," Art said.

"It's a mess in Cameroon. Rebels, warlords, corrupt government troops—you name it. I looked it up when Brian told me a little about it. It's not in the news since it's too dangerous for the foreign press, the government has clamped down on internal journalism, and the U.S. has no economic interests there."

"That's a bit cynical, don't you think, Ivy?"

"What do you know about what's going on in Africa versus elsewhere? Are Europeans or Middle Easterners intrinsically more important or interesting?"

Art shook his head, but I sensed it was for some reason other than disagreement. Disappointment that I'd turned out to be cynical? I'd thought, as an African American, he'd readily agree to my premise. Perhaps he felt little connection to the continent. After all, I didn't feel Swiss at all.

"Anyway," Art said, "you're saying maybe Brian's trying to help one side or the other for this woman's sake? If he knew Dennis was—or is—a smuggler, he could've flown this woman here to make a deal of some kind. That could be what Dimitri was talking about when he said Dennis wasn't really retired."

I thought that over. "It's possible, but I don't think women in Africa get to be dealmakers." I tried to remember more about my uncle's history in case that was relevant. "Brian did get involved in a situation in Central America once. They deported him."

"Tell me more about that."

"That's all I remember. You can probably find out more about it."

I suddenly realized I was very tired. With an effort, I sat up straighter, matching Art's current posture. He didn't appear to notice.

"Sure, we'll check it out. Do you like the guy?"

"My uncle?" I shrugged. "I've never really thought about it. Family's family."

"Would you choose him as a friend?"

He'd rephrased his question to get an answer, and the new prompt was easier to respond to.

"Well, no. Like I say, he preys on women."

"You didn't say that. You said he was a womanizer."

"Whatever term we use, he works to charm women in order to have sex with them. That's a very different wavelength than mine. It's his life and he can choose whoever he wants to be, but if I'm picking friends, he wouldn't be on my list."

"How do you think he'd react if I confronted him about his role in all this?"

"I'm not sure."

"No idea at all?" Art asked.

"Do you want me there? Would that help?"

"You'd be willing?"

"Sure."

"Let's just knock on the door of his B and B early tomorrow," Art suggested. "We might catch the woman in there with him. At the least, he won't have time to prepare for us."

"Okay. You're the boss."

"Why don't I feel that's the case? Why do I keep feeling like I need to do what you want, Ivy?"

"Maybe you're in love with me," I joked.

He peered at me intently and didn't respond.

****

As I lay in bed, hoping to instantly fall asleep, I wondered why so many people seemed to think I was attractive or special. When this had happened with Dee, I'd glibly denied it. With Art, I'd attributed it to an impersonal phenomenon—energy.

I'd been taught we're all equally amazing beings and all equally shmoes. Of course, Bhante had used a Tamil idiom for the latter before I taught him the Yiddish term. After that, he hunted up more Yiddish words and taught them to the entire community.

Whether special or schmo is more accurate in a given moment depends on one's vantage point. From the usual human perspective, we're a messy, bumbling species. Some of us hide this better than others, but no one's immune—not even my deceased teacher. He regularly binged on ice cream, for example, making himself sick.

On the other hand, viewed from a spiritual vantage point—atop a mountain, so to speak—looking down—everyone is perfect the way they are. There's tremendous room for improvement, of course, but the imperfectness is not something going wrong. It's *right* that we should be the way we are, warts and all.

Anyway, my investigation of why I was suddenly being admired was guided by this perspective. I knew I was just another person whose life path happened to be different than most. Were people sensing my chi—my internal energy signature—as I'd claimed they could? Perhaps. Was my level of awareness reflected in my eyes? I guessed it could cause me to stand out. Lastly, I tried to open up to the idea that I was physically attractive. I had never thought of myself as that before. Had I grown into beauty while at the temple?

I fell asleep without arriving anywhere with all this. In the morning, it seemed self-indulgent to have wondered.

At six thirty, well before anyone else in my family arose, I was out the door. I'd eaten an overly sweet yogurt and a handful of almonds from the kitchen in the main house, which would sustain me for a while.

Then I drove back to the police station in downtown Palo Alto, parked the Jaguar, and met Art, who sat on the front steps gazing at his phone. He wore the same blue sport coat as he had on our last outing, this time over new-looking jeans.

"Looking at photos of cute kitties?" I teased as he stood.

"Playing Scrabble. It's my only addiction."

He pointed to the right, and we headed that way.

"I love Scrabble," I told him. "I used to be good at it too, but I haven't played in years. I'll bet there are all sorts of new words now."

"There are, and I know most of them. We need to play. Beating the app isn't nearly as satisfying as trouncing a self-described good player."

Art turned and smiled. I still loved that smile. We strolled around the building toward a parking lot behind it.

"Oh, it's like that, huh?" I responded. "Self-described? I happen to be very modest. When I say 'I'm good at it,' I mean I have world-class, soul-crushing skill, the likes of which you've never encountered in your puny, meaningless life."

Art stopped, beat his chest like King Kong, and roared at the top of his lungs.

I laughed. "Shh. It's early. Don't wake the whole neighborhood."

"You've awakened the beast in me. Fear my wrath!"

"It's definitely going to be an interesting game," I told him.

Art drove us to Brian's in an unmarked car, which was obviously a police vehicle, markings or no markings.

"Can you sneak up on criminals in this thing?" I asked after a few blocks. There was very little traffic.

"No, I use confiscated vehicles when I want to lurk. And I don't sneak. I lurk."

"I'm sorry. Any skulking?"

"Occasionally. And sometimes I snoop."

"I like that one. It's more personal, implying curiosity about what you might find."

"Oh, I'm always curious. I want to know everything. In fact, let me ask you some things. Okay?"

"Sure."

"What were you like before you became a Buddhist?"

"Good question. Let me see…I was depressed a lot. I had low self-esteem. I read incessantly—mostly novels. I thought too much, blocking direct experience." I paused for breath. All of that had come out in a rush. "I weighed a lot more too. I loved to dance. I was scared of other people's judgments, so I tended to stay quiet. I was a good student and I tested well, but I wasn't any sort of brainiac. I just worked hard."

"Not me. I sat in the back of the classroom and tuned out the teacher. I had a learning disability, which stayed undiagnosed until I was a junior in high school. So I thought I was too stupid to get anywhere in school. Why bother trying? That was my motto."

"What a shame. Does that interfere with your Scrabble game?"

"You wish. And I've got a lot of workarounds on the job."

We were both quiet for a while. I was thinking about my past self, and how harshly I had described her. I was tempted to tell Art what I admired about her—how brave and thoughtful I'd always been. I decided that was too Ivy-centric. I'd be doing it for me, not because he needed to hear it.

"So what's the plan at Brian's?" I finally asked.

"I'll take the lead. Just listen and pay attention. If you think there's something you need to add, go ahead, but otherwise..."

"Gotcha."

Brian came to the door in a fuzzy blue robe. "It's a bit early, isn't it? Hi, Ivy. Hello, Detective Petrie. I'd ask you in, but I have company."

"Would that be Grace Kamgaing?"

Brian stared at Art for a long moment. "I guess you'd better come in, after all."

He stepped to the side, Art brushed past him, and I followed.

The B and B was messy, with a few empty beer bottles on a low table beside the couch. Two pairs of shoes sat haphazardly just inside the door, one pair much smaller than the other.

As we lowered ourselves onto flimsy director chairs at the wooden kitchen table, Ms. Kamgaing emerged from the doorway beside the kitchenette and stood with her hands on her hips.

Nearly six feet tall, slim, with cropped hair and very dark skin, she could've been a fashion model except for several scars. The thin, raised one on her forehead mimicked the arc of one of her eyebrows. Another one on her neck hinted at a more serious wound. Jagged scar tissue snaked down under her chin, nearly reaching where an Adam's apple would've been if she were a man. I knew these were not due to skin cancers.

She wore one of Brian's white dress shirts, which she'd left unbuttoned enough to display cleavage, and it only covered the top half of her lithe thighs. Grace seemed oblivious to this, or perhaps so comfortable in her skin that our presence didn't matter to her.

Her facial features were actually hard to discern in the underlit room, due to the hue of her skin. I could make out dark pupils against the white of her eyes, and generous lips that were slightly lighter than what looked like a wide nose above them.

"Who are these people?" she asked Brian in a delightful accent. She spoke slowly, hunting just a bit for the word "these."

I was struck by the musicality of her voice. Lower in pitch than I would've expected, a liquid lilt came along with her words. I was charmed, and I could readily see why Brian had been attracted to her.

My uncle introduced us and gestured to the chair beside him for Grace to sit. True to her name, the African woman walked over gracefully and then lowered herself with a dancer's poise. I was glad for her sake that the table blocked Art's view of her lower body. Well, for mine, too, actually. How could I compete with someone like her, even without glimpses of her private parts?

"I am so glad to meet you, Ivy," Grace told me. "I was very sorry when Brian said he needed to keep his family separate."

Closer now, I saw that her nose was concave at the top, widening out right near the bottom. Her eyebrows were almost the same color of her skin. I still couldn't see them clearly. Her prominent cheekbones created creases on their inside borders, as though the middle of her face was a parenthetical aside.

"I'm sorry, too," I told her. "I didn't know you existed, or I would've welcomed you."

"Separate from his family? Why did Brian say that?" Art asked.

"Who are you again? You are with Ivy, yes? Her husband?"

"I'm a policeman investigating Dennis Sorenson's murder."

"Oh, yes. A terrible thing."

Art persisted. "So why has Brian been keeping you a secret?"

"My husband can explain."

"Husband?" I blurted out. I did not see that coming.

Brian spoke up. "Grace is my wife, and we're here to secure funds for her people in Cameroon."

"Congratulations," I interjected, despite my abject surprise.

"Thank you. If we're not successful, I fear outright genocide. The government has built a dam that's left her tribe with a permanent drought. And that wasn't by accident. The northwest part of the country has been trying to secede for a long time, so the army considers them rebels."

"You see this as a humanitarian thing?" Art asked.

His tone was skeptical. He didn't care if they were married. He cared about the case, and he wasn't sure he was being fed the truth.

"Absolutely," Brian answered.

"How have you been going about this?"

"We have brought items to sell," Grace said. "Dennis was going to help."

"How could he help with that?"

"He said he knew a lot of rich people—all over the world. He told us if we came here, we could go home with enough money to save my people."

She squinted, frowned, and shook her head, each one competing for my attention.

"What sort of items?" Art asked.

"My people's things."

"Their heritage," Brian explained, "which is a shame. The Tikari people are well-known as artisans, and traditionally they've kept the best pieces for themselves."

I took the opportunity to watch Grace again. Her scrutiny of her husband didn't evidence love or even fondness. Her fiery eyes and the tension of her mouth exuded intensity—passion. It didn't seem personal or related to my uncle. The topic of the conversation had fired her up.

"Pieces?" Art asked.

"Pottery, wood carvings, and intricate basketwork," Brian told him. "You've never seen anything like their baskets. We're talking museum quality."

Grace spoke up. "Yes, our items are very beautiful. Very valuable."

"I've known Dennis for years," Brian explained, "and he knows wealthy collectors—people who bought specialty things from him in the past."

"You mean exotic animals?"

"Well, yes. And art from around the world. I know about Dennis's checkered past. At one time, we were close. We dated sisters."

"Your Croatian girlfriend?" I asked. "The one at the Rusty Snake?"

"That's right." He looked at Grace. "I've told my wife about Ana. We have no secrets."

"It sounds like you have plenty of them," Art commented. "Just not between the two of you. Why did you feel it was necessary to hide all this? Why couldn't you present Grace to your family and tell them you were already in the country before your sister's death? You could've said goodbye to your sister if you'd stayed in touch."

"I know. I've been beating myself up over that. Clearly, it was a mistake. And when the proverbial shit hit the fan, I should've come forward. I should've known you'd find out. This puts us in a very bad light, as though we're doing something wrong."

"Aren't you?"

"What do you mean?"

"You still haven't come clean, have you? Your *items* were smuggled out of the country, weren't they? That's another reason you needed Dennis, and another reason to keep your activities secret."

"Please don't mock my wife. English is her third language, and there's nothing wrong with the word 'item.' "

My uncle was focusing on something other than the question to gather himself.

"Answer my question. Governments don't let their

ethnic history leave the country, do they?"

"No, you're right. Dennis told us to keep everything secret because he knew the legal consequences. He said we'd never be able to go back to Cameroon, and the government here might seize our things and return them." He ran his hand through his thick head of hair. "You've got to understand. This is a matter of life or death. Wouldn't you cut corners to save thousands of lives, Detective?"

"This is your idea of cutting corners?"

Brian turned to me, imploring with his eyes. "Ivy, you get it, don't you? This is an act of love—not just for Grace, but for all the people at risk of being exterminated in Cameroon. I have to try. I couldn't look at myself in the mirror if I didn't. And I'd never be able to look at my beautiful wife again. I can't betray her."

Grace smiled wanly and nodded her head slowly when Brian turned his eyes to her.

"Let's move on," Art said before I could respond.

I'm not sure what I would've said. My heart understood. But had Brian's actions led to murder? How could that be okay, whatever his motives?

"Do either of you know Joseph Hamadou?" Art asked. "We got a tip he was involved in this, and we've checked him out. He's also African."

It took me a moment to remember this was the name that Dimitri had given me. The African connection was probably more than a coincidence.

Grace spoke up. "Whoever that is, that's not his real name."

"Why is that?" Art asked.

Brian answered. "That's the most common first and last name in Cameroon. It's like calling yourself John

Smith. A lot of people use it as a pseudonym over there. Once a squad of soldiers all called themselves Joseph Hamadou as they stripped our clinic of painkillers, laughing all the while."

"Okay. Thank you. What have you done to try to sell the artifacts now that Dennis is dead?"

"There's a man in East Palo Alto who Dennis told us to call if we couldn't get in touch with him. We talked to this man. He said he could help."

"What's his name?"

"Dorian Boukar."

Boukar aka Hamadou? I wondered. How many people in East Palo Alto could be involved in this? Had Boukar killed Dennis to take over the sale of the artifacts? And what did any of this have to do with my mother? That remained the real mystery.

"Can I ask a question?" I asked Art.

"Sure."

"Brian, why was Dennis helping you? The guy's not a humanitarian, is he?"

"Far from it. No, it was all about money. He said he was going to farm out some of the work to someone who really needed it—who was still in the business and had current contacts. He and this other person were taking thirty percent."

"Do you think Boukar could be Dennis's partner—the one he was going to farm things out to?" Art asked.

"It could be," Grace answered. "He speaks a very low tongue. And he is very dark inside. His soul smells bad."

I didn't know what to make of that.

Brian added, "Boukar didn't mention he was already involved. I think he would've if that were true, since it would've helped his sales pitch when we were trying to cut a deal."

"Which you haven't yet, right?"

"Right."

"Where are these artifacts?" Art asked.

"They're safe," Brian asked, as though Art was worried about that.

"Safe where?"

"In a secure storage facility in San Jose."

"I may need that address later. I'll let you know. Now, let's get to the meat and potatoes here. How is Dennis's murder mixed up in this?"

"Honestly, I don't know. It probably isn't."

"Let's say it is. You can make better guesses about that than I can," Art told him. "If it is, then what can you come up with?"

"Well, let's see…" Brian half closed his eyes and rocked forward and back a few times.

Once again, I studied Grace's face. Now that she wasn't directly participating in the conversation, her expression was almost blank—seemingly indifferent. Didn't she care about the murders? Wasn't she at least curious about who had committed them?

I realized I was interpreting her expression from the vantage point of my culture. Perhaps the Tikari had a different attitude about death, or maybe Grace had experienced so much violence that she was inured to it.

From there, I thought about my own relationship to violence, which was shaped by my Buddhist beliefs more than the culture I was born into. The first of Buddha's five basic precepts that all Buddhists are supposed to follow is that we should avoid killing or harming any living thing. In studying this simple doctrine, I was struck by the word "avoid." It's hard to know if this is just a vague translation from Pali for a similar word, but Buddha didn't say "never" or even "refrain from." "Avoid" implies that sometimes violence is necessary. I knew that historically, a lot of Buddhists committed violence in the name of religion, as other faiths did. Were they taking advantage of this loophole?

The not harming any living thing always struck me as impractical. Plants were alive. Insects were alive. What about bacteria or viruses? Where did you draw the line? So I've always tried to live according to my sense of the spirit of the precept. Don't be violent. Don't hurt anyone or anything unless you have to.

Brian finally spoke. "I want to stress that I have no idea who committed these crimes, but if I'm guessing, I'd say it was whoever Dennis was working with. Maybe they got greedy or had a falling out over something. Another possibility is the man he was in partnership years ago—in the Caribbean. I can't remember his name. He probably holds a major grudge."

"Morin," I supplied.

"Yes, that's it."

"You seem to know an awful lot about Dennis's past," Art commented.

"I used to drink too much, and so did Dennis. He became rather disinhibited when he did." He spread his arms and grimaced. "Look, I know this doesn't reflect well on me. I'm just trying to tell you everything and let the chips fall where they will."

Grace looked puzzled. That wasn't an idiom she knew.

"Anyway," Brian continued, "you told me to guess. This is my guess."

Art paused and then spoke in a more aggressive tone. "How do I know you're not lying—about all of it? Can you prove any of this?"

"Brian has told you the truth," Grace asserted in a steely tone.

She seemed offended that someone would call her husband a liar.

"This sounds like a story you've dreamed up," Art said. "When I hear something this complicated, it's almost always a pack of lies. Liars think that making something complicated or giving a lot of details makes something more convincing. It doesn't. The truth is usually pretty straightforward, isn't it?"

He glared at my uncle and my new aunt—one by one—taking his time.

"Are we under arrest?" Brian asked, edging his chair noisily away from the table and holding his hands up in front of his chest. Clearly, he was intimidated by Art's words.

"How about you tell me the truth," Art directed. "I don't want to have to check to see what laws you two have broken. I don't want to have to tell my lieutenant about this. You seem like nice people. I respect the work you do, Brian. And I admire you, Grace, for your bravery in coming to this country on this mission, assuming that's really why you're here. But that only goes so far. I need cooperation!"

He was virtually yelling at that point. I was seeing Detective Art in action—doing police work on the frontline—trying to break a suspect, or a witness, or whatever Brian was. His behavior seemed inappropriate—a mild form of violence. Did he really have to act like that to get the truth from my uncle and his wife?

Brian shrank back even farther and shrugged, clearly at a loss.

I finally stepped in. "Art, let's suppose they're telling the truth—just for a minute."

He wrinkled his brow and frowned at me.

I plowed ahead, looking him in the eye. "Your head-on approach hasn't gotten anywhere, has it? I think that's because there isn't anywhere to get to. Let me try something."

"You might as well, now that you've interrupted what I was doing." His frown deepened.

"Brian, ask Art again if he's going to arrest you? I think he might answer you now."

"Are you arresting us?" he asked in a shaky voice.

Art sighed. "For what?"

"Lying to you? I don't know. You seemed to think we're guilty of something."

"Everyone lies in investigations like this," Art told him. "The prisons would be overflowing if we arrested them all. And there are no local laws about smuggling things out of Africa or selling illicit artifacts. That's a federal matter. They can find out about this on their own. Or not. It's a one-way street with them. They want our help, but they won't give us any. As for my earlier threat, I have to say things like that to see how you'll react."

"We passed your test?" Brian asked.

"For now."

"Thank you," Grace said softly.

Art waved away her gratitude.

"What about Mom?" I asked my uncle. "Could any of this have something to do with her?"

"God, I hope not. I just don't see a connection,"

Brian said. He paused to think about it more. "If her death was a murder connected with Dennis, I suppose it could've been a warning to him. But then why kill him? Wouldn't they do that first if they wanted him dead?"

Art responded. "Maybe he didn't heed the warning. Maybe your sister knew too much about Dennis's business. There must be a lot of people in his past who wouldn't want their name revealed—not if they were involved in crimes with Dennis. Or it could be that Boukar or Morin were worried your sister would raise a fuss after one of them killed her husband. She was rich. She could pursue an investigation far beyond what the police could."

"That sounds unlikely—not something she'd do," I interjected.

"Well, the killer wouldn't know that. It could also be one of the people Dennis contacted for your sale. Maybe they held a grudge about a previous deal. Maybe once Dennis or his partner reached out to that person, they found out he used to be Anton."

"All that sounds possible to me," I said.

Brian hung his head. Grace shrugged. Her face was blank again.

I realized there was something off about her. She'd been damaged by what she'd been through in Cameroon. Her reactions were out of step with what went on around her, even accounting for cultural differences. A lot of psychology was universal—evolution-based.

"We're almost done," Art told the two. "Have you ever heard of Bruce Peralto?"

They both shook their heads.

"Agnes Murphy?"

"No," Brian responded.

It took me a moment to remember Dennis's sister's last name. She'd been married.

"Is there anything else I should know that I haven't asked about?" Art tried.

Both Brian and Grace shook their heads.

I was struck by the fact that they were pretty much out of words at this point. I was glad I hadn't been on the other side of Art's interrogation.

We waited while Brian texted Art the contact information for Boukar, as well as the storage unit's address.

Chapter Fifteen

In the police car on the way back to the station, Art suggested we stop and have breakfast.

"I know a great little cafe. We can discuss the interviews," he told me.

"And get to know each other better?"

"Well, sure. Why not?"

The Omelette House sat on a corner, sharing walls with a dry cleaner and a skateboard shop. From the ratty exterior, I would've never guessed how delightful the interior was. Fresh bouquets of pink sweet peas brightened each table. The ceiling was arched, its narrow oak slats forming a half barrel above us. Wide maple planks under our feet showed their age with dents and scratches, but someone had recently waxed them. They reflected the dangling globes that were distributed every ten feet or so. Plain wooden tables and chairs were scattered around the medium-sized room in no particular pattern. There was more space between them than usual.

"Art!" the middle-aged woman standing next to the register called.

She wore an old-fashioned white waitress uniform, replete with a yellow half-skirt apron. Her hair was a bird's nest with two black chopsticks stuck through it. Her worn, friendly face broke into a big smile.

"Betsy!" he called back. "This is Ivy."

"Hello, Ivy. Welcome to the Omelette House."

"Thanks. You've got a beautiful place here."

"Oh, it's not mine. I'm just the head grunt." Betsy put her hands on her hips and studied me. "I never see Art in here with a woman. And you don't look like a cop."

"No, I'm not."

"So what's the story?" she asked Art, turning to face him.

"You're even nosier than I am, Betsy."

"Everyone tells me that. Has this Ivy person ruined my chances with you?" She grinned.

I could tell this was a game they played.

"Never, Betsy. Ivy and I have confidential police business," he told her. "She's an informant for the New Jersey Mafia—oops!"

"Sure. And I'm the first woman pope. I see the way you look at her. Go sit wherever the hell you want if you're not going to dish."

Dee called while we were walking back to an empty table.

"It's my niece," I told Art as I took the call.

"Where are you?" Dee asked. "Where did you go off to so early? I thought we were partners. I've been worried about you."

"I'm sorry. I got caught up in things and didn't think. I'm with Art Petrie. We just talked to Brian."

"What about last night? How did it go with that gangster?"

"I'll tell you everything when I see you. We've found out a lot. What do you have for me? I'll share it with Art."

"Art, huh? What? Did you sleep over at his house last night, Aunt Ivy? Is he what you're 'caught up' in? Is he why you forgot all about me?"

"No, I slept in the guesthouse, Dee." I rolled my eyes at Art. "It's the investigation. I'll make it up to you. I promise."

"Well, all right. Here's what I found out—"

"Hold on. Can I put you on speaker—for Art?"

"Sure." She paused to let me do it. "There are two guys in the bay area who have ever been arrested for big-time smuggling—besides Dennis, I mean. One is in prison—some Swedish guy who used to be a diplomat—and there's another one right near here in East Palo Alto."

"What's the second one's name?" Art asked.

"Dorian Boukar."

"Did you run across the name Joseph Hamadou?"

"No. Why?"

"That's probably be the same man," he told her. "We think Hamadou is a pseudonym."

"I'll check into it. There's more."

"Go ahead," Art said. "And thank you for your help."

"So this guy Dimitri owns a bunch of businesses, including a gun store in Redwood City and a pet store in Santa Clara. Maybe he and Dennis did stuff together. Maybe he bought Dennis's hippos to sell at his store."

"You found out he smuggled hippos?" Art asked. "That sounds kind of impossible, Dee. Do you know how big they are?"

"No, that was just an example of an exotic animal. It could be that Dennis sold Dimitri guns, too—or smaller animals."

"We know about the stores, Dee," Art told her, "but we can't find any business connection between Dennis and Dimitri. We've never been able to tie Dimitri to any criminal activities."

"They're both from the same place in Bulgaria," she said. "That's suspicious, right?"

"Sure," he replied.

"That's all I've got for now."

"Thanks."

Our server, a younger version of Betsy, sidled over. She'd been waiting until we got off the phone to approach us. Her name tag actually read "Betsy Jr." "What can I getcha?"

I glanced at the menu on my paper placemat. Art spoke up.

"I'll have my usual, Laura. And make sure you bring cornbread for my friend, whatever else she orders."

"Sure."

I settled on an omelette, a cup of tea, and the de rigueur cornbread, which proved to be the highlight of the meal.

"Why does your name tag say you're Betsy Jr.?" I asked.

"Betsy keeps switching it out with whatever she thinks is funny. Last week I was Betsy's Mom. I'm pretty sick of it, but our manager says I have to wear a tag and this is all I've got."

"I remember one time you were Betsy's Biggest Fan," Art said.

"Yeah, that was a bad one. I'd better go get your order in."

"This is a fun place," I told Art. "I can see why you like it here."

I looked around a bit more, taking in the faded, blown-up photos of breakfast foods adorning the walls.

One of them reminded me of what had happened in a diner my dad had taken Jan and me to when we were quite young. Back then, a giant depiction of a bagel beside our booth had spawned a nightmare in which a twenty-foot-tall bagel chased me down the street, rolling faster than I could run.

"So what do you make of the interview with my uncle and Grace?" I eventually asked Art. He'd been watching my face, perhaps trying to figure out why I'd frowned at the innocent-looking photos.

"I think I need to contact the State Department to find out more about what's going on over in Africa. I don't think Brian or Grace were lying, but I also don't think they were telling us everything, either. I thought about asking them more about the politics in Cameroon. It's hard to know who are the good guys and who are the bad guys in this kind of conflict, but I figured I'd just get more of their side of it." Art shook his head. "What a story. I was certainly surprised by what they had to say."

"I was shocked my uncle was married, let alone all the rest. And I agree they probably know more than they told us. The way the information came out in fits and starts makes me think Brian was divulging as much as he felt he needed to from moment to moment. When you directed him, he came through. When you didn't, he didn't volunteer anything. At the same time, I doubt they were withholding anything related to my mother. She was Brian's sister, and I know he loved her." I thought a moment, gazing at the ceiling. "Do you think my uncle and Grace are in imminent danger? Do the police need to assign them protection or something?"

"No, I don't think so. I was pursuing all the potential African leads with them—and I'll continue to do that to be thorough—because that's their angle on this thing, but I'm not worried about them. That's the plot of a thriller or a spy movie. In real life, this kind of crime is more personal—less complicated—like I said to Brian."

"So you've eliminated my uncle as a suspect? Is that what you mean? That makes sense to me. I really can't see him killing anyone—no matter the circumstances. He's a good person devoted to charity work."

"He's still a possibility in my mind. I haven't ruled out many suspects yet, and I don't imagine you have either. Look at what Brian's done for love so far. And how much he's lied to both of us. Suppose he had to kill Dennis to save Grace—or her whole tribe?"

"I see what you mean. It's hard for me to look at motives for murder. In my mind, there aren't any that make any sense."

"Good for you. I wish everybody thought that way."

"Grace is quite beautiful, don't you think?" I asked. I don't know where that came from—not my rational mind. I guess some part of me wanted to gauge Art's interest in other women. And he was an African American and she was African, after all.

"I suppose. When I'm on a case, I don't really think about people that way."

"Except for me."

Art grinned. "Yup. Except for you. Look, I've made myself clear how I feel. What about you? What do you think of me—besides saying you like me? Give it to me straight. Are you saying you're not ready to go on a date just to be nice?"

"No, I don't do that. And I don't actually know if I'm ready or not. If I were, you'd be my guy."

"That's great, but don't wait too long or

somebody'll snap me up. You've seen my terrific smile. If I hold it for more than five seconds with Betsy, for example, she'd be on me like flies on rice."

"That's a very unattractive simile, Art, but at least you get to be the rice."

Our food arrived at that point, and we both focused on eating. The moment we were done—we finished at the same time—Art told me he needed to get back to the station.

"I've got a meeting with Lieutenant Cline. I'm not looking forward to it. I wish we could stay here all day."

"Thanks. I enjoy spending time with you, too, Art. Of course, your preferring to be here instead of at a meeting with Cline is a faint compliment, isn't it?"

"Yup."

Chapter Sixteen

Mercifully, Dee wasn't home when I arrived back at Jan's, so I was able to meditate and catch up on sleep with a long nap. Lately, she'd been waylaying me as I headed for the guesthouse.

I was surprised by the lasting effects of jet lag. If memory served me, I hadn't experienced anything like it traveling in the other direction.

My youngest niece woke me by jumping on the king-size bed.

"I found him! I found him!"

"Who?"

"The French guy."

It took me a moment to remember who Dee meant. "Morin?"

"Yup. Jacques Morin."

"So where is he? Could he be the murderer?"

"He's dead. In a New Orleans cemetery."

"And this makes you happy?" I sat up and smiled at her.

Dee climbed off the bed and stood over me. Her overalls looked even bigger from close up.

"I bet the cops haven't found him. It wasn't easy. And now we can eliminate him from our list of suspects."

"We have a list?"

"Of course. Here, it's on my phone. I'll read it to

you."

She took a moment to find it and then started reading.

"Maria the ex, the men out on Grandma's street, the lady who saw them, that Dimitri guy, Uncle Brian, the East Palo Alto guy, Morin's son, Dennis's sister at the hospital, Mom, and you. No offense. I wanted my list to be comprehensive. You said you were taking a nap, but nobody saw you during the time of the murder."

I smiled again. "That's okay, but back up a minute. Why do you suspect the woman who saw the men near Mom's house?"

"We've only got her word about them, right?"

"Holly said she saw the car when Dennis was using binoculars."

"Yeah. She thought he was perving. Anyway, she saw *a* car, not necessarily a car with murderers in it. And there's something about that lady I don't trust."

"You didn't meet her, Dee. Why do you say that?"

"I dunno. Just from what you said."

"Okay, what's this about the Frenchman's son?"

"He lives in Medford, Oregon. He's a rabbi."

"Why do you suspect him?"

"Well, it's a coincidence he only lives one state away—you know, when he's from France and all. Maybe he wanted revenge for his dad."

"Okay, that's theoretically possible, Dee, but he's a *rabbi.*"

"Are they all good people? Every single rabbi? What about all those crooked ministers who steal money?"

"I don't think we can put rabbis in the same category," I said.

"That's racist."

I stared at her.

"Okay, maybe it's not racist. But I'm keeping him on my list."

"Sure. It's your list. Tell me about Agnes—Dennis's sister. What else have you found out about her?"

"Her employees complain about her online. She's not a nice person."

"That doesn't make her a murderer." I was playing devil's advocate so Dee could make her case.

"She was there, she knows about medical stuff, and she's Grandma's sister-in-law. So that's opportunity and means, and they say most murderers are family members. Oh, and then there's her background back in Bulgaria. I guess I need to find out more about that. What if she was a sniper or something?"

"I'm sure the police looked into all that. And Agnes probably has an alibi. If she didn't, I think Art would've mentioned it."

"You think he's telling you everything? Just because you like him doesn't mean he's telling you everything."

"That's true. Good point." I paused and pondered how to respond to her putting her mom and me on her suspect list. "I don't think I'll investigate myself or your mom," I told Dee. "But I'll confess I wasn't really taking a nap. Jan and I were busy at the time of the murder robbing a bank, so we have alibis from the CCTV footage. I'm the one wearing the Donald Trump mask."

"Don't be silly. And don't worry. If it turns out it's one of you, I promise I won't tell."

"Sure. I appreciate that."

"I was supposed to collect you for dinner, Aunt Ivy. They're probably wondering where we are. You can tell me everything you found out after."

"Goodness, it's dinner time already? How long was I asleep?"

"I have no idea. I don't know when you started. Shall we figure it out?"

"No, that's okay."

The meal was once again dominated by Jan's monologues. This time I recognized her behavior as a symptom of her bipolar disorder. Her speech was pressured—she *had* to talk—driven by the energy her biochemistry dictated. Sometimes this meant she was cycling into mania. I hoped that wasn't the case.

Her kids seemed used to it, and I didn't mind—as long as that was as far as it went. Since Jan didn't demand a response to what she said, I just let her words wash over me.

After dinner, out on the patio, Dee and I continued our conversation. It was the warmest evening yet, with a slight breeze. The fresh, dry air was a treat. It had taken me months to get used to the humidity in Asia.

When I filled Dee in on what I'd found out at Brian's and in conversation with Art, she added Grace to her suspect list. She seemed to want the list as long as possible for some reason. My goal was to whittle it down.

"What about Betsy and Betsy Jr.?" I asked.

"Huh?"

"Never mind."

When Dee took off to do homework. I retreated to my living room to keep working on the case. If Dee could make a list, I could make plans—or at least brainstorm some possibilities.

I could talk to Brian again without Art. A policeman

may have inhibited him. I could try to find Boukar. That one didn't seem like a good idea—too dangerous. I could go on a date with Art. *Wait a minute*, I thought. *How did that one get in there?* I could take Grace out for lunch and get to know her, and possibly find out more about her role in all this. I could interview Agnes at the hospital. I could talk to people like Maria or Dimitri again. I could try the Rusty Snake bartender without Brian.

The list was overwhelming. I decided I'd take a break from the case and then check in with Art first thing in the morning to see what ground the police had already covered. Why duplicate their investigation? I could share Dee's information as well.

Was I inventing excuses to talk to Art? I decided I wasn't, but I could see I needed to keep an eye on that. I didn't want to turn into an infatuated teen. As a sophomore in high school, I'd developed a series of crushes on upperclassmen—at least once every few weeks. Then I made sure I manufactured excuses to be near them so they could discover their feelings for me, which never happened. Once a basketball player asked me my name and said he liked my butt. I couldn't sleep for three nights.

After an uneventful afternoon and evening, I slept well, rose early again, meditated, and then went for a walk. I met another walker at the corner—an older woman clad in workout gear, jiggling for all she was worth in her purple leggings.

"Good morning," she said. "You must be Jan's sister. I'm Gilda."

"Ivy." I offered her my hand and we shook. Her voice was familiar.

Gilda's face, wrinkled and leathery, didn't match her fit body, which could've passed for someone in her thirties. Soulful brown eyes were embedded under an unusually heavy brow. Her mouth was kind, even beyond her half smile. It was something about the way her lower lip moved with her words.

"Would you like to walk together?" she asked. "My dog is being groomed this morning. I'm used to company."

"Sure. Molly is wonderful. We met recently."

"Oh, that was you. Sorry about that."

"I very much enjoyed our encounter."

We were silent for half a block, and then Gilda spoke.

"I worry about Jan. I don't think her erratic behavior is good for Dee and Holly."

"Erratic in what way?"

"For example, last time we talked—I live next door—the green house—she told me she'd stopped paying her mortgage, even though she easily could. She said the people who had bought her mortgage from her bank were bloodsucking leeches who only cared about money. I said, 'Of course that's true. They're in the finance business. It's nothing personal.' Then I asked if she was worried about foreclosure, and she told me they wouldn't ever do that because her daughter was so special."

"My goodness. Did she seem hyped up—overly energetic?"

"I'm a therapist, Ivy—an LCSW. She seemed somewhere between hypomanic and manic."

"Yes, she suffers from bipolar, and she doesn't take her meds as regularly as she ought to. I suppose she may have some sort of personality disorder, as well."

"This has been a pattern," Gilda told me. "Another time she spent hours scraping her driveway with a wooden spoon. And when Jan gets triggered and yells at someone, watch out. A man who put a bag of his dog's poop in Jan's garbage bin called the police when Jan came at him. I had to intervene to prevent a physical altercation, and I certainly didn't enjoy putting myself at risk."

"I understand. Do you experience her as rapid or slow cycling?"

"You're a therapist?"

"No, I was in grad school to be one for a while. It stuck to my ribs."

"I don't have enough contact with your sister to answer that. I'm sure you know more about her illness than I do. I just worry."

"I'll talk to her," I said.

"Please don't mention me. I don't need her wrath. We've managed to be good neighbors for many years. I'd hate to ruin that."

"Of course."

We were silent for the rest of the mile-long walk. I was comfortable with it, and she seemed to be, too. Perhaps only a Buddhist and a therapist would be.

I took Jan aside after breakfast. We sat side by side on the couch in her office. She smoothed her navy skirt and then frantically picked lint from her black sweater. She had pile of it in her palm before I'd even organized my thoughts and spoke.

"How are you doing with your moods?" I asked. "You seemed a little wound up at dinner last night."

She seemed even more so in that moment, but I

didn't need to point that out.

"I'm up and down, as usual. Nothing special." The pace and pitch of her speech belied this.

She peered at me, not sure why I was concerned. That wasn't promising. At a certain point, Jan lost self-awareness about her symptoms. Her sense of normal shifted to encompass whatever state she was in.

"You're taking your meds?"

"Ivy, I don't appreciate being interrogated like this. Everyone always wants to know if I'm taking my meds. If I was emotional for one second, Mom asked me. All my doctors ask me even when I go in for a sinus infection or something. I'm surprised the gardener doesn't ask."

"If you can afford a gardener, why aren't you paying your mortgage?"

"Aha! That's what this is about. How did you know?"

I pointed to the table in front of her. "It's in plain sight. I was in here the other day. I don't remember why. So what's the story?"

"Oh, I'll get around to it. Some creepy outfit bought the mortgage, and I want them to sweat."

"You think they will?"

"I don't know. It seemed like a good idea at the time."

"I've heard that before, Jan—right before things fell apart for you."

I reached out and held my sister's hand. When I squeezed, she squeezed back.

"Okay, I get it," Jan replied. "You're worried. Maybe I would be too if I were you. But really, I'm okay. Nobody coasts through their mom's death and a murder in the family the same week. Except you, I guess."

I paused to come up with something positive to offset what Jan probably heard as criticism. "I appreciate how you're handling yourself during this conversation," I told her.

"Well, I don't want to demonstrate what you're accusing me of—being crazy and out of control. Because I'm *not*."

She pulled her hand away and tightened it into a fist beside her hip. It was an effort for her to stay under control.

"I care about you. I'm not accusing you of anything," I told her.

"It sure sounds like it."

"Sometimes we need to be suspicious of the way things sound to us, especially if we have a mood disorder."

As soon as I said this, I realized how preachy and condescending it was. I expected heat from Jan. She surprised me.

"What do you mean 'we,' white man?"

I was momentarily confused. "That's the joke about Tonto and the Lone Ranger?"

She nodded. "Remember those reruns we watched as kids?"

"Sure. You had a crush on Tonto, didn't you?"

"Of course not. I just liked his outfit."

"So you say."

She grinned. We were sisters again.

****

I called Art a little later.

"Did you know Jacques Morin is dead?" I asked.

"Good morning to you, too, Ivy."

"Oh, sorry. Hi."

"Hi back. Yes, we did. Of natural causes."

"Did you know his son lives in Oregon?"

"No. That's interesting. I'll bet your mysterious consultant told you."

"Yes. Shrouded in a black, hooded cape, this guy has a bank of computers hidden in the basement of an old missile silo in Idaho. His mom comes once a week with casseroles."

"I think I know that guy. Does he also enact James Bond villain scenarios and put them on online—you know, lasers heading for sensitive areas and all that?"

"Exactly, that's him. I pay him in collectible action figures."

"I'm glad we got that squared away."

"Did you find the East Palo Alto guy?" I asked.

"We did. Dorian Boukar. I sent an officer to roust him out of bed yesterday afternoon. He has a solid alibi. I don't like the guy, but he seems to be a dead end as far as being our perp. He says he uses the Hamadou pseudonym sometimes because he doesn't want people to confuse him with his brother, who's an accountant in Redwood City. Anyway, Boukar's wife is from Sofia, Bulgaria. That's a connection to Anton and Dimitri I didn't expect, so we're going to keep looking into him. I tried to interview the wife, too, but she's on vacation in Mexico."

"Without her husband? That might be significant."

"Yes. There could be something there."

"Did you ask him about Dennis's deal with Brian and Grace?"

"Yes. He says he didn't have anything to do with it. It was only after Dennis died that he heard from Grace. But he knows some things about Dennis's history that we weren't aware of. Dennis bribed officials in the Dominican Republic to let him do whatever he wanted. Apparently, he imported contraband in freighters, and then shipped them from the Caribbean to corrupt customs officials in other countries."

"How did Boukar know all that?"

"He worked for Dennis for a while, although Boukar says his import operation is strictly legal now."

"Why do you think Boukar told you all this?"

"I threatened a thorough investigation into his business—including an IRS audit. Of course, I can't actually get the IRS to do anything, but he doesn't know that. There's no way anybody in his line of work is completely legit, so he was happy to tell me what he did."

"Are you going to question Dimitri? If you do, ask him about this: he told me Boukar and Dennis partnered on deals. That goes against what Boukar told you."

"Well, if he was talking in the past tense, that would fit."

"That's true."

"Dimitri's coming in at two. I definitely want to take a run at him. I'll bring that up. Anything else you can tell me?"

"No, that's it."

We both paused before Art spoke again.

"What are you up to today?"

"I'm not sure. I've got a list. Would it be okay if I talk to Dennis's sister?"

"Sure. Why not? You still think she's got something to do with this?"

"She runs the hospital where Mom died, so maybe."

"I doubt she'll agree to it. We had a hell of a time

getting her to sit down for an interview. I wasn't there, by the way."

"I'm sure you could've charmed her into submission."

"Of course. I'd have used my devastating smile and a ready wink."

"A ready wink?"

"That's right. Have I used my wink on you yet?"

"Maybe. I don't remember."

"Well, there's something to look forward to," Art told me.

"Can I ask who you've ruled out—who I don't need to keep on my suspect list?"

He paused for a moment. "This will surprise you. It seems very unlikely that Dimitri was involved in the murder. I want to talk to him about what he knows about the other players in this. He has an airtight alibi and a complicated history with the man June Vormelker identified—Peralto. There's no way he'd hire that guy. In fact, if he saw him on the street, he'd probably have Jerry—his bodyguard—beat him up."

"Did you investigate Jerry?"

"As far as it goes. One of our sergeants knows him and says he's a good guy. Apparently, Jerry's all about being big. He doesn't have to get violent to control a situation."

Chapter Seventeen

Dee found Agnes's direct phone number, and she answered immediately when I called. We sat in my niece's room.

"Who is this?"

Even her greeting was hostile—as if every phone call was an attempt to hassle her. Of course, this one was.

"Lois Sorenson's daughter—Ivy."

"I have nothing to say to you. The police have already disrupted my hospital with their so-called investigation. Your mother had a massive stroke. That's all there was to it."

Her voice, accented and clipped, was also loud.

"I'd just like to ask a few questions. It won't take long. I'm sure you'd rather I do that than file a lawsuit about your nurse's dereliction of duty."

"He's been disciplined. There's no need to waste your money."

Now she spoke quickly, trying to dismiss me as soon as possible.

"Which is it? A lawsuit or ten minutes of your time?" I asked.

"Fine. Go ahead."

"Did you know your brother was a smuggler?"

"Of course he wasn't. I know what he did with those hippos, but it was all strictly legal."

"Hippos? Really?"

"The drug men wanted them."

I paused to gather myself. "If what he used to do was legal, then why did he change his name and lie about his background?"

"He dealt with many corrupt people. After all, who buys strange animals? Who buys art that doesn't have good papers? They're all crooks, these people."

"You think criminals wanted to harm Anton?"

"*He* did. That's what he told me."

"Okay. Let's leave that for now. I understand you have an interesting background."

"So what? That's not relevant."

"Perhaps not, but I'd like to know more about you. If I don't know who you are—if I can't put these answers of yours in context—they don't mean much."

"Whatever. Get on with it."

"You were in the military in Bulgaria?"

"Yes."

"What rank, what was your job?"

"I'll tell you because you can find out online, anyway. And it doesn't matter. I was a colonel in Internal Security."

"That sounds like an important job."

"Yes, it was."

"How did you go from that to being a nun?"

"Oh, you know about that? That is not common knowledge. It was the way I could legally emigrate. I joined an order that was persecuted, and then I became an asylum seeker. It worked. I have always been successful at everything I did."

"So you left your order after you got here?"

"Yes, as soon as my paperwork went through. Then I went to school to be a hospital administrator. As you see, I have risen up the ranks as I always do."

"Yes, what you've accomplished is amazing. Now let me ask you about hospital protocol and procedures."

"No, that is privileged information. Imagine the lawsuits if everyone knows how we do things. Then what happens when we don't do it that way? Your threat, your forcing me to talk to you because of our nurse—that's an example of what can happen. This is my job. I must do my job and not tell you. And I need to do my job right now, too. Goodbye. Sue me if you must."

She hung up.

Dee had wandered off while I was talking, which surprised me. I would've thought she'd have been interested in following my side of the conversation. She returned with a half-eaten doughnut in her hand and white powder on both her lips and the bib of her overalls.

"So what's the story?"

"Well, Agnes was unpleasant—no surprise there— but I convinced her to talk a little."

I told Dee about Agnes's nun ruse to move here. "Maybe her background in the church was why she could run a Catholic hospital, too," I added.

"What about being in the Bulgarian army?"

"Actually, she was high up in what she called 'Internal Security.' That sounds foreboding, doesn't it? She said there's information about it online."

Dee jumped up and ran to her desk, where her laptop sat.

"Let's just see." She typed and clicked for a while. "Hmm, here it is. I just had to look under Bulgarian Internal Security instead of her name like I was doing before."

She read for a minute or two.

"Okay, you're right. She was a colonel, and she got kicked out. Internal security is like the secret police or Homeland Security or something. You'd have to do something pretty bad to get kicked out of that, I think. And it was worse back when she was there. Hold on, let me get Google to translate a newspaper article."

I breathed and emptied my mind. I needed to release the energy I'd taken on from Agnes. It felt corrosive as it roiled inside me.

"Aha! It was a big deal. She took money to give contracts to certain companies, and then she locked up people who could testify against her. Her boss went missing, too."

"What kind of companies?"

"A gun company, a uniform company, and—get this—an import-export company." Dee grinned. "Import-export," she repeated.

"That seems significant. Good work. Was she arrested?"

"No, she skipped the country and went to Turkey. That's where she became a nun. This Agnes person is bad news, Ivy."

I mused out loud while Dee kept typing. "It's hard to sort out, isn't it? So many people we've investigated are involved in crimes. And they all seem to know one another."

"Yeah, that's weird. There's Dennis, this Boukar guy, and now Agnes. Maybe Dimitri, too." Dee looked up from her laptop and shook her head.

"Of course, it was years ago with Agnes," I pointed out.

"Yeah, but still. Maybe she's trying to hide her past. That could be a motive."

"She told me herself the information was online."

I watched Dee scrunch up her face as a way to return my attention to the moment. Throughout my investigation, I retreated up into my head much more than I needed to.

"I'll bet hospitals don't go online and do an international-level search when they hire people," Dee finally said. "They may not know about her. Maybe she'd lose her job if they did."

"Would you murder someone to keep your job?"

"No, probably not."

I stared at her.

"Okay, definitely not."

I thought a moment. "From what I know about her work, I can't imagine Agnes has the free time to be involved in anything besides running a hospital."

Dee scrunched up her face. "I don't get why she'd steer you to the internet. Why make it easy for us to find out this stuff?"

I didn't answer immediately. I liked having these pauses between our responses. It was a more familiar pace.

"Maybe it wasn't a mistake," I said." Maybe she was trying to intimidate me—to get me to back off. Her history is alarming, isn't it?"

"Yup. Are you intimidated?"

"Actually, yes. She scares me more than Dimitri did."

"Can I go with you when you talk to the next person—or whatever you end up doing?"

"Absolutely not. It's too dangerous. We don't want anyone else knowing you're involved—not even the police. Well, besides Art Petrie."

"What do you mean besides him?"

"He knows, but he's looking the other way. He was teasing me about it earlier."

"Can you trust him, Aunt Ivy? I mean, *really* trust him?"

"Yes."

After leaving Dee's room and lying on what I thought of as Holly's chaise on the patio, I called Art again and got his voicemail this time. I left him a message about my conversation with Agnes, and Dee's research into her background. So far, it was the only element that linked Mom's death and Dennis's murder. Perhaps it would light a fire under the police.

The more I thought about it, the more I believed Agnes wanted me to know she was dangerous—that her past was beyond checkered. Other people had encouraged me to back off my investigation. Agnes was trying to scare me to stop.

I didn't want to. *Why?* I wondered. *Why is it so important to me to continue?*

If I were a therapist and a client came in and asked for help figuring this out, what would I do? That's what I asked myself.

One path would entail looking at whatever emotion might lie behind the choice. I brainstormed. Guilt over abandoning my family for my spiritual ambitions? Anger about someone committing a murder? Some sort of emotional distress around tolerating an unresolved puzzle? Stubbornness? Pride?

The last two weren't really emotions, and for that matter, guilt might be more of a mental construct, too. Fortunately, I didn't get bogged down with semantics.

Of that list, mental or not, guilt seemed the most

likely. For over a decade, I never gave myself an opportunity to tell my mother in person that I loved her, or say goodbye, or be there for significant family events. I'd missed Mom's wedding to Dennis and Jan's thirtieth birthday party—an extravagant celebration on a huge, rented yacht. As Holly had reminded me, I hadn't been there when she and Dee needed me—when their mom's disorder impeded her from truly mothering them as young teens.

Would finding Mom's killer—if she had even been killed—assuage my guilt? Probably not. So what else could be going on?

I remembered that the last time I'd thought about this, I determined that having something to focus on in my new life was part of the equation. I'd read that people who left cults, nunneries, or the military—odd bedfellows there—felt adrift—lost—for a time when they returned to the world. It seemed likely that obsessing over the two deaths was a preemptive attempt to ward that off.

And it was working, at least short-term. Since I'd assigned myself a mission, carrying it out gave me a purpose—a role in the world. I didn't have to face how to build a life worth living outside the temple. I didn't even have to determine where to settle down.

What I needed to realize was that I was only postponing the inevitable. At some point, I'd need to go through a legitimate adjustment period—however rocky—and come out the other side. You can't get away with suppressing, avoiding, or trying to leapfrog over what your life curriculum brings you. It'll always comes back to haunt you in indirect, hard-to-work-with ways if you try.

I decided to stop thinking and tried to return my attention to the moment, which I'd visited far less lately than I was accustomed to. Thoughts, after all, are just passing science fiction stories we concoct, and then tend to believe. My teacher said we all have drunk monkey minds and need to be suspicious of what they come up with.

So I sat and just noticed what there was to see, hear, smell, and feel.

Just from reclining a few lower feet in the chaise than the lawn chair I usually sat in, the view was different. Now the water in the pool created no sparkling reflections, and the hedge behind it resembled a row of soldiers guarding the woods beyond them.

By embedding myself in the moment, I smelled pine and lighter fluid from someone's backyard barbecue. These had certainly been in the wind five minutes earlier. I simply hadn't noticed them.

A misfiring motorcycle blatted in the distance. When it was out of my hearing, a bee buzzed by en route to the garden on the side of the house. I could also—just barely—hear the gentle sloshing of the pool water.

When I tuned into body sensations, I became aware of the way the chaise's plastic webbing held me, my butt and back squeezing just a bit into the gaps between its intermittent horizontal support. One of my ankles lay on the other one—I'd crossed my stretched-out legs. I felt the weight, both on my lower ankle and on my heel against the chaise.

My muscles had relaxed while I observed my senses, especially my face. I felt peaceful, satisfied, and wonderfully slowed down.

After a soothing half hour of this, I reflected on my

experience and my recent state of mind.

I'd been so caught up in investigating, I'd forgotten to notice half of what was right in front of me. When someone sat across from me and spoke, for example, I'd filtered out whatever part of the encounter hadn't served my quest for the truth. I'd missed out on truly experiencing everyone I'd met.

For that matter, what items were on Art's desk? That would've been a way to get to know him better. What aromas had there been at the Omelette House? Surely a restaurant was full of them. I'd tuned out the display on the Jaguar's dashboard, most of my surroundings at the airport and the Stanford shopping center, and basics such as the clouds in the sky and what type of ground lay beneath my feet.

I'd ignored whatever hadn't immediately struck me as relevant or interesting to the case, with no conscious discrimination. This was *not* what the Buddha had advised. Who was I to preemptively rule out whatever experiences the universe had brought me? Who was I to narrow down the richness of life?

I needed to think when I needed to think, and otherwise I needed to remain in observation mode. What use was noticing something if I immediately started processing it ad infinitum, pulling me away from the next thing to notice? In Asia, I'd been in the moment ninety percent of the time. In the States? Maybe forty, probably more like twenty percent.

Why had I been this way since returning home? Was I nothing more than the man in a story who thought he'd achieved enlightenment from meditating in a cave for years, then walked down to the village marketplace, and cursed a man who jostled him? Why had I abandoned mindfulness, or at least limited it to what I'd willfully chosen to pay attention to?

I saw again how this could be a natural reaction to leaving the sangha—a protective mechanism in the face of too much stimuli. So when I started investigating, I was already halfway to being stuck up in my head, and my efforts compounded the problem.

I hoped to do better, but I knew that as the case continued, I was likely to pull away from the moment again and again—and rightly so in some cases. How could I protect myself from a criminal if I was busy observing a butterfly fluttering beside me?

Art called me back at this point. "Thanks for the info about Anton's sister," he told me. "I'm having to farm out more parts of the investigation now that you're feeding us so much information. And there's been a major break in the case. We're sure now that the men in the car down the street from your mother's place committed the murder—on orders from an unknown individual."

"Tell me about it." I felt energy surge up my spine.

"The guy June and Maria identified—Bruce Peralto—bragged to a friend in a bar, and the bartender heard. It's always something really stupid that trips up these guys. We haven't located him, but when we do, we can probably turn him—get him to tell us about the other guy, and who their boss is."

"So he said he'd been hired to commit the murder?"

"Yes. Can you believe it?"

"Why do you think it took two guys to carry out the murder?"

"Who knows? Maybe there were only two at the surveillance stage. Maybe the tall one was just the driver."

"So in essence, you've solved the case?"

"Well, that's premature. The guy could've lied to his friend to impress him. It happens. People even come into the station and confess to things they didn't do sometimes. The bartender seems like an honest guy, but we need to look into him more to be sure. And we still have to find Peralto. Sometimes we don't. Sometimes the perp is out of the country by the time we start looking."

"Our guy's stupid, though."

"Yeah, at least when he's drunk. We'll see." He paused. "I'm sorry this doesn't seem connected to your mother's stroke, Ivy. I know you were hoping it would be."

"Oh, no. I don't want it to be one thing or another. I just want to *know*—on behalf of my sister. I don't think she'll be able to truly grieve and move on without resolution."

Bingo! There's the strongest reason for me to continue. Why didn't I realize it earlier?

"Okay, fine. We're doing what we do in these situations—talking to family and known associates, checking the trains, buses, airlines, customs at the Mexico border, putting out an APB on his car—all that. There's really no room for you on the case anymore. I'm sorry."

"What about finding out who's behind this—who hired these guys? What if you don't find this Bruce guy, or he won't talk? How could it hurt for me to keep looking into that part?"

"The closer you get to someone, the more likely they'll take off before we get enough evidence to arrest them. It's important not to tip off suspects that we're closing in."

"Oh, I don't think my talking to anyone is likely to scare them into running off."

"Don't underestimate yourself. Some people find you formidable."

"Really? Who?"

"We questioned several people after you did—thanks for nothing for that, Ivy. Two of them mentioned they were impressed by you—by your presence. Dimitri told me—let me check my notes—I want to get this right—uh…that he's decided not to screw you, but he still thinks you're an amazing woman and he wishes he could screw a different head onto your shoulders so you didn't talk so crazy. I think he likes the word 'screw.' "

"Apparently."

"So please don't spook anyone if you won't listen to me—if you won't stop."

"I was just looking at that a few minutes ago—why I want to continue. It's important to me for various reasons."

"I can't stop you, but Lieutenant Cline can. Don't get on his radar, Ivy. I want to arrest bad guys, not someone like you."

We were both silent for a moment. Then I spoke.

"Suppose I look into who on my suspect list might've had a way to contact lowlife accomplices—or knew this Bruce guy beforehand. If I can connect a suspect to him, that would help, right?"

"We've got someone on that, Ivy. Like I said, we know what we're doing."

"My consultant came up with things you didn't find, though." I could hear the whiny tone of my voice.

"We would've. And let me ask you this. Is your

consultant fourteen years old?"

"I'd rather not answer that, Art."

"Okay, I understand."

"Will you let me know if you find the missing shooter?" I asked.

"When, not if. Let's stay optimistic. Sure, I'll keep you in the loop about any major developments. And please let me know about anything you find, even though I don't think we'll need it."

"You never know."

"That's for sure."

****

I hunted for Dee, but she wasn't in the house, on the patio, in the garden, or anywhere else. I did run into Holly, who lay on the couch in the living room, partially covered by a multi-colored afghan. As usual, she had her phone in her hand. I sat down across from her.

"I'm sick," she told me, and then coughed unconvincingly.

"Practice that cough for your mom," I advised. "Have you seen Dee?"

"Mom drove her to school on the way to work."

"Of course. I keep forgetting about school." I started to slap myself on the side of the head—an old habit—but I managed not to.

"I wish I could," Holly said wistfully.

"What do you dislike about it?"

"Most everything. Be honest, Aunt Ivy. Did you really like high school?"

"No. I was overweight and scared everyone would think I was a loser. Most of my classes were filled with kids who weren't interested in learning, and a lot of teachers were only marginally interested in teaching."

Holly nodded along with this, although she couldn't possibly have identified with being an ounce too heavy.

"That was me," I continued. "Why don't you like school?"

"It's like we're slaves and plantation owners are bossing us around all day. Be here at this time. Be this other place now. You have to pee? No, you can't go unless the bosses give you permission. It's Fascist. This country is supposed to be all about freedom. Well, I don't have any. What if I want to do something besides listen to some fat guy talk about angles and degrees? There are actually laws that make us sit there and waste our time. It's ridiculous."

"What wouldn't constitute a waste of time? What do you want to learn?"

"I dunno. I've never thought about that. Maybe stuff about how to live. You know, doing relationships, or buying a car, or maybe where to go on vacation."

"More practical things."

"Yeah, I guess so."

"How could you learn what you want to know on your own?"

"I dunno."

"Think about it. You don't have to miss out on those things just because schools are academically oriented."

She grunted and returned her attention to her phone. I'd been dismissed.

I replied to emails and then meditated in Dee's room until my phone rang.

"This is Ivy Lutz, right?"

The low-pitched male voice was rough, both in the sense of unrefined, and in timbre—a smoker.

"Yes. How can I help you?"

"That's the right question. We've got your smart-ass niece, and you can help us by backing off what you've been doing."

"Investigating?" I was stalling for time to gather myself. This didn't feel real. I was frozen.

"Whatever you want to call it. It needs to stop if you want the kid back."

I breathed deeply and gathered myself. I needed to keep it together for Dee's sake. "In the movies, I'm supposed to ask for proof you really have her."

"We're not doing that."

"Then I'm not backing off. Dee's probably at school."

He didn't respond for a stretch. Then he said, "I just sent you a photo."

"My phone doesn't do that. How did you get my number, anyway?"

"What do you mean? Everybody's phone does that."

"Mine cost thirty dollars."

"All right, all right," he said impatiently.

A minute later, a familiar voice spoke.

"It's me, Aunt Ivy. I'm okay. They're—"

"So here's how it's going to work," the man told me. "You call your pal on the force and tell him you're done. Then you throw away anything you wrote down. We have eyes and ears everywhere. If you talk to anyone connected to the case, if you go somewhere like the Rusty Snake or the hospital, we'll know."

"Okay." It was hard to get this out. My poise—based on nothing more than bravado—was dissolving.

"After we give you back your pain in the ass niece, you need to remember how it easy it was for us to grab her. It's just as easy to grab her again or kill you. Oh, and when you call the cops to say you're done, if you say anything about this, well, I wouldn't want that on my conscience if I were you."

"I understand. All that's fine. I'll do as you say."

"Good girl."

He hung up.

I flopped on my niece's bed. Quick, shallow breaths were all my tight chest could manage. My hands shook, and my face heated up. I was too scared to think or notice anything besides my intense apprehension.

After a time, I got my brain back online. Of course I'd do whatever they wanted. But would that be enough to keep Dee safe? Didn't kidnappers sometimes fail to return hostages even after their demands were met?

I dutifully called Art after I'd calmed down a bit—twenty minutes later.

"I just wanted to let you know I've thought it over, and I won't be investigating anymore. Could you spread the word at the station? I know your lieutenant will be relieved."

"Yeah, Cline really doesn't like you, Ivy. I don't know why. It goes beyond the fact that he thinks you're meddling."

"Is he a Christian?"

"Actually, yes. Some fundamentalist church. How did you know that?"

"Some of those folks believe that Buddhism is blasphemy—a threat to their one-way-or-the-highway approach."

"That could be it. Why did you change your mind?"

"You're right about it being dangerous. I understand that now. Speaking of which, you mentioned that Dimitri wasn't a murder suspect anymore. Does that mean I'm safe from him? He scares me."

"He's got no beef with you, Ivy. Unless you start interfering with any criminal activities he's got going, I don't see why he'd bother you. And I'm not sure he's a criminal, anyway."

"Thanks."

"You sound stressed. Are you okay?"

"It's just family stuff. I'm fine."

He paused and then spoke in a more casual tone. "So if you're completely off the case, there's no conflict of interest about us seeing one another, right?"

"There never was. I explained why I'm hesitant."

"I know, I know. I'm going to keep trying, anyway."

"That's fine. I'm flattered."

"I've gotta go. Let's talk later."

"Sure."

I'd asked about Dimitri because he'd said I could call him if I needed his help. I nervously dialed his number. Was this a mistake? Could word get back to the kidnappers?

"Ivy! You called."

"Yes. Did you mean it when you said you'd help me if I needed it?"

"Yes. Since then, the cops made me waste my time at their station. I want this thing over. Are you getting anywhere?"

His voice was as growly as ever. Now he sounded more serious than he had before. The investigation had come to his doorstep.

"Somebody kidnapped my niece to get me to back off, so I guess so," I told him.

"That's not right. That's terrible. How can I help?"

"Can you find out if your corrupt cop passed on

information to the murderers? Or maybe it's another cop. I don't know. It's the only way I can see how these people know my phone number and what I've been doing. They said they'd know what I said to the police, too."

"You think I pay a bad cop? Why do you think that?"

"When you called me, you said you had my number from either a spy in my family or the police department. I know it's not my family."

"You remember that? Good for you. I was showing off, Ivy—playing the big man. I'm sorry. I wanted more dates. Women like men who have connections. Here's what really happened. Your crappy phone shows your number on that little screen. When I took your phone to try to put my number in, I saw it.

"Oh, I didn't think of that." I felt very foolish. "I'm sorry. Do you have a way of looking into whether there's a corrupt police officer?"

"I think so. Jerry—you remember Jerry?"

"Yes. He's hard to forget."

"Jerry knows a cop. He used to be one. He'll find out."

"Great. Do you think you can find out anything about the kidnapping itself?"

"We don't want to go there. Not good for your niece."

"I'm just supposed to let them do whatever they're going to do?"

"Yes. To keep her safe. That's it."

"Okay. I appreciate this, Dimitri."

"I like you, Ivy. You are weird, but you have a big heart."

"Thank you."

Chapter Eighteen

I felt horrible that I'd risked Dee's life. As Art had predicted, if I kept talking to people, it could be dangerous. Only it was Dee, not me, who was paying the price for my stubbornness. I couldn't even imagine what she was going through. Did she think they were going to kill her?

Since there was still scarce evidence that Mom's death and Dennis's were linked, I had no business getting involved in Dennis's murder. I hardly knew the man.

When Dee didn't show up after school, what would Jan do? She'd panic and call the police. I could only hope the kidnappers, via their likely police contact, could differentiate a mother worrying about a missing child from a report of a kidnapping.

While I was still fretting and second-guessing myself in Dee's desk chair, I heard footsteps coming down the hall. A moment later, Dee walked in.

I rushed to hug her. "Thank God you're all right!" I burst into tears.

"What do you mean? I'm fine."

"You've been at school?"

"Sure, just like every weekday. What's going on?"

My phone rang. It was the same voice.

"We've made our point. Stay out of this or next time…Well, use your imagination."

"But I heard her, and you said you had a photo."

"Ain't technology a wonderful thing?" he said. Then he hung up.

Dee stared at me and raised her eyebrows.

"I thought you were kidnapped," I told her. "How could they have rigged up things to fool me?"

"It's not that hard, Aunt Ivy—not if you know what you're doing. Once my nemesis in the gifted program photoshopped my head onto someone wrestling a pig. Carol. I can't stand her. Another time, she recorded my voice in class, I guess, because she pieced together something awful and found a way to play it over the school PA. I won't even tell you what it was."

"God, I'm so relieved you're okay, Dee. I was so worried."

Some of the tension in my body dissipated, but my metabolism was still revved up. My fear subsided, replaced by deep gratitude. I felt like clasping my hands together, bowing, and thanking the universe. Tears streamed down my face.

"I've never seen you like this," Dee said, pulling back to watch me. "I thought you could be calm about everything."

"I have limits like everybody else. I've told you I'm just a person. What kind of monster doesn't care if her niece is kidnapped?" I started to cry harder—releasing more of my pent-up energy.

Dee moved forward and held me. "You can be a person, Aunt Ivy. I'm sorry."

A moment later, she led me by the hand to her bed, sat me down, and then plunked down in her desk chair. When she swiveled to face me, she asked me if I was ready to talk about the case again. I didn't really know if I was.

I just nodded. Dee could talk. I'd listen.

"Well, we know more now," she said. "Or we might, anyway."

"Like what?" I still wasn't thinking clearly.

"Where would they get my voice? It sounded like me, right?"

"Yes."

"So where? It's not online anywhere. At least, I don't think it is. Could they have hacked my phone?"

"You're asking me?"

"I'm just thinking out loud. Unless these people are serious techies, hacking my phone would be too hard to do. It used to be easier, but I tried it with Carol, and even I couldn't do it."

"What about your police interview? Do they record those?"

"Yes! They had a device on the table—that thing that looked like a mouse."

"Really? A mouse?"

"A computer mouse. It doesn't matter. What does matter is that maybe a cop supplied my voice."

"I was thinking there had to be a cop involved, too, even aside from your voice. The guy on the phone knew things he had no business knowing. For that matter, how did he know to call again right when you got home?"

"Someone's watching the house, I'll bet."

"Stay here. I'm going to go look."

"No, don't do that!"

I took off before Dee could talk me out of it.

I headed out the back door and sidled along the side wall of the house, feeling as though I were in a spy movie, which was both thrilling and scary. Or maybe the remaining adrenaline in my system lent it that vibe.

From behind a bush, I spied a silver pickup truck parked next door—in front of Gilda's house. I wasn't close enough to make out the license plate, but I could see the back of a man's head behind the wheel. There wasn't much cover between my bush and the truck, but it still seemed like a good idea to try to get closer to see the plate, if only to rule out the possibility of foul play. It could be Gilda's gardener, after all.

As I snuck up on the truck, I saw eyes in the rearview mirror notice me. The truck roared off. I only caught the first few figures of the plate. 8CBH.

I ran into the house and called Art.

"There was a truck monitoring our front door. It just took off. Maybe you can catch him."

"What type of truck?"

"A silver pickup truck. I don't know what kind. The beginning of the license plate is 8CBH."

"Got it. I'll see if we have a car in the area. There's really only one way out of Woodside onto the highway."

"Thanks."

Back in Dee's room, we continued to discuss what we'd found out from the fake kidnapping while we waited to hear back from Art.

"They must be pretty desperate," Dee said. "I mean, you don't go to all that trouble unless you think someone's getting somewhere, right?"

"That makes sense. I wonder which thread I pulled that triggered this. Talking to Agnes?"

"I dunno. Maybe."

"What would happen if I called back the number that called me?" I asked. "Dimitri made me learn how to do that to call him."

"I'm sure they're using a burner—you buy them at

the store so you don't have to identify yourself to the carrier."

"Then you burn them?"

"Not literally, Aunt Ivy. Jeez. You mentioned Dimitri. Could he be behind this?"

"Art says no. I forgot to tell you I called Dimitri when I thought they had you."

"Why? You think you can trust that guy?"

"I was desperate, and the kidnappers said they'd know if I contacted the police. Who else could help?"

"I don't know. Are you going to call him back and let him know I'm okay?"

"I guess I ought to. I hope he'll still want to help with the rest."

I called Dimitri. "She's back. My niece is okay. I could still use your help, though. I'm pretty sure now there's a police officer involved, and maybe you could ask around in the Bulgarian-American community about Agnes—Anton's sister."

"Why do you want to know about her?" His tone was aggressive. Had I struck a chord with this?

"Do you know her background?"

"She was a nun. I think she was bad at it."

"She was also a colonel in Internal Security—before that."

"Really? Those were nasty people. But that must've been a long time ago. Now she helps people get better at her hospital."

"Even so. She may be mixed up in this."

"Okay, I'll see what I can do. I know a guy in San Diego who was in Internal Security. I'll ask him. Maybe he knows her better than I do. This is like a full-time job you gave me, Ivy. You're going to owe me."

"Is that a problem? Do you mean more dinners?"

"Maybe. Maybe something else. I like it when people owe me."

"That sounds ominous."

He laughed. I liked the sound of it despite myself.

"You think I'm such a bad man. You don't know me."

"Do you need a bodyguard because you're so nice?"

He sighed. "I am not my business. My business needs protecting." Then he hung up.

Without thinking about it, I walked over to Dee, pulled her to her feet and hugged her again.

"I'm so glad you're safe," I whispered in her ear.

"Hey, I was just at school. You're the one who went through all this."

I just kept hugging her. I didn't let go even when she started squirming. "I can't breathe down here," she had to say before I'd release her.

Art called. "We didn't find him on the road, but there's only one vehicle in the area with those digits that's a silver truck, so we've got guys heading to the owner's place in Milpitas."

"Who is it? Can you tell me?"

"I'm not supposed to, but since this is about you, Ivy, it's only fair. It's a guy named Thomas G. Dawson, according to his registration. Hold on a minute."

I waited.

"Okay, a colleague just handed me his rap sheet. This guy was actually a cop—in Vegas—but he got kicked off the force for taking bribes. He served six months, which wasn't long enough, in my opinion. That was eight years ago. After that, we've got nothing. You're sure he wasn't just visiting someone in the

278

neighborhood?"

"No, he saw me and took off."

"But you didn't see him? You can't identify him?"

"No, sorry."

"We've got enough on the guy to bring him in if I tell Cline a little white lie about what you saw. Is that okay with you?"

"Sure. That's up to you."

"I want June Vormelker to get a look at him. I could show her a photo, but if she picks him out of a lineup as the tall guy who was driving the car in front of her house, then we've got our two killers. Like I said with Peralto— the one still on the run—we can probably get this guy to cut a deal and find out who ordered the murder. We might need him to, actually, because Peralto might be dead."

"Dead?"

"Yeah, I'm afraid so. We've got a badly burned body in the morgue that might be him. I'm waiting to find out. They're backed up from that shooting at a nightclub last Saturday."

"That's a sad comment on our culture, isn't it? A backed-up morgue."

"Yeah. Listen, I need to get off. I'll call you later."

"Okay."

I spent the rest of the afternoon reading in an armchair across from where Holly was still ensconced on the couch. She'd switched to reading *On The Road*, an English assignment. When I asked her about it, she told me she was pretty sure the guy in the book was doing meth.

Dee fussed in the kitchen preparing dinner. "Mom called and said she's going to be late. I don't mind making dinner. I'm a much better cook, anyway. Do you want to help?"

"Sure."

We chatted about our favorite novels while we gathered salad ingredients, switching to which politicians were the biggest idiots—her words, not mine—as we chopped vegetables.

When Jan finally got home, she asked if we could talk, so I trailed her to her office.

"Don't be too long," Dee told us. "The casserole comes out in twelve minutes."

Once again, we sat side by side on the leather couch. I guess that was our serious talk place. The stern look on Jan's face let me know the tenor of what was coming.

"I've been too busy to ask you this before, but what have you found out about Mom and Dennis?" Jan asked. "It's been days now since you told me anything. I don't appreciate that, Ivy. She's my mother, too."

"They've identified one of the shooters in Dennis's murder—apparently two men were involved. The one they know about is either on the run or dead, and they may find the other one today."

"Why'd they do it?"

"They were hired by some unknown person for unknown reasons."

"That's a lot of unknowns. And what does that have to do with Mom?"

"Maybe nothing. I'm still looking into that."

"Do you think Dennis killed her?"

"At this point, no. But we'll see."

"Dee said you made a friend on the force—that detective Petrie. He's got a thing for you?"

"He does, and I admire him, too. We're lucky he was

assigned to the case. He's been willing to collaborate."

"But that's all you found out?"

I pondered how much to tell her. "I've got my eye on several suspects, and there's a guy in the Bulgarian community who's doing some work for me."

"How are you paying him? I'm not a bank, you know. I've already given you hundreds of dollars to help you get on your feet."

"No, he's just doing this as a favor."

"It's a man who's also smitten with you, isn't it? You need to realize you've become very attractive, Ivy. Don't abuse that. Don't take advantage of men."

"I won't." I couldn't help but smile at her admonition.

"It's not funny, Ivy."

"No, sorry."

"What about at the hospital? Are the nurses suspects?" Jan asked.

I shook my head.

"And what about Dennis's sister? I still don't think Mom just suddenly dropped dead. After the first stroke, someone said she regained consciousness for a while before she supposedly had another one. I wish I'd been there for that. So she was getting better. Why would she get better and then immediately get worse?"

"I don't know enough about strokes to answer that, Jan. But here's an important question. Who told you Mom was conscious? Who was there to see that?"

"Hmm, let me see. I think Agnes told me that—or maybe Dennis. I'm sorry."

"Supposedly, neither of them were in her room at that point. That's what they told the police."

"So one of them was lying!"

"Or both, for all we know, but Agnes is the only one still alive. I wish you could remember who told you."

"I'll say it was her if that helps. Maybe the police would grill her if I say that. Maybe she'd break down and confess."

"That won't happen. She was high up in the equivalent of the secret police back in Bulgaria. She's tough."

"I definitely think she did it," Jan said. "All this adds up to her."

"There's a lot more to this. It's a complicated case, but I agree that she's capable of it, and she may have had the opportunity. On the other hand, I can't imagine what her motive would be."

"Maybe she knew Dennis was going to get murdered and wanted to inherit his money that would've gone to Mom."

"I didn't think of that. Maybe. I'll look into it. Art has access to the will."

"Art?"

"Art Petrie."

"It's like that, huh? Well, he *is* good-looking, isn't he?"

Dee called us for dinner, and we trooped back to the kitchen.

Later, in the guesthouse, I called Art again. I hoped he wasn't getting sick of me. I still got a tingle whenever I heard his voice. He was home watching a basketball game. He said he'd call me at halftime, which he did.

"So what's up, Ivy?"

I told him what Jan had mentioned and asked about Dennis's will.

"Nothing goes to Dennis's sister. Apparently, they

didn't get along and hadn't for a long time. I think it went back to something that happened back in Bulgaria. So cross that off as a motive as far as your mom goes. I'll certainly talk to Agnes, though. She definitely said she was never in your mother's room—she told one officer early on that she didn't even know her, in fact. That seems unlikely since it turns out she was her sister-in-law. Do you know if she was at your mother's wedding?"

"I don't. Does this mean you're open to the idea of foul play?"

"I always have been, but more than before now."

"I appreciate that, Art."

"How's your sister doing? Has she calmed down?"

"More or less. About the case, anyway. She's been busy at work, and I think a lot of her passion was about Dennis, who's no longer around to hate. But there might be a storm brewing internally."

I detailed Jan's bipolar disorder.

"I understand. That's rough. Listen, halftime is mealtime."

"Sure. Enjoy your game. I hope a lot of baskets go in for your team."

"Uh, right. How about lunch tomorrow?"

I thought about that. "Sure, lunch sounds good. We can discuss the case in person."

"That's great! I'll be the guy wearing a big smile, and if you treat me right, there might be a ready wink coming your way, too. I'll text you directions to a place I know."

"Okay, bye. No, wait. I can't get texts, remember?"

"Sorry. Got a pen and a piece of paper?"

"Hold on."

I found them, and he told me the address.

So now I had a quasi-date with a man I was attracted to. If one of the nuns back in Asia had asked me if such a thing was possible so soon after leaving the temple, I'd have laughed.

What was happening?

It wasn't lust. I'd tamed that beast years ago. Was it my commitment to following the choreography karma dealt me? That was certainly a pretentious way of looking at it.

What else might be in play? Ego, of course. It felt good to be pursued—desired—and presumably that element added to my enjoyment of spending time with Art. Was there a surplus of pride, vanity, or another illicit variety of ego satisfaction involved?

I decided I couldn't know the answer to that question without further exploration. Lunch with Art could serve as another experiment of sorts. I was bound to find out more about my motives by simply being with him and paying attention.

I realized I was working hard to find reasons that having lunch with Art made sense. It didn't need to. I could just want to do it without all the thinking. I'd been quite unmindful for the last ten minutes.

I spent the following morning doing research on the computer myself while Dee was at school. She showed me some things to try before she took off with her mom and a miraculously cured Holly. I think Jan knew her oldest daughter had simply needed a day off and had uncharacteristically cut her some slack.

So I perused social media sites using Dee's passwords, starting with posts from Agnes. Now that the police were successfully sorting Dennis's murder, and I was keeping a low profile about that because of the threat to Dee, turning my attention to Mom's death seemed like the best plan.

Unfortunately, Agnes's posts revolved around mundane life events such as restaurant visits, TV shows, and a Hawaiian vacation. No help there. When I clicked on where I thought her photos were supposed to be, nothing happened.

I emailed Dee to see if she could help, asking her to only reply if she wasn't currently in a class. I think I knew she'd ignore that.

In a few minutes, she wrote back. *Photos are encrypted on that site. Only people she puts on a list can see them. Let me see what I can do.*

While I searched fruitlessly for more background information about Dennis's sister—probably covering the same ground Dee had, my niece must've been at work at her end. She phoned me twenty minutes later.

"She's got a boyfriend! They went to Hawaii together two months ago. There's a photo of them standing in front of this cool-looking beach at sunset. Either she's tiny or he's huge. He's kinda scary-looking too. I wonder how they can do it with such a height differential."

"Do what?"

"Aunt Ivy! Come on, you know what I mean."

"Oh, I get it. What else did you see?"

"She likes cats. She's got several photos of this weird-looking one named Gidget. How's that for a stupid name?"

"I wouldn't pick it. I'm planning to name all my future cats 'Dee' in your honor."

"Ha, ha."

"What did the cat look like?" I asked. "Maria—

Dennis's ex—raises a rare cat breed, remember?"

"Oh, yeah. Let me send you all the photos to your email. I know your phone can't get them. Oops, my teacher's coming. She's gonna take my phone. Over and—"

I'd have to wait to check whether Agnes and Maria were connected. If they were, it could be an innocent cat-lover commonality. They were likely to know each other via the Dennis connection, anyway.

****

I worked out some exciting things en route to meet Art. Finally, after examining all the relevant evidence, I felt I'd figured out the core of the case.

Art's restaurant selection wasn't a restaurant. It was a brightly decorated food truck whose lettering declared it specialized in Indonesian burritos. The truck sat in the corner of a big box store parking lot. A few white plastic tables and stackable chairs had been placed nearby.

"I know it looks weird," Art said as he met me at the end of a short line by the side of the truck. "But what they do here is really amazing. Basically, it's authentic Jakarta street food served in tortilla wrappers, which keeps it from being a big mess. I usually get it to go and bring it back to the station or go to a park."

"Is there a park nearby?"

"Hey, you haven't been gone so long that they've changed all the parks, Ivy."

"Good point. We could go to Mitchell Park."

"Sounds good."

"Am I late?" I asked. "I hope I didn't keep you waiting."

"No, I'm compulsively early to keep from being late myself. You're right on time."

I ordered vegetarian *nasi gola*, mostly because the English translation on the menu poster called it crazy rice. How crazy could rice be? I needed to find out. Art asked for *soto tangkar*, a beef ribs stew.

We sat at an empty table to wait. After a moment, he reached up to brush off a shred of a wrapper that had scooted across the parking lot and now rested on the shoulder of his corduroy jacket. His rust-colored pants almost matched the jacket, and he wore dark brown, cushy-looking shoes that almost matched his skin tone. The black soles of the shoes looked to be about two inches thick, which made them oddly bottom-heavy.

"Those look like very comfortable shoes," I commented. In a recent phone conversation, Art had called me out for ignoring social mores when I'd jumped right into police business.

"They are. Plus I get them a size larger and put in extra spongy insoles. The bones that go out to my toes are a little sideways when they're supposed to be straight. The older I get, the more the ball of my foot hurts when I walk."

"Can't they do anything?"

"Not now. Have you ever seen little babies with their feet in casts?"

I nodded.

"That's when they can fix it. Nobody noticed in my case."

"I'm sorry."

"Hey, I still came out way ahead in the genetic dice roll. Not everybody can wink like me."

I laughed. "And those shoes are bound to come into style someday. If a room full of monkeys can eventually type the complete works of Shakespeare, anything's possible long-term."

"You think the monkeys will beat me to it?"

"I do, but don't give up hope."

"Thanks for your support."

Our number was called, so I grabbed our bag of food and drove separately to the park. Several empty picnic tables sat under a wooden pergola not far from a playground. As we strolled there from the parking lot, I took Art's arm, evoking his warmest smile yet.

I was disappointed with my meal, which was basically fried rice with vegetables and an overly bland sauce. When we finished eating, I spoke.

"Shall we get to it? What did you find out? Did you find the second shooter—the guy in the truck? Did Frizzy June identify him?"

"Frizzy June?"

"Oh, sorry. That's the shorthand name I have for your witness in my head."

"I like it. It fits."

Art unfolded his napkin and wiped the corner of his mouth. Then he blew his nose in it.

"Sorry," he said. "Spicy food makes my nose run."

"Well?" I asked.

"You're impatient, aren't you, Ivy. It's nice to see."

"Why's that?"

"If you never were—if you didn't ever get annoyed, or impatient, or whatever—I'd never be good enough for you."

"I really want to hear about the case right now, Art."

"Sure, sorry. We haven't found him yet, but June positively identified Dawson as the other man in the car from a photo. Peralto's dead, by the way—shot and then burned. So we've got one perp who bragged about the murder and another one who was with him on the street shortly beforehand. We're bound to find Dawson. We know where he works—who he hangs out with—all that. And there's a surprise there."

"I think I know the surprise."

"I'll bet you don't."

"He works for Dimitri, doesn't he?"

"Yes. How'd you know that?"

"You said his middle initial is G, right?"

Art nodded.

"And it stands for Gerald? He goes by Gerry?"

"Yes."

"He's Dimitri's bodyguard. And I think he's Agnes's boyfriend. I can confirm that with a photo later."

Art was silent as he assimilated this. Then he nodded several times. "Wow. That explains a lot. Well, it might, I mean. How did you figure that out?"

"I guess it was a lot of little things. When we went to the Rusty Snake, Gerry told Brian he had a Bulgarian girlfriend with an important job in San Francisco, for one thing. Sizewise, I kept hearing about a great big guy, or a tall guy, or however else he was described. Who fit that description in the cast of characters I ran into? Gerry. And then there was Dmitri telling me that Gerry had been a police officer and he had a friend on the Palo Alto force. You said Dawson had been a cop in Las Vegas. There's more, but I don't remember it all. Even so, I wasn't sure it was him until Dee found a photo online, and I considered the odds that Agnes's boyfriend happened to be huge. Without even seeing the photo, I knew from her description what I was going to find. It fit."

Some children squealed with delight from the

nearby playground across a small lawn. Then one of them ran over—a little African American boy. He was probably four.

"Uncle Greg?" he said to Art. "Push me on the swing!"

His mother rushed over and swept him into her arms. While harried and a bit out of breath, she took a moment to swing the boy around before facing us

"Sorry. My son loves his uncle, but he's been stationed in Bahrain the last year."

"No worries," Art said. "Just let me say goodbye."

The woman had started to walk away with the boy in her arms. Now she returned and set him down.

"What's your name?" Art asked the boy.

"Arthur."

"Me too!" Art told him. "They call me Art."

"Me too!" the boy said, imitating Art as best he could.

"Well, you be careful going up to strangers, okay? I'm a police officer. I'm one of the good guys. But maybe the next man you want to be your uncle won't be so nice."

"Okay."

"Thank you," the woman said. "Maybe he'll listen to you."

Art pulled a business card out his wallet and handed it to her. "Call me if it doesn't take. I'll show him around the station and talk to him again."

The woman took the card, tears in her eyes. "No one else has been kind when Art runs over. He does this all the time—well, whenever he sees a Black man. People think he's a pest."

"Oh no," I told her. "This has been delightful. I'm

so glad we've met you both."

Out of words, the woman and little Art turned and walked away hand in hand.

"Where were we?" Art asked.

"I think Agnes is behind this, working with Gerry and his corrupt cop friend."

"A corrupt cop?"

"Yes. Whoever warned me off knew things they couldn't know otherwise. And they had a rigged-up recording taken from Dee's interview with you. She remembers what she said—what words they cherry-picked."

"Warned you off from what, Ivy?"

"Oh. I can't believe I forgot to tell you. At first, I wasn't supposed to." I filled Art in about Dee's fake kidnapping. "Sorry," I finished.

"I don't know what to say, Ivy. I warned you." His frown was devastating, conveying both strong disapproval and disappointment.

"Once again, I'm sorry, Art."

"Noted," he said crisply. "Tell me more about why you think Dennis's sister is behind this."

"It's the Gerry connection on top of all the rest. How could it just be just a coincidence that Agnes's boyfriend killed her brother? And the fake kidnapping warning came after I talked to her, and Agnes is the one who had access to my mother in the hospital."

"We're back to that, Ivy? I can imagine somebody at the station taking bribes—just barely—but I still don't see a connection to your mother. Plus we're short on motive here in Dennis's murder. Agnes had her own brother killed? Why?"

"I don't know, but you said they were estranged.

And remember, she probably lied about being in Mom's room while she was awake."

"Well, it's possible," Art conceded. "But Gerry is Dimitri's employee, and Dimitri isn't a former nun running a Catholic charity hospital."

"But it all adds up when you consider Gerry and Agnes are a couple. You really think that's a coincidence?"

"Maybe there's so much money to be made selling artifacts that Dimitri's eliminating people so he doesn't have to share the proceeds."

"Let me call my uncle. Let's see how much money we're talking about."

I reached for my phone and dialed. "Brian, it's Ivy. About how much are the artifacts worth?"

"Maybe four million in total. We're hoping for that, anyway."

"Wow, that surprises me."

"That's because you've never seen them. Some date back to the fourteen hundreds. They're remarkable. We'll take you down to see them before they're gone. Okay?"

"Thanks. That would be great. I've got to go."

"Bye."

"Four million," I told Art.

"Good to know. That's more than enough for some people to kill. I brought in a guy once who'd committed a murder for eight hundred dollars."

"Getting back to the case, I don't see why you're pushing for Dimitri when I've laid out such a good case against Agnes. Have you found out something new about him?"

"No, there still isn't any evidence against him for

anything, actually. We don't know exactly what Dimitri does, beyond his import-export business, which seems to be legit. He might be trying to cash in on a reputation as a bad guy without real credentials."

"Maybe. He did that with me, it turns out. He pretended he had a police officer in his pocket." I thought things over. "I guess there are other angles about this that I wasn't considering. I still like Agnes for this, though."

"That's cute, Ivy. 'Angles.' 'You like her for this.' That's real cop talk."

I shrugged.

"I still don't get it, Ivy. Why are you zeroed in on Agnes? It's more than just the evidence, isn't it?"

"She scared me just from talking to her on the phone—in a different way than Dimitri does. I think that was her intent. I'm sure she's mixed up in this somehow. Call it intuition if you want. And I've read about the so-called Internal Security outfit in Bulgaria. They disappeared people, tortured people—they were like domestic terrorists. She was a colonel. That wasn't a ceremonial title. She was right in the middle of it all."

"I read that she was fired and then had to flee the country," Art said.

"For being worse than her peers. What does that say? Agnes is dangerous."

"Okay, let's say she is. I've said it before, but I'll say it again. Where's her motive? Why kill anyone? What does she gain from it? In police work, this isn't a little detail. It's usually the key to catching and convicting perps."

"It's got to be about money," I said. "And there's lots of it here—millions, it turns out. Suppose she was the missing partner with her brother while they pretended they didn't have anything to do with each other? Or maybe the two siblings really did hate each other and their history finally came to a head. Maybe there's a recent trigger that set Agnes off. You don't have a motive for Dimitri being involved, either, do you?"

Art grinned. "Maybe you're sweet on him from your fabulous date. Maybe you dig old men. After all, you wore that sexy dress for him, and for me, here you are in jeans and a T-shirt."

"You don't need inducements, do you, Art? I should be in a burka and a hijab to de-induce you."

"I'm picturing it." He looked up and away to the right for moment. "Nope. Still looking great, Ivy."

I smiled. "So let's look at what we know for sure."

Art's phone chirped. "I need to see who this is," he told me.

He held the phone up to his ear after pressing a few buttons and listened for a moment.

"Thanks, Bert. Yes, I'll see you there."

He put the phone back in his pocket and spoke to me. "I'm sorry. I've got to go. They found Gerry Dawson."

"That's great."

"No, not so great. He's dead, too."

Chapter Nineteen

I found out later on a phone call with Art that Dawson's body got hooked by a fisherman in the San Francisco Bay. He'd been shot in the head. They brought Dimitri in for questioning. He had a solid alibi and seemed quite grief-stricken. Gerry had worked for him for over six years. I told Art he needed to ask about Gerry's friend on the force. He told me he already knew who it was—the guy who'd vouched for Gerry early in the investigation. He wouldn't give me a name.

"It's an internal matter," was all he'd say.

I asked him if the corrupt cop had technical skills—could he have faked the photo of Dee I hadn't seen, and the voice I'd heard? Art said yes.

I talked to him the following morning as well, having spent the intervening day emailing, shopping for the family's groceries, having lunch out with Jan, hiking in the foothills, and then playing board games with my nieces in the evening. Holly called them bored games, but she seemed to have fun beating us.

"So what's next?" I asked Art. "Have you questioned Agnes? You got that photo Dee forwarded to you, right?" Gerry and Agnes were kissing on a beach on Maui. They looked happy.

"We're gathering more evidence before we bring her in. A couple of patrolmen broke the news of her boyfriend's death and asked her if she knew anything that could help us find the killer. They said she was cold as ice—like she didn't care—and she said she hadn't seen him in a week because she was especially busy at work—which checks out. The government's been conducting an audit of the hospital."

"But you'll take her in as a suspect soon?"

"To be honest, I'm not sure. Cline doesn't like the idea. At this point, putting aside your mother since there's still no hard evidence of foul play, all we've got is her background—nasty stuff from decades ago—one inconsistent statement, and the fact that her bodyguard boyfriend was murdered. He might've been a murderer himself, but that doesn't make her responsible for what he did, Cline says."

"Does she have an alibi for when Gerry was shot?"

"That's tricky. The coroner can't fix the time of death very well because of the body being in the water, plus I didn't tell you the gory part, but maybe I need to now. The body was chewed up pretty bad by a boat propeller."

"Ugh. So she could've done it?"

"We don't know. She was at the hospital, but by herself in her office for quite a while. We're looking into where the body got dumped, based on where we found it and the currents and the tide. If that tracks back to somewhere Agnes could've gotten to from the hospital quickly, that gives her opportunity."

"Does Agnes own a gun?"

"Ivy, I'm uncomfortable going into all these details. Cline doesn't want you involved—especially now that he thinks you've got a vendetta going against Agnes. He wants us to go back and look into Brian's deal, Boukar, and Dimitri. Oh, and we never got around to looking at

Jacques Morin's son in Oregon. We're also still waiting on the State Department to fill us in on what's going on in Cameroon. Maybe I'll try to goose them today. We only have Brian and his wife's word for what's happening there. Maybe it's not the way she says it is."

"I can't let Agnes get away with this, Art. I can't let it go."

"How many murders have to happen before you see how dangerous this is? Everyone who could help us figure this out has gotten murdered. Do you want to be next?"

"Art, I have a different relationship to death than most people."

"You don't care if you die? Is that what you're saying?"

"No. Obviously, I prefer to live, but I believe death is just a transition that will bring me to my next life, and then I'll die again. And live again. And so forth."

"Being reckless has nothing to do with any personal philosophy. Being reckless is just foolish. Stupid. Pigheaded."

"Pigheaded?"

"Sorry. Maybe muleheaded. Pick an animal you like."

"I'll be more careful. I promise."

"Look where your earlier idea of careful got you. Mine is based on in-the-trenches experience with murderers. I don't know where you get yours from. Books? Movies? Come on, Ivy. Be sensible. How am I going to do my job if I have to worry about you?"

"I don't want to argue. I've explained myself, and you can make of it what you will. I'm not responsible for your feelings."

"That's kind of harsh, isn't it, Ivy? I'm trying to tell you I care about you. I care about what happens to you. And you tell me you don't care about that?"

"I'm sorry. I wasn't focused on the impact of my words. When I think my motives are good, I forget how things come across sometimes."

"All right." He paused. "Do whatever you want, but promise me this. If you make any progress, let me know so I can assign someone to protect you. Progress means danger."

"No promises," I told him. "There may be a situation in which it won't make sense to do that."

"You don't give an inch, do you? Have you always been so stubborn?"

"You know, I guess I have."

He was silent.

"I'm sorry, Art."

"I'm going to keep an eye on you, Ivy. If you cross a line with this, I'll tell Cline, and you'll get hauled in on some bullshit charge. I'd hate to do it, but if it's the only way to keep you safe, I will."

"I appreciate your caring. I hear it as that now. Thank you."

After we hung up and I gave it some thought, I decided to go back to the Rusty Snake that evening to see Dimitri. I hadn't heard from him since he promised to find out what he could. I called Brian to see if he'd go with me. Like Art, he tried to talk me out of continuing to investigate. Eventually, he agreed.

After she came home, Dee and I discussed our other options at length. Depending on what I found out from Dimitri, we'd pick one and see where it took us.

Brian drove. Apparently, that was important to him.

He wore khaki pants and a black fleece pullover similar to mine.

I asked him about his wife on the way to the bar, and he was happy to share all the reasons he loved Grace, as well as the multiple tragedies that had befallen her family.

I also asked him what the truth was about Dimitri. "Is he really a criminal, or did you make that up to deter me from finding out what you were up to?"

"The latter. I like Dimitri. I always have. He might be a bit on the wrong side of the law—I don't know— but he's not some major villain. And if you're worried about tonight, the Rusty Snake is his office. There's no way he'd do anything untoward there. We'll be safe."

We arrived, and I led the way into the dim space. Sure enough, Dimitri sat at the back of the room, with a new giant man across the table from him. Once again, the older man was gazing at an iPad on the tabletop.

The bodyguard rose as we neared. If anything, he was bigger than Gerry had been. He adopted a fierce expression that looked unnatural, replete with major squinting and scowling.

"Where do you find these guys, Dimitri?" I asked. "Is there some big-and-tall bodyguard store?"

The bodyguard grunted and started to move forward. Brian stepped up beside me.

"Ivy! Good to see you." Dimitri called. "It's okay, Ivan. But why don't you take this man to the bar and buy him a drink. Maybe get some peanuts. The peanuts are good here."

Ivan jerked his thumb at the bar, and Brian followed him. He knew the drill.

"Sit, sit. It's almost good to see you," Dimitri said.

I sat. "Almost?"

"I'm not happy. Once again, I had to go waste my time at the police station. You told them about Gerry, didn't you—that he worked for me?"

"They already knew. What I told them they didn't know was that Gerry's girlfriend was Agnes—Dennis's sister."

"So?"

This wasn't news to him. He'd been holding back on me. I don't why I was surprised.

"You know Gerry and another guy murdered Dennis?" I tried.

"No, he didn't. He never did things like that. Maybe he was involved, but he didn't shoot anyone. I know Gerry."

"Okay, let's say he was involved. The police have proof of that. Did they tell you?"

"They told me nothing. *Nothing.* What else do you know, and why are they telling *you*?" Dimitri asked. He was dumping anger. It was radiating into the room, but it wasn't directed at me.

"The detective likes me."

"Petrie?"

"Yes."

"That's funny." No smile or laugh accompanied this remark.

"It is?"

"To me." Dimitri continued to stare at me without any vestige of humor.

I took a deep breath. "Okay, here's what I know," I told him. "See if you can help me with this. Agnes may have had an opportunity to kill my mother, and both the men involved in Dennis's murder ·are dead. I think she hired the shooter and had Gerry do whatever he did for her. You know Agnes, right? She's capable of this, isn't she?"

"But why? Why would she do all this? She has a good job. She had a good boyfriend."

"I don't know. I thought you could help with that part."

"Why should I?"

"Don't you want Gerry's killer caught?"

"I do."

"Do you think it could be Agnes?"

"It could be." His face was still stony.

"So?"

"Let me think."

I did, looking around the bar. Several men openly stared at me. Skip the bartender waved and held up a beer bottle. Did I want a drink? I shook my head just as Dimitri began speaking.

"All right. Here's the real story." He relaxed his face and spoke much differently. "Agnes and Boukar are partners—smugglers. She makes the deals. He gets whatever you need from other countries. They both learned how to do this from Anton. Basically, he sold them his business and sent them clients for a finder's fee."

"Like Brian and Grace."

"Yes. Brian approached Anton."

"So Anton wasn't directly involved?"

"Agnes cut him in for a bigger piece of the pie if he'd play frontman. It lowered their risk, and they were trying to do something different this time—selling all that African art they snuck in."

"How do you know all this?"

"That's my real business. I'm an information broker. I pay people for information, and I use it to make money. Gerry knew that, of course, so he brought this to me, and I paid him well. If things hadn't gone wrong, I could've had a good-sized piece of the pie myself by threatening to expose Agnes and Boukar after the deal went down. Naturally, I would have thrown some of that Gerry's way."

"So he wanted to make money by betraying his girlfriend? Really? And where did your accent go? Why are you speaking like you were born in Texas?"

"The Dimitri act helps. I was scarier before, wasn't I? In my business, you need to be scarier than everyone's other options. People need to think that paying me is better than trying to kill me. And I went to college at the University of Texas. Good catch."

"Why did you steer me to Boukar? Wasn't that against your own interests?"

"I knew you wouldn't get anywhere with him. The police talk to him all the time, and they don't get anywhere. Besides, we had a deal. I didn't think you'd go out with me, to tell you the truth. So I didn't think I'd have to tell you anything. But then I did."

"What would happen if people knew all this?" I asked. "Is this something Agnes would kill for?"

"Maybe. Boukar wouldn't. He's a little worm. No guts." Dimitri paused. "I told Gerry many times that Agnes was no good. He wouldn't listen. He liked older women. He liked her. Go figure. I'd rather kiss a man than be with her."

"Your Dimitri accent is back."

"I think I'll stay with it. It's fun."

"So it's dangerous that you know all this?"

"Of course. That's why I've got Ivan, and some other precautions that are none of your business.

"And it's dangerous for me, too?"

"Oh, yes." He paused and then pointed toward the bar. "Ivan has a brother. A big guy. Maybe bigger. I'll make a call."

"It's hard to imagine anyone bigger."

"Big is good. Bodyguards are for scaring."

"Thanks. I'll think about it."

"What are you going to do? I'm telling you all this so you don't go bother these people. It would be stupid. You're a lamb. They're sharks."

"I can't picture a shark eating a lamb. Maybe if the lamb fell into the ocean."

"They would if they could. Sharks definitely would eat lambs. They'd say, 'Yum, yum, yum. I love eating this nice lamb.' "

"Dimitri, you're right about one thing. You're definitely an interesting man."

"I told you! And you're growing on me, Ivy. Maybe I'm willing to sleep with you now."

"In your dreams."

He laughed. "You sound like a regular woman now."

"Thanks, I guess."

Chapter Twenty

Back at Jan's, Dee and I discussed the case in the guesthouse. It still felt odd to treat a fourteen-year-old as a peer, but she'd certainly proven her mettle during my investigation. And she came through once more in our conversation.

"How about you wear a wire again, and you confront Agnes with what we know? You could have your policeman boyfriend nearby."

"Officially, the police won't let me be involved anymore, Dee. Art's talking with me informally, but that's it, so no wire." I thought it over. "I suppose I could present something to him at the last minute—as a fait accompli. He wouldn't refuse to protect me if he knew I was going ahead regardless. But wearing the wire is out."

"I could lend you my phone," Dee said. "If I enhance the microphone, you could keep it in your pocket and record everything."

"That's a good idea."

Dee scrunched up her face, her snub nose getting even smaller. "How would you set up a meeting? Why would she agree to talk to you?"

"I could call her and say I was going to tell the police about her role in this unless she met me."

"Aren't you the kind of person who'd tell the police right away if you knew something? Why would Agnes believe you? And why wouldn't she just go ahead and kill you if you did that?"

"Dee, do these murders feel real to you? Are you clued into the danger here? How are you doing with all this? I'm concerned that when we talk, you don't seem to appreciate the gravity of all this."

"I get freaked out at first when something happens, then I get used to it. I've always been that way."

"I don't think you should ignore your feelings when you've been exposed to trauma. That's not something you want to ignore."

"That's the thing, Aunt Ivy. I haven't been exposed to anything. It's just stuff I keep hearing about. I'm sure I'd be a mess if I discovered a dead body or something."

"Okay, I see what you're saying. It's conceptual as far as you're concerned."

"I guess so. I mean I cried about Grandma and I'm worried about Mom's moods, but I don't care that Dennis is dead, and I never met the other dead people."

"Okay."

"You didn't answer my question," Dee told me. "Why would Agnes think that someone like you could be a blackmailer?"

"Not everyone can read other people, and I've found that immoral types expect others to be that way, too."

"That's interesting, Aunt Ivy. I didn't know that. What about her killing you right away? Why wouldn't she do that?"

"I could tell her I left a letter at a lawyer's office. That seems to work in the movies."

We were both quiet for a bit. For my part, I was noticing how much of my planning was based on movies and TV shows—as Art had said. And I still wondered how Dee could talk so blithely about murders.

"Do you think there's a safer way to get to her?" Dee finally asked.

"You mean besides threatening her with exposure?"

"Yeah."

"I guess I could waylay her at the hospital or as she leaves work—surprise her and see what happens. For that matter, you could find out where she lives."

"Oh, I know where she lives. It's right near the hospital, where hippies used to live back in the day. Now it's all hipsters and homeless people."

"What's a hipster? That sounds like a cross between a hippie and a hamster."

"I don't know how to describe them, but I know one when I see one. I guess you could say they look pretentious in a hip kind of way."

"Hmm. So what do you think I should do?"

"Let's use the threat about exposing her to get you and Agnes in some public place where Art can watch you and get to you easily. She's not going to shoot you in a coffeehouse, right?"

"I wouldn't think so."

"She may not want to shoot you at all since she's got a crooked cop in her pocket and he probably told her they won't let you be on the case anymore."

"I think it was Gerry who knew the cop. I don't know if Agnes is still connected to whoever that is."

Dee paused to think. "I can rig up my phone to send live audio to Art while we're recording. Then he'll know when you've gotten her to confess so he can swoop in. Or if she gets too scary."

"I very much doubt she'll confess."

"Then why are we doing this?" She threw her hands up in the air. "Isn't that the whole idea?"

"It's to get more information—to see her reaction to what I say."

"Well, she might let something big slip."

"She might. Do you think she'll check to see if I'm recording her?"

"Maybe. Hold on. I think I can make your phone look like it's not doing anything, and if she goes looking for a microphone on you, she won't find one."

"I like this plan," I told her.

"Me, too. And I want to listen in. I can send out the audio in a conference call. And maybe I can watch from across the street or something."

"Absolutely not on the watching part, Dee. Agnes knows what you look like—they had a photo when they fake kidnapped you. And no matter what precautions we take, it's still dangerous."

"I could wear a disguise."

"Dee, no."

"It's not fair. You go out there and do all this stuff, and I'm stuck at home."

"That was our deal. You agreed to it."

"Aren't Buddhists supposed to live in the moment and be flexible? You have to change things up sometimes. Didn't Buddha talk about that?"

"You're not going to get anywhere with this, Dee. Give it up."

She sighed and nodded.

****

Brian called a while later while Dee worked on setting up her phone. I'd spent the time since concocting our plan chatting with Holly about a school trip to Yosemite, and then reading when she became bored with that.

"Ivy, Grace would like to get to know you better. How about you join us for a coffee?"

"Sure. When?"

"What about now?"

"Okay. Where?"

He named a coffeehouse in downtown Palo Alto, and we agreed to meet in a half hour. I could scope out Bean Buzz as a possible meeting site with Agnes while I was there. And I certainly reciprocated Grace's interest in connecting. She was Brian's wife, as well as someone likely to open my eyes to life in Africa. For that matter, she probably knew more about the case than she'd let on earlier.

"I'm off," I told Dee.

She didn't look up from her phone. "Okay."

I took the opportunity to be mindful to my surroundings as I drove. Although other cars periodically demanded my attention, I stayed as rooted as I could in the full range of sensory experiences being presented to me through the windshield.

What probably looked mundane to most eyes—including mine lately—was revealed to me as detailed patterns of light and dark, an awe-inspiring sense of space, and an ever-changing array of forms. It didn't matter what the shapes were—what names we gave them. They just looked the way they looked.

At one point, on Sand Hill Road, I spied a small carcass by the side of the road—a cat? Ordinarily, I'd have felt a rush of revulsion and would've turned my eyes away. Now I simply saw it as a particularly interesting shape and a jumble of subtle colors—another element of my experience.

I felt incredibly calm. I'm sure my heart rate was

under fifty beats a minute. I was actively meditating while I drove. I made sure I came back to earth a mile or so before the coffeehouse. Mindfulness to the senses could be a self-centered activity when socializing was called for.

Bean Buzz was squeezed between an organic grocery and a smoothie shop on University Avenue, which was, not surprisingly, only a few blocks from the Stanford campus.

Students stared at laptops throughout the large room, and another interracial couple sat in the middle of the huddle of small round tables. I had no trouble distinguishing Brian and Grace from them. Even a casual glance toward that side of the room fixed on Grace's ebony skin tone. They sat at an isolated table near the front window.

"I ordered you a black tea," Brian told me as I approached.

"Thank you." I lowered myself onto an uncomfortable wooden chair. "Grace, thanks for reaching out. I'm sorry I've been busy and didn't do it myself."

She was even more striking than I remembered. Perhaps it was the way the multi-colored scarf on her head contrasted with her skin.

I loved her black and brown top and matching skirt. Although I'd never seen the pattern of tight spirals before, it was easy to recognize it as African. I could see no sign of makeup. Gold hoops hung from Grace's ears and silver bangle bracelets ringed both wrists.

I have no idea what Brian wore.

"It is nice that we are meeting now," Grace told me. "Brian says you are working on finding criminals?"

"Yes."

"How is that going?"

"Actually, pretty well at this point."

"Tell us about it," Brian said.

I filled them in on my progress and plans—the parts that had nothing to do with them. Periodically, Grace asked questions, sometimes to have me define a word and sometimes to find out more. I was struck by the magnitude of her curiosity. And I remained delighted by her accent and musical voice.

"Don't go meet Agnes," Brian said when I'd finished. "If she's a killer, what's to stop her from killing you?"

"Several reasons. We'll be somewhere such as here—in public. And I'll tell her if I don't make a phone call in a half hour, my information will be passed on to the police."

Dee and I had decided that was better than the letter at the lawyer idea.

"What's the point, though?" Brian said. "Do you think she'll reveal anything? Why would she?"

"To gloat? By accident? I don't know. People do it all the time in movies."

My uncle shook his head. I heard myself and followed suit. Movies? Really? That was my argument? It was one thing to be motivated by fictional events, but to offer them to someone else as an argument?

"I agree with Brian," Grace said. "This is foolishness. Look around. If you meet her here, why are you so safe?"

I glanced around the room. "What could she do here and get away with?"

"I don't know. Can we think of every way better

than someone like her could? I have seen killing—too much killing. It comes in many forms—more than you can imagine. This Agnes cannot be trusted."

"Have you met her? It sounds like you have."

"No, no," she protested. "I am basing on what you said. You said this."

Her careful English had deteriorated for some reason. She spoke faster now, with more of an accent.

"Well, you've got a point. I guess there's risk."

"Grace is right," Brian said. "Agnes could hold a silenced gun under the table, shoot you, and then walk out."

"She could poison you," Grace said.

"What about a knife?" Brian added. "Or a stun gun set on high? Who knows what she could come up with."

"I need to hold Agnes responsible for her actions. It's a kindness to Jan, and something I've committed to do. I don't break promises."

Of course, I was breaking my promise to Art to stay safe.

When I asked Grace to tell me about herself, she shared anecdotes about growing up in a small village, her brother's rise to power in her tribe, and what sufficient funds would mean to her people. After a half hour of this, she turned the tables and questioned me.

"Tell me about your religion. We do not have this in my country."

"It's about kindness. And paying attention to be able to manifest it."

"Manifest?"

"I'm sorry. To be able to do it. No one can be kind or compassionate without noticing what's going on around them. Many people sleepwalk their way through life. Do you know what I mean?"

"They walk in their sleep? We have this, too."

"I'm sorry again. I shouldn't use American idioms. What I mean to say is that a lot of people don't live in the moment. They're not learning about life. They're just noticing their own thoughts."

"Oh, you must live in the moment where I come from. You will not survive if you don't."

"I understand. May I ask you another question?"

"Of course."

"This is your first time here, right?"

"Yes."

"What are your impressions?"

"Impressions?"

"What do you think about the people here?"

She paused and thought. I was struck by her dark eyes. They were unreadable. Beautiful, but mysterious.

"They are very much concerned with themselves. They seem to be greedy and think they know everything. Many are unkind—bad Buddhists, you must think." She smiled. "And they stare at me like I am a strange animal. The men stare at my body. I am used to that. But the women look at me with hate."

"Really?"

"Oh, yes. I see it in their eyes. I'm sorry to talk this way about your country, but you asked."

"What else?"

"Everyone is rich and has nice things. Everyone wears nice clothes and drives expensive cars."

"That's true in this area. Housing is so expensive now that only people with a lot of money can afford to live here. But I suppose by African standards, even poor Americans in other parts of the country would seem rich, too.

"You are wrong." She raised her voice and leaned forward. "There are no 'African standards.' It is different everywhere you go."

"I'm sorry. I know very little about Africa."

"That's right. You don't!" Her vehemence ramped up, her words tight and controlled. "That's what I mean. People here think they know everything important, but they don't. There's a whole continent that people don't want to know about. If they did, they would have to do something. We have wars like Ukraine. Do Americans care? No, because we are a different color. Because no one gets rich from us. I could tell you more about this, but I see Brian is giving me the evil eye so I will stop."

Grace's passion was on display. I didn't even get a chance to agree with her. I could picture her in a war-torn region, fighting alongside the men of her tribe. Underneath her striking exterior was a steely, intense person. I understood now why she was the one here trying to sell her tribe's art. I wouldn't want to negotiate with her around anything that concerned her people's welfare—or even where to go out to eat.

Despite his so-called evil-eye, Brian smiled. "I found someone special," he told me. "It's hard to argue with any of that, isn't it?"

"Yes."

"I am so lucky a beautiful, strong woman has an interest in a broken-down old man like me."

I took a risk. "What attracted you to Brian?" I asked Grace. "Why are you with him?"

This was clearly a step beyond the depth of our current conversation, but I was curious how she'd answer. I suspected he was her ticket out of poverty and a route to protecting her tribe. Brian was good-looking for a septuagenarian, but he drank, womanized, and the age disparity was huge. Actually, it didn't seem likely that a woman from her culture would find any White man attractive.

Grace wasn't prepared for this question. Her eyes darted around as she tried to respond. "He is kind like you talk about," she finally said. "Very kind. Very big heart. Helps many."

Once again, her speech had devolved into less skilled English, which was interesting.

"How about on a personal level?"

She had to work to come up with an answer for this, too. Then she looked at her husband and smiled. "He is a wonderful lover."

Brian beamed. I dropped the subject.

I asked her about her experience trying to make a deal for the art.

"We met with Dennis and he said he would arrange things. He said he was close to someone who could do what we wanted."

"You didn't talk to anyone else?"

"No, and Dennis died before we could sell anything."

"I've told you all this, Ivy," Brian admonished. "Please don't badger my wife."

"I'm sorry, Grace. Do you feel badgered?"

"I don't know this word."

"Am I making you uncomfortable?"

"A little. Please stop."

"Of course."

Brian regaled us with stories of his time in South America for the rest of the visit. I'd heard most of these suspiciously tall tales before, and I suspect Grace had too. My uncle was most at ease when he was talking about his exploits.

The two of them were an odd match. There was no question about that.

My tea never arrived. I didn't miss it.

Chapter Twenty-one

Surprisingly, Agnes didn't need a lot of convincing to meet me. When I called and hinted I knew she was involved in smuggling, she immediately agreed to meet me at Bean Buzz the next morning at nine.

I turned to Dee when I got off the speaker phone.

"That was easy," she said. "Why do you think that is?"

"It sounded like she already wanted to get together. Maybe she wants to scare or threaten me again. In person, I hear she's even more formidable."

"Maybe. I guess we'll find out tomorrow. Let's test my phone modifications," Dee suggested.

We ran into a problem right away. "If I use your phone because mine is dumb," I asked, "how can I send audio to you? You won't have one."

"I can't believe I didn't think of that. That's not like me."

"Can you borrow Holly's?"

"Maybe if *you* asked her."

"I'll try."

I hunted Dee's sister up in her room, which I hadn't ventured into before. It was an incredible mess, with clothes strewn all over the floor. Several surrealist prints hung askew on the pale pink walls. I recognized Magritte and Dali's work. I didn't know the others. One of them looked like a mechanical elephant standing near a headless woman. The imagery was vaguely disturbing to me.

Holly sat at her desk. She looked up from a tablet in her lap when she saw me and frowned. "So I guess Dee's busy, huh? It's time for your obligatory visit with your second-choice niece."

"I'm sorry you feel that way. I've tried to spend time with you, Holly. I think you have to take some responsibility for why that hasn't happened more."

"Like what? What did I do?" Her nostrils flared and her lips thinned.

I sat down on her bed. "For one thing, your attitude. You're angry with me for not being around when you needed me. You're angry right now, aren't you? It's time to let that go, don't you think?"

"Maybe." Now she crossed her arms and leaned back in her chair.

"And when we talk, I feel dismissed after a while. In almost all our one-on-one encounters, I've initiated things. All you have to do is say, 'let's take a walk' or 'tell me about Sri Lanka,' and I'm there. Have you expressed any interest at all in me or my life? Almost all our conversations are Hollycentric."

"So I'm just a total fuck-up? Everything's my fault?"

I shook my head. "You're not listening if you think I said that. I don't believe there's anything wrong with what you're doing—it's developmentally appropriate. The important thing is to be aware of it—to be honest with yourself. Think for a minute. What have I done wrong since I got here?"

"You spend all your time with Dee."

"Obviously, that's an exaggeration, but yes, I've

spent much more time with her. Why do you think that is? And why do you think there's something wrong with that?"

"It makes me feel bad." Holly made an I-feel-bad face with some effort, looking like a toddler who'd been denied a cookie.

"And?"

"And that's why it's wrong."

"Your feelings tell you the moral value of things?"

"Yes." She nodded furiously. She was sure of this, although I'm not sure she understood what I meant. She'd started nodding before I'd gotten to the end of my sentence.

"Who's creating those feelings?"

"You are by liking Dee better."

"Who said I do? Listen, I want to run an idea by you. I say *you're* generating your feelings by how you interpret what I'm saying and doing. And I say emotions are subjective and not very reliable sources about what's happening."

"That's ridiculous. Anyway, I don't care." Holly threw her hands in the air and snorted.

I was reminded of what Dee had said—that snorting wasn't likely to help her sister's social life.

"I think you do." I leaned forward and raised my voice for emphasis. "I think your not-caring schtick is just a pose you've adopted because you care a lot. It's hard to endure such strong caring, so you adopt a persona—a false front."

"You think you've got me figured out, don't you." Her tone was scornful.

"Yes, I do. What's more important is what do *you* think? Stop a moment and consider what I've said. Try

318

to be open and accepting. Try the ideas on for size. Do any of them resonate—ring true?"

She closed her eyes and was quiet for a minute or two, which surprised me. I'd expected ten seconds worth of assembling justification for her point of view. Her tight face gradually relaxed as she thought. When her eyes finally opened, they were clearer and softer.

"I can see I haven't done much from my side to be with you, Aunt Ivy. That's true. But I'm the kid and you're the adult. Isn't that your job?"

"Up to a point. You can't have it both ways. You want your mom and me to treat you as an adult, but when it's convenient—like now—you play the kid card."

"Okay, fair enough. And I guess I don't have a right to complain if I haven't made a bigger effort to get to know you."

"Thank you. I appreciate your saying that." I truly did. It looked like Holly and I might be able to salvage our relationship.

"But you have to admit that things between you and Dee are really different than between you and me."

"Sure. Your sister and I have a lot of similar interests, and she reached out right from the start to find out what I know that might be helpful to her. That's her personality. You have a different personality—not worse or better—just different. Do you want to find out everything in the world and run circles around everyone else while you do it? That wouldn't suit you at all, would it? Our culture rewards extroverts, athletes, and other types of people. That's culturally determined. Other cultures do things differently, so once again, who's really better than anyone else?"

"Like what do other cultures do?" She was

genuinely curious, accepting the premise.

"Well, in Sri Lanka, no one would appreciate Dee for who she is. It's not okay there for a young woman to act the way she does."

"Okay, I see what you mean. But why are you coming at me like this? You're not my therapist or something."

"I don't want to miss out on truly getting to know you. I need to help you dismantle whatever you've got in place that blocks that. This is self-interest, Holly. You're an amazing person. I can tell."

"How can you tell?"

I grinned. "I have mysterious Buddhist powers. Didn't you know?"

"Can you spike a volleyball so it bounces up to the ceiling? I can. Well, I did it once."

"That's a cinch for the likes of me. I can do that with one hand tied behind my back."

"It only takes one hand, Aunt Ivy."

"Good point. I guess I'll have to stop tying that other arm back. It's a waste of good rope. Listen, I need a favor."

"What?" She seemed wary.

"Can you lend Dee your phone tomorrow morning—just for an hour or so?"

"I've got stuff on there I wouldn't want her to see."

I thought for a moment. "What if you were there while she used it—keeping an eye on what she did?"

"What does she need it for? She's got a better phone than I do."

"I'm going to use her phone to send audio to her from a meeting I'll be having with someone," I told her.

"Do you have permission from the other person? I

think it it's illegal if you don't. Don't let Dee make you a criminal like she is—all that hacking."

"I'd better tell you something, Holly. I'm meeting with the woman who might have ordered Dennis's murder and may have killed your grandmother, too. Recording laws are beside the point."

"Holy shit! Why are you meeting her? Is it safe?" Her eyes widened and she grimaced.

"To try to get evidence. And I sure hope it's safe."

"What about the police? Isn't that their job?"

"They're looking in a different direction."

"I'll help however I can. But be careful."

After that, we discussed surrealistic art, which Holly knew a lot about. One thing led to another. I didn't leave her room for another forty-five minutes. When I did, our epic hug warmed my heart.

Chapter Twenty-two

Dee showed me how to use her phone the next morning. It was surprisingly simple. All I had to do was start a conference call to Art and Dee, and then leave the line open while keeping it in speaker mode. They'd keep their phones muted. Dee made a cute Buddha icon for me to tap to make the phone look like it was turned off. She also put 911 and Art's cell number in her speed dial, making them number one and two so it would be easy for me. I practiced doing what I needed to do while I waited to leave.

Holly sat with us in Dee's room—it was a Saturday. I thought we'd be attending Mom's memorial service that day, but it had been pushed back a week for reasons the country club refused to tell us.

They wore similar outfits—the first time I'd seen that. Both had on black hoodies over jeans; Dee wore red plastic sandals, while Holly wore what I surmised were white volleyball shoes. The contrast in size, body configuration, facial features, and internal energy were as marked as ever.

While we waited, the girls discussed whether their mom had entered one of her "phases," which I knew to be their word for her cycling into mania. Holly told me that earlier that day she'd seen Jan dancing around on the patio in her underwear—with no music on. Dee noticed that Jan hadn't bathed for a few days.

I wondered how I could be so caught up in my own agenda not to have noticed anything awry. That was exactly what I'd vowed to work on. I promised the girls I'd evaluate my sister myself later to see if I needed to intervene. But first things first.

Despite all our planning, or perhaps because of it, I was nervous. I felt it as a fluttering in my gut and ragged breathing.

There was no guarantee Agnes would reveal anything useful. I could be putting myself at risk for no reward. And my attitude toward death might very well be tested at a new level. Perhaps I'd fail to live up to my supposed fearlessness.

Ordinarily, I found it helpful in the long run to be humbled by corrective life experiences. The more accurately I knew myself, the better, especially about something like dying. Now, there was a short-term event to survive, and fear could affect my ability to do so.

When it was almost time to leave, I called Art to let him know I was meeting Agnes and enlist his help. I got his voicemail and left a detailed message. Then I set out in Jan's Jaguar and faced traffic—something I hadn't accounted for on a weekend. When I finally parked— fifteen minutes late—I set up Dee's phone. She answered the conference call and muted her end of the call. Then I included Art on the call; I got his voicemail again.

Not reaching Art presented a dilemma. Should I go ahead with the plan, assuming he'd get the message and tune in? Or did I need to reschedule? Now that Art knew what I was up to, I probably couldn't reschedule, unfortunately. He'd have to tell his lieutenant that I hadn't stopped investigating, and there'd be consequences. He'd made that clear.

I decided to leave my phone connected with his voicemail. That way, he could monitor my conversation on his way over if he was late.

I disembarked from the car and strode toward Bean Buzz. In hindsight, had I been armed with a little more familiarity with modern devices, I certainly wouldn't have.

When I entered the coffeehouse, I saw Agnes glowering at me from a table across the room near the restroom doors. As her photos had shown, her oversized head was almost overshadowed by her even more oversized nose. I couldn't make out the rest of her features from that distance. Agnes wore a gray cardigan sweater and a long black skirt. Her hair was clipped short enough that I'm sure some people assumed she was gay. Even seated, I could see she was built like a football player, with square, broad shoulders and a thick neck.

Frowning now, she stood as I approached, and gestured for me to follow her. I was definitely not going out a back door again, so I didn't budge. I'd learned my lesson from Dimitri.

Turning, she spoke sharply. "If you want us to talk freely, I need to check you for a wire, and if you don't want to disrobe right here, follow me into the ladies' room. Okay?"

"Okay." I hadn't really thought about how looking for a wire would work. What she said made sense.

So I followed her into the two-stall, two-sink bathroom, which was larger than I would've thought the coffeehouse needed. Agnes called out to see if anyone else was in there. When no one responded, Agnes reached into her voluminous black leather purse and pulled out a rubber wedge, which she jammed under the door.

"You've come prepared, haven't you?" I said.

"Always. Strip."

"Down to my underwear will be sufficient, I think."
I didn't relish what I was about to endure.

"That's fine. And empty your pockets."

"Okay."

Agnes was thorough. Clearly, she'd done this
before. Her manner was professional, at least—no
comments on my body or clothing choices. No gratuitous
handsiness. She didn't pay attention to my phone when
she saw it was shut off.

"Okay. Get dressed."

I did. Agnes leaned against the vanity counter,
keeping her face as neutral as she could. Her hostility
was still apparent, anyway. Now I could see that despite
her distractingly bulbous nose, her eyes were a lovely
shade of pale blue and her sensuous lips were quite
attractive.

I stood a few feet away, facing the mirror above the
sinks behind her. I looked scared. My green eyes were
open wide, and my compressed lips were tense. I held
my body stiffly, with my arms crossed over my chest.

"You have been a pain in my ass since the start,"
Agnes told me. "You and your crazy sister. Why
couldn't you let this go?"

"To be honest, I'm not sure. Why couldn't you?
Why kill anyone? Your motivation is still a mystery to
me."

"Who said I did? You have a witness? You have
evidence? The police don't."

"Let's not play games, Agnes. It's just us in here,
and I know what you did."

"Fine. Do you want to be next?"

She said this unemotionally, as if she were asking me if I wanted salt on my food. It was chilling. I felt tentacles of fear snake out from my gut, spreading throughout my body.

"No." I was hanging in there despite my fear.

"Then listen. You need to leave. Take a nice vacation. Go back to China. Whatever. If you're here the day after tomorrow, more people will die—maybe your family this time."

She wasn't bluffing. My stomach continued to churn, and an electric shiver ran up my spine. My chest tightened painfully. It was hard to breathe.

"All right, I will," I told her in a weak voice. "But before I go, tell me what's going on. How have you managed to outwit the police? Why have you done all this?"

Here was the moment of truth. Would Agnes answer me?

She stared at me a while. "I owe you nothing, but there's no harm. You know that Dorian Boukar and I are in business together, right?"

I nodded.

"And that Brian's wife Grace is here to sell art?"

"Yes."

"Well, we are right on track with that. When I say *we*, I don't mean me and Boukar. Fuck Boukar."

"That's rather cryptic."

"Whatever. I suppose you want to know about your mother."

"Yes."

"I met Anton when he happened to be in her room and I'd come to check on her as a courtesy to him. Lois was unconscious. I needed my brother's cooperation to cut Boukar out of the deal so I could skim money from the art sale. Your uncle wouldn't have known a damn thing about it. When my brother agreed—for a piece of the action—and we'd discussed the details, I happened to look at your mother. She was wide awake, listening.

"Right then, I knew she had to go. She was halfway dead, anyway—in ICU. Who would suspect anything? But my brother knows me. He told me if I hurt her, he'd kill me. I told him I wouldn't. The idiot believed me. Marriage made him soft."

"How did you do it?"

"Easy as pie. After we both left the room, I came back and put a little cocktail in your mother's IV drip. No one else saw her awake, so everyone assumed the strokes killed her. Everyone but my brother—and your fucking sister."

"So then you killed Dennis, too?"

"Not personally. What was I to do? Wait around until he killed me?"

"Later, you killed your henchmen to cover your tracks?"

"Yes. It was a shame about Gerry. He was a fun guy. But his moron friend had to shoot his mouth off. They had to go."

"You said, '*We* were still making a deal' before. Who did you mean?"

A stall door swung open, and Grace strode out, holding a huge revolver.

I couldn't think. I couldn't move. I wasn't in my body or my mind. I don't think I'd ever seen a gun in someone's hand before in real life, let alone one pointed at me.

"Agnes," Grace said with only a hint of her previous accent, "this is foolishness. Now we have to kill her."

"You think?"

"It's one thing if you tell your secrets. That's up to you. But my name is almost here now. This woman is smart. She's going to figure it out. That's not okay."

I came back online. I had to. Even more adrenaline surged through me. I trembled all over. I struggled to get words out.

"You two were both taking a cut of the money?" I asked.

"Yes," Grace answered. "A million each. Your uncle has no idea. I've been playing him since day one." She smirked.

Her accent, like Dimitri's was entirely gone now.

"Are you even African?" I asked.

"None of your business." She turned to Agnes. "I'll handle this. You go. You're going to need an alibi. No one will suspect me."

Agnes nodded, turned, removed the door wedge, and edged the door open.

Jan burst in. "I heard everything! The cops heard everything!" Then she saw the gun in Grace's hand. "Oh, shit."

"Shut up!" Grace demanded.

I looked into Jan's eyes. She was manic and revving up as I watched. There was no telling what she might do.

"You animals!"

She rushed Agnes and tried to claw her eyes. Agnes crouched into a fighting stance and warded her off with a forearm. Grace lunged forward and drew back the pistol to hit Jan in the head. I tackled Grace, bringing us both down onto the linoleum. The gun skittered across the floor, ending up near the door. For a moment, time stopped. We all froze and looked at the gun.

Then a young woman walked in, saw what was happening, and picked up the gun before anyone could react. She was probably a student, so frail-looking the revolver looked too heavy for her to even hold.

"Everybody stay right there!" she shouted. She waved the gun around with a shaky hand. It looked as though she might shoot one of the sinks.

"Thank God you're here," Grace said in a thick African accent from a prone position.

"Don't listen!" Jan called. "They work for Satan! We are the righteous ones!"

I stood and told the woman to call the police.

"I certainly will." Her voice shook.

"I'm a police officer," Agnes said, also struggling to her feet. "Give me the gun."

"Don't do it," I said. "Just call the police. Let them sort it out."

Agnes walked toward the woman with her hand out. The terrified woman either had to shoot her or hand it over, or so I thought. Instead, she ran out of the ladies ' room, gun in hand.

"What now?" I asked as we all stared at one another.

"Is it true?" Grace asked as she scrambled to her feet. "Did your crazy sister speak the truth about the cops hearing us?"

"She said she did. Test her—ask her what she heard."

I could only hope Jan was coherent enough to confirm the truth. She'd wandered over by the sinks, where it looked as though she was contemplating her appearance in the mirror. Her crazed eyes stared at her crazed eyes.

Agnes nervously asked her what she'd heard.

"A million each. Mom was awake. Satan's slave killed her own brother. Grace's heart is black like she is. My sister can kick all of your asses. She's a Shaolin monk. Her kung-fu saved Hong Kong."

The stress had triggered a severe decompensation. Jan was truly out of it. But she'd proved I'd transmitted our conversation.

"How?" Agnes asked me. "How did you do that? We checked the room. I checked you."

"My phone. Well, not mine. It just looks like it's off. It's on—still recording and sending out live audio even as we speak. You two are finished." I paused and let that sink in.

Now that I had the upper hand, I began to calm down—emotionally. Physically, energy still roiled within me in sickening fashion.

"Don't make it any worse by what you do next," I continued. "And Grace, you haven't murdered anyone— as far as I know, anyway. There's hope for you. You can put on that poor-little-African-me act. It's very convincing. And if you provide evidence against Agnes, they'll probably cut you a deal."

"I like the sound of that," she replied.

A familiar voice spoke from outside the door—Art.

"This is the police. I want all of you to come out with your hands on the back of your heads. Don't make me come in there and shoot someone. Ivy, are you okay?"

"So far. You can come in. Nobody's armed."

Jan attacked Art as soon as he entered. She'd sidled toward the door as he spoke. When he grabbed her in a bear hug, gun in hand, Grace tried to run out the door. I tripped her. While she was down, Agnes leaped on her back and began choking her.

Art shoved Jan to the side, and I grabbed her arm and held tight. He separated the women, and three more officers streamed in and cuffed them. Jan sank to the floor in an inert puddle, and I began crying and couldn't stop.

Chapter Twenty-three

"Where *were* you?" I asked Art as we sat in his car much later. I'd been crying in the back seat for God knows how long, waiting for him to get around to me. "Why didn't you come to the coffeehouse sooner?"

"I was getting a dressing down from Cline in his office when you called. Then when I checked my messages after I survived that, I headed straight here. The first two minutes of your audio is on my voicemail, but that's the longest message it'll take. I figured out you were in the ladies' room when that woman ran out holding a gun. So tell me what happened. I'll listen to what you've got on Dee's phone later. I want to hear it from you first."

I told him, occasionally taking a break to cry. I wished Art would put his arm around me or say something empathetic, but he was in detective mode and just waited for me to continue when I paused. When I'd gotten through it, I asked how Jan had ended up at the coffeehouse.

"She happened onto her kids listening in early on, grabbed the phone, and took off. She's with our mental health officer now, so don't worry about her. If need be, she'll be hospitalized for a few days to keep her safe. The gal who grabbed the gun is in bad shape, too. She can hardly talk."

"Thank God that woman needed to pee," I said.

"And Agnes and Grace?"

"We've got them cold, Ivy—thanks to you, you idiot."

I smiled wanly.

"They won't get bail. They're gone," he added.

"What about Boukar?"

"The feds will deal with him. Hopefully, they'll let us use him as a witness when they're done with him."

"Has anyone contacted Brian?"

"Someone's bringing him in for questioning. He's still a suspect until we know more. Grace is his wife, after all."

"I'm sure he's not involved."

"I hope you're right, Ivy. I hope Grace was telling the truth about him, but we've got multiple murders. This is the biggest case the city's had in years. We're going to be thorough. You're going to need to come in, too. You'll have to sign paperwork that you were present and witnessed what the recording has on it. And other detectives will need to question you further about everything. I'm off the case now. That's what Cline was doing this morning—reassigning me. He wasn't happy. I didn't always include what you were up to in my reports and he found out."

"I'll try not to get you into more trouble, Art." I should've realized he'd gone out on a limb for me. I should've known I'd endanger his career. I felt awful.

He looked me in the eyes. "You let me worry about that. Just tell the truth."

"Of course."

"What about my nieces?" I asked. I'd been worrying about Dee and Holly for the last twenty minutes.

"I tried to call them. The phones you and Jan

surrendered rang in my pocket. There's no landline, right?"

"I don't think so."

"There's an officer en route to the house. He'll fill them in and make sure they're okay. They'll need to come in to make statements, too. It's all by the book from now on. If we don't follow protocol, we'll give a defense attorney ammo in court."

"You'll probably find other evidence now that you know the story, right?"

"Absolutely. If Cline had let us investigate Agnes more thoroughly in the first place, it wouldn't have come to this."

"Could he be the corrupt cop—the one feeding information to her? I forgot to ask her about that."

"No, he just had things wrong. Cline's pretty arrogant. It's not the first time he overrode the evidence trail based on his own opinion."

"So who is it? Can you tell me now?"

"Yes. Gerry's friend—the one who helped them—is one of our tech guys—a sergeant. We used to be close. He didn't know anyone would end up dead, but that doesn't matter. He's part of a conspiracy to commit murder."

"So it's all wrapped up?"

"As far as I know."

"What about the artwork? What happens to that?"

"I have no idea."

Art's phone rang, and he took the call. "Petrie here. Uh, huh. Oh, my lord. I'll be there as soon as I can." His face was slack.

"What is it? What's happened?"

"Ivy, I'm sorry. I've got to go."

"Tell me, Art."

"The corrupt cop just hung himself. Flannigan had a family—two kids. I spent Christmas with them a few years ago." Art began to cry.

I leaned over and hugged him. "Oh, God. I'm so sorry."

After a few moments, he wriggled like a fish, and pulled away. "I really do have to go," he said hoarsely. "Thank you."

I clambered out of the car.

"Do you have someone to be with, Ivy?" he asked through the open door. His face was still ashen and now streaked with tears. Yet he was thinking about me.

"I'll head back to the house to be with Dee and Holly."

"All right. Take care."

Chapter Twenty-four

"Cline's been demoted," Art told me on our first official date two weeks later at Herb's Grill. "The whole case has been a mess—terrible PR for the department. And Palo Alto isn't exactly a cop-friendly town in the first place."

He wore a brown fedora with a red feather, which he didn't take off until I complimented him at our table.

"Will you end up with a better boss?" I asked.

"I hope so. It's me. I'm Lieutenant Petrie now. I'll only answer to the captain, and he's a hell of a guy."

"That's wonderful, Art."

"They want to hold a ceremony to give you a commendation, too."

"No, thanks. I'm not proud of myself. Maybe the police screwed up, but I screwed up worse. I endangered my family, I triggered Jan's breakdown, I almost got killed. And there are two extra dead people because of me—Gerry and Peralto. If I hadn't been so stubborn and foolish about investigating, it would all have turned out differently. My uncle's barely keeping it together. Jan is still in the hospital, and she thinks the psych nurses there are poisoning her. I could go on, but you know all this."

"That's one way to look at it. What about your Buddhism? Has that gone out the window? When I first met you, it seemed like it was right there at the surface. You brought it up all the time."

"I'm not sure how my beliefs help with this. I guess they've been beaten out of me by all this intense drama. It was easy to hang onto Buddhist principles at the temple. This is another story."

"Listen, they put me on leave while they investigated me. I get that. I was involved in a way I wasn't supposed to be. So I had free time and I read a lot about Buddhism—a crash course. I want to understand you, Ivy. I'm serious about you and me. Here's what I think, and correct me if I'm wrong. Buddhism says there are causes and circumstances behind everything that happens, right?"

"Yes, that's a basic precept. Even if you don't know the back story of something, you can assume there is one."

He nodded. "So how did you cause any murders? Just because evil people did what they did in response to you doesn't mean you need to feel guilty. You're not the backstory here."

"I don't believe in evil or guilt," I told him.

"Do you hear yourself? You're ignoring the meat and potatoes of what I just said—seizing on a couple of words you have an opinion about. People do that all the time in the interview room."

"You're right. I guess I don't really want to be looking into this right now."

"Maybe not. But you need to. The way I see it, whoever starts the chain of events that leads to a major crime is who's responsible. Why did people get murdered in this case? Because Grace set out to steal money from her tribe by conning Brian. She started this, and she got Agnes involved. She may not have known who she was dealing with there—someone even more

ruthless than her. I don't know all the details about that—
that's for the DA to worry about now.

"The point I'm making is this. What if I went
looking into something shady you're doing and you
decided to shoot me. Is that on you or me? Did I do
something I should get killed for? In your case, is trying
to solve a murder case such a terrible thing?" He paused
and let the weight of that sit with me. "There are almost
no actions that justify killing, Ivy. Believe me, I've heard
every excuse in the book."

"Yes, but suppose you could've predicted the
outcome and you went ahead anyway." That was me. I
was warned and I didn't stop.

"You predicted ·ll the murders? You thought Agnes
would keep killing?"

"No, but I shoul·l've listened to you. You knew what
I was doing was risky."

Art paused and studied my face. "You're doing it
again. You're veering away from what we're really
examining here—your religious values. Buddhism is
your deal, Ivy. It's what made you the remarkable
woman you are. So let's get back to it. What would
Buddha say?"

"I don't know. I just feel lost, Art." It was hard to
follow him as waves of hopelessness rippled through me.

"All right. I'll give it a shot, which is a little
ridiculous after only a week and a half of reading about
it."

For some reason I was moved by his words—even
heartened a bit. What he'd said earlier had hardly made
a dent.

"Go ahead," I told him. "Don't worry about getting
everything right. I need help, and you're helping me.

That's what matters."

"Okay. Here goes. Life changes all the time. We have to keep accommodating the changes as best we can. Buddhism says that to do that, we have to pay attention and roll with the punches—not fight against the way things are. Have I got that right?"

"More or less. Another way to say it is that we suffer when we can't accept the way things are."

"Exactly. That's what I mean. This stuff is bottom-line truth, Ivy. It matches what I've learned as a cop. So here's my point. I think you made some big life changes and had others foisted on you. Then all the crimes and everything showed up on top of that. It's been really hard to accommodate. It's warping the way you're thinking about things. If I asked you a few weeks ago about a hypothetical situation like this, you'd have told me you wouldn't second-guess life and you'd try to find out what lessons are coming out of what happened. Am I right?"

I had to smile, hearing my own words coming back to me out of Art's mouth. "Yes, you're right."

"Do you still think that's a good way to deal with this?"

"Yes, but I'm not there."

"Have you got anyone to talk to about this?" Art asked softly. "Losing your faith is a big deal—especially when you've been a nun."

"Do you mean a therapist?"

"Or a spiritual teacher. I don't know. Someone. I'm hardly the best person to be talking to about this."

"You're doing great, Art. Let me take a minute and think over what you've said."

"Sure."

He was patient while I thought for several minutes,

breathing deeply as though I were meditating, which reminded me of something.

"I haven't been meditating regularly," I told Art.

"Is that a big deal?"

"Actually, yes. Maintaining a practice is essential for me. And I see now how else I became so lost—so disconnected from my core self."

"Attagirl. Now you sound like you."

I smiled. "Let me think a little more." I spoke again when I finally had more to say. "I let personal desire con me into thinking I was on a congruent path with karma," I told Art.

"You lost me. I know what karma is now. What do you mean by 'a congruent path'? And by desire? You mean your attraction to me?"

"No. I do find you attractive, Art. Very. But that's not what I mean. Let me try again. I'm used to talking about this with students who grew up with Buddhism. I need to use different language now that I'm back in the States.

"Sure. Very attractive, huh?" He grinned and raised his eyebrows.

I nodded. He winked.

"What I mean is that instead of doing what was called for—what my reading of the circumstances told me would work out the best for everyone involved—I let my ego rule me. I made choices as a selfish individual instead of as a member of a collective."

"But you *are* an individual."

"In one sense. It depends on what level you look at this from. Yes, I'm in a separate body and I'm maneuvering through my individual life—my unique spiritual path. Who could argue with that?"

"Not me."

I was back. I was on a roll. I was teaching. It felt great. "On a deeper level, aren't we all in this together? Nothing means anything unless it's in relation to something else. And our bodies—and everything else—are made of the same stuff—atoms and molecules and all that. If you think about it, you and I are connected by air molecules right now. We're not separate. We just can't see air. So we're all just different arrangements of the same stuff, which is all interconnected."

"I wouldn't go that far," Art said, "but I get what you're saying. If you keep in mind that we're all in this life deal together, you don't get as selfish and you make better decisions."

"Yes. I should've just said that. I tend to be long-winded about this."

"No, no. It's fascinating. But I disagree that you were acting selfishly when you investigated your mother's death. What was wrong with that? Wasn't that to help your sister?"

"Originally. But even so-called helping can become self-serving. Suppose it made me feel good and it wasn't really helping? Or what if my attempts to help harmed others—like this did?"

Art nodded. "I get it. I'm not saying you made great decisions, and I don't know all your motives. I just know you did your best, and criminals committed the crimes—not you." He was thoughtful for a moment before he continued. "Ivy, can I ask you something?"

"Of course. Anything."

"Okay, how's our date going?"

I laughed and he joined me.

"Well, it's different," I told him. "Maybe we should

switch to other topics—something less philosophical. Tell me about your most embarrassing middle-school moment."

"Sure, as soon as you tell me about yours."

"Fair enough. I laughed so hard in Spanish class once, I wet my pants."

He smiled. "I've always found irregular verbs hysterical myself. Here's mine. I tried to kiss Cheryl Klaussen at a dance when everyone else in the school knew she was gay."

"What did she do?"

"She kicked my ass. I was pretty scrawny in seventh grade. Cheryl had about six inches and thirty pounds on me."

"So do you think we're ready to move our relationship on from crime to more of these lovely biographical topics?"

"Sure. Tell me about your nose-picking history."

I laughed. I felt like myself again—when I'd thought I never would.

"I can see we're off to a great start, Art."

"The sky's the limit, Ivy. Or maybe past there. Who knows?"

Epilogue

I'm living in Jan's guesthouse, attending graduate school again to become a psychotherapist, and leading a meditation group several times a week. My inheritance is substantial enough to both bankroll me and create a foundation to provide educational opportunities for girls in Sri Lanka.

Art and I are happy with one another—except when we're not. Our conflicts tend to revolve around who gets to accommodate who—a gold-plated problem. But we also still mix it up sometimes when either of us gets triggered. For example, Art might say something with a certain authoritarian edge—like my father did right before…well, I don't want to get into that. The longer we're together, the harder it is for me to tolerate Art's problem behaviors because each new iteration comes on the heels of my having asked him not to do it again the last time. He tries. I appreciate that. And I try to never laugh at any sincere effort of his, however comical it might be. That's a big trigger for him. Art's willingness to cook certainly ought to outweigh whether he remembered to put beans into the chili.

On balance, the relationship is something sublime that neither of us have ever experienced. And sex is a million times better now that I'm awake to it.

Unfortunately, Art regularly trounces me at Scrabble.

I repaid Dimitri for his help by setting him up on a date with Maria Kostova's sister. Last I heard, they were on an Alaskan cruise.

Jan is stable and seeing a crackerjack therapist. Dee is Dee. And Holly remains Holly. I feel as though I'm a surrogate mother to all of three of them. It's a role I'm hardly qualified for, but I'm learning.

I've realized that for all my talk about compassion, my spiritual path has been relatively loveless for years. At the temple, what passed for loving kindness toward others were kind actions without the love—a willful decision to act like a good person.

My heart-centered connection with Art provides a drastic contrast to this, and to all the mental chatter I endured while investigating the murders.

Where had the love been as I'd first stayed with my family? Had I ever been in my heart with Jan? Had I felt a flood of loving energy at any time besides watching TV with Dee, hugging Holly, and meeting Molly the dog— a total of three times. What did *that* say about me?

Even with Art, it wasn't until we were together for a few months that I began to rest in my heart when I was with him. Our early encounters pulled me into my head as I watched, evaluated, and tried to take my cues from him—all of this in pursuit of establishing a partnership. Once again, where was my heart?

These days I'm working on undefending my heart— dismantling my defenses. It no longer needs armor. My father's dead. I'm a grown-up with an array of skills and tools to navigate life, and Art is emotionally safe. The worst thing he's done on purpose so far is tease me about my ears. I retaliated by pointing out that his taste in ties was atrocious. Fortunately, he rarely has to wear one.

Would I play detective again if the opportunity arose? Who knows?

A word about the author...

Verlin Darrow is currently a psychotherapist who lives with his psychotherapist wife in the woods near the Monterey Bay in northern California. They diagnose each other as necessary. He barely missed being blown up by Mt. St. Helens, survived the 1985 Mexico City earthquake, and (so far) he's successfully weathered his own internal disasters. He maintains a website, verlindarrow.com, and encourages readers to contact him at verlindarrow@gmail.com.

Thank you for purchasing
this publication of The Wild Rose Press, Inc.

For questions or more information
contact us at
info@thewildrosepress.com.

The Wild Rose Press, Inc.
www.thewildrosepress.com